A Jolt from the Blue . . .

The sound of waves slapping the breakwater suddenly intruded on Liam's thoughts, brought into focus by another noise closer at hand. A thin, dry coughing whispered from out in the corridor.

"Fanuilh," Liam whispered. He was thinking of Tarquin's familiar, a miniature dragon. Where was it?

Without a thought, he rushed from the bedroom. Another whispered cough came from behind the second door in the corridor. He pushed open the door and stepped in.

He had a glimpse of a workroom, three long tables, a wall lined with books, another lined with jars of murky fluids and dried things. Another cough.

Then there was a jolt that traveled the length of his body. The pain swelled like blossoming light, flooding to his head. Something within him was being stretched, racked beyond its limits. Frozen upright by the pain, he felt the thing in him begin to split, torn in two. Absurdly, he thought part of it slipped through him and out the leg where the pain began.

Soul? he thought, and fell.

FANUILH

DANIEL HOOD

ACE BOOKS, NEW YORK

This book is an Ace original edition,
and has never been previously published.

FANUILH

An Ace Book / published by arrangement with
the author

PRINTING HISTORY
Ace edition / May 1994

ISBN: 0-441-00055-X

ACE®
Ace Books are published by The Berkley Publishing Group,
200 Madison Avenue, New York, New York 10016.
ACE and the "A" design
are trademarks belonging to Charter Communications, Inc.

PRINTED IN THE UNITED STATES OF AMERICA

10 9 8 7 6 5 4 3 2 1

SOUTHWARK

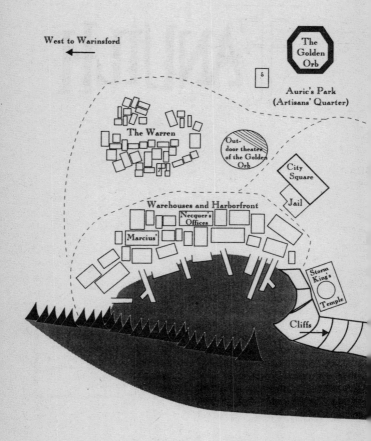

West to Warinsford

The Golden Orb

Auric's Park
(Artisans' Quarter)

The Warren

Out-door theater of the Golden Orb

City Square

Jail

Warehouses and Harborfront

Necquer's Offices

Marcius'

Storm King's Temple

Cliffs

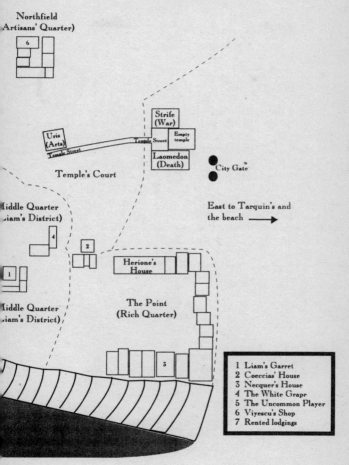

North to Duke's Seat

Northfield
(Artisans' Quarter)

6

Uris
(Arts)

Temple Street

Strife
(War)

Empty
temple

Temple Street

Laomedon
(Death)

City Gate

Temple's Court

East to Tarquin's and
the beach →

Middle Quarter
(Liam's District)

4

2

1

Herione's
House

Middle Quarter
(Liam's District)

The Point
(Rich Quarter)

3

1 Liam's Garret
2 Coeccias' House
3 Necquer's House
4 The White Grape
5 The Uncommon Player
6 Viyescu's Shop
7 Rented lodgings

CHAPTER 1

THE FEAST WAS a thing Liam Rhenford had never thought to see in Taralon and because of that, and his general feeling of being an outsider, he allowed himself a little too much of the hot, spiced wine.

Of course, the merchant Necquer was not really Taralonian; he was an expatriated Freeporter, and their sensibilities were less easily offended. Liam had spent a fair amount of time in the Freeports himself and was not offended, but he found himself wondering if any of Southwark's other merchants, Necquer's competitors, would consider such a feast with anything other than disgust.

Clerks and overseers in their rough best drank noisily in Necquer's home; stevedores and sailors, shorn to the ears in the traditional haircut of Taralon's lower classes, ate his food and sang dirty chanteys in his hall; spinning and weaving girls danced, giggling, to the minstrels Necquer had hired. Even in Southwark, the southernmost city of Taralon's southern duchies, position and the bounds of class distinction were well observed, if not as rigidly as in more northern parts. The merchant, however, had thrown propriety to the wind.

In his own home, Liam could hear other merchants saying, *he let them dance in his own home*, and smiled to himself over the social outrage.

Necquer's home was beautiful in a cramped way; a high, narrow wooden building nestled in the Point, Southwark's tiny rich quarter. Gleaming parquet floors shone under vibrant, imported rugs; light and warmth radiated from countless silver candelabra and roaring fireplaces. Fine food piled high on trestle tables disappeared almost as

1

soon as it was served, and wine and ale flowed in silver and pewter mugs. Freihett Necquer was entertaining his lowborn workers in a style normally reserved for his social equals as if it were nothing and his workers, in turn, accepted it without question. Glass-paned doors at the rear of the house opened onto a rain-dark stone porch overlooking the harbor; a group of sailors formed a circle there, encouraging two wrestling men with catcalls and shouts. A trio of musicians played loudly, and the sound of Necquer's employees dancing, eating and celebrating was louder than the rain or the surf crashing below.

I had no idea he was so rich, Liam thought, casting admiring eyes about the merchant's home. *I should have charged him more for those maps.*

Ostensibly the feast was in honor of the upcoming Uristide, but the real reason was that Necquer was alive and well, and in a mood to celebrate. He had survived one of the worst storms in Southwark's memory and—by a miracle—come home with a cargo of immense value.

When Necquer's workers talked, which they did only rarely between laughing and eating and dancing breathlessly, they talked of that miracle, and many slyly hinted that Necquer had never kept a Uris-tide before, and probably did not know who Uris was.

The miracle was the disappearance of Southwark's Teeth, the towering, jagged rocks that guarded the city's harbor. Rising black and ominous from beneath the sea like the spine of a submerged sea-dragon, they stretched for miles from the west to close off most of the harbor, leaving only a small entrance to the placid harbor. They took a greedy toll for the protection, however, in the form of ships smashed against their unyielding sides, keeping many safe in return for the occasional wreck sent down to the Storm King. A week before, another merchant's caravel, bearing a fortune home from Alyecir, had been crushed into the Teeth. Three men out of a crew of sixty had escaped. Four days later, Southwark woke, blinked its eyes, and saw the Teeth gone. The sea rolled unstopped into the roadstead, and the coast looked barren, for all the world like an old man without his

natural teeth. A day after that, Necquer had led four mer-
chantmen limping into port. Experienced seamen declared
it a miracle: battered as the ships were by the late season
storms, they could never have negotiated the Teeth. And that
morning, the day after Necquer's safe arrival, Southwark
woke to find that the unknown thief had repented, and the
Teeth were back, resuming their posts as if they had never left.

Necquer had more than enough reason to celebrate, and
his employees—common sailors, poor clerks, burly stevedores and longshoremen, the girls who spun and wove his
trade goods—accepted it wholeheartedly.

Liam listened to everything he could, circulating aimlessly around the noisy, crowded house, taking long sips
of wine. He spoke to no one, because he knew no one,
and thought more than once of the invitation extended to
him by Necquer's wife.

He had arrived almost an hour after sunset, delayed as
much by the fact that he would not know any of Necquer's
employees as by the rain. The house was already full of
people celebrating, and though the music had not started
yet, the noise was deafening. He took a deep breath and
shouldered his way into the feast.

Necquer had spotted him after a few minutes and jostled
his way over.

"Rhenford! It was good of you to come!" The merchant
was almost as tall as Liam, but far broader. Almost forty
years old, in many ways he was a typical Freeporter,
dark of hair and skin, easygoing and unpretentious. He
clasped Liam's hand and shoulder, smiling broadly. Over
his shoulder, he called out: "Poppae! Poppae! Come over
here! There's someone you should meet!"

An expensively dressed young woman separated herself
from an obviously painful conversation with a weaving girl
and threaded her way through the press. She was beautiful in
a quiet way, finely formed, porcelain features framed with a
mass of curling, glossy black hair. She was young, barely
into her twenties, and she looked almost childlike compared
to her husband. Necquer watched her make her way towards

them, and it struck Liam as he bowed over her hand that the merchant was carefully scrutinizing their introduction.

"Poppae, this is Liam Rhenford, the gentleman who drew the maps that have made us rich! Rhenford, my wife Poppae."

"Sir Liam," Poppae murmured, a slight smile playing over her lips.

"I'm afraid I'm not a knight, Lady Necquer," Liam corrected politely. He had grown used to the southern habit of indiscriminately applying titles of respect. In the north, where he was raised, the degrees of rank were carefully delineated and scrupulously denoted with countless specific names, each signifying a slight difference in class. Southerners, on the other hand, tended to use whatever title came to mind, as long as it broadly approximated the subject's position.

Necquer suddenly breathed hard, as though disappointed in the conversation, and turned away abruptly. Liam watched him go, slightly surprised. Lady Necquer showed no interest in leaving. In fact, she gazed at him curiously.

"I suppose I owe you my husband's long absences, Sir Liam?"

He let the honorific pass this time. She spoke the southern dialect, but not as thickly as most he had met in Southwark, and her eyes were disturbingly enormous, sad and blue.

"I am afraid you are correct, madam. I did draw some maps for your husband, but had I known they would cause you pain through his absence, I'd never have done it." He had, in fact, given her husband a secret few others knew about. Alyecir and the Freeports, the main trading destinations of ships from Taralon, lay to the west. But to the east and south a number of cities existed on coasts undreamed of by Southwark's merchants, unvisited because of a Taralonian superstition about sailing the Cauliff Ocean. Liam had reached them by traveling overland, but he knew they could be reached from the sea. Late in the summer, it had occurred to him to sell the maps he had made, and he had chosen Necquer primarily because he was a Freeporter, and might not share Taralonian superstitions.

As hoped, Necquer had no objections to trying the Cauliff, and on Liam's assurance that the journey would be short, had departed as soon as he could ready four ships, even though the fall storms were approaching. That had been a little over six weeks before, and already he was back, and if the size of his feast was any indication, the trip had been very successful.

Lady Necquer looked at him with new respect, and edged a little closer, giving in to pressure from the ever-growing crowd.

Liam let his eyes rove over the crowd, nervously refusing to meet her eyes. It had been a long time since he had had to deal with anyone of even Lady Necquer's station, and the social pitfalls their conversation presented loomed large in his mind. On the other hand, he had noticed the discomfort with which she spoke to Necquer's more common employees. He supposed that, clean-shaven and well dressed as he was, he represented a far more interesting companion than longshoremen and tars straight off a three-month voyage. And bowing over her hand had probably not hurt his image.

"You speak passing fair, Sir Liam, and with a Midlands tongue, 'less I'm mistaken."

"You are not, madam. I was born in the Midlands." He could not help feeling that he sounded stiff and stilted to her, but it had been a long while since his breeding had been required of him.

"My husband's tongue was schooled Midlands," she said with a smile, "though a very Freeporter he is. He learned in Harcourt and the other western ports. But tell, how does a Midlands tongue come to speak so far south? And to draw maps of lands even further south?"

Liam dropped his gaze to his boots, taking in the tooled leather, uncomfortable speaking about himself. "When I was a youth, certain . . . family problems forced my departure from home. I have traveled widely since," he finished lamely.

"No first son's legacy for you, then?" she said sympathetically. "You were a second son?"

"Yes," he lied. It was far easier to claim the anonymity of a lesser position than to explain to the curious woman that he was an only child, and that his birthright had been stripped from him in war. And far less painful.

"And so you traveled. But not as a sailor?" she asked, and he detected a note of hope in her soft voice.

"No, madam. Sometimes as a surgeon, or navigator, and twice as captain. Most often merely as a passenger. The charts I drew your husband were taken from my notes."

"Navigator, captain, surgeon, e'en? You are a man of several parts, Sir Liam, though you are no knight." She laughed brightly. Liam caught on only after a moment, and then laughed with her.

"It would very much agree with me to hear further of your travels, Sir Liam."

"Even in a Midlands tongue?" he asked with mock humility, beginning to warm to Lady Necquer's sad eyes and gentle manner. She smiled at him.

Necquer suddenly loomed up behind his wife, smiling as though he had heard the joke.

"Eh, Poppae, we seem to be ready for the minstrels, don't you think?"

The question was asked without any detectable overtones, but Lady Necquer paled slightly, and caught her breath.

"Faith, I suppose we are, lord." She made to move away, but Necquer took hold of her tiny waist and kissed her soundly on the cheek. She snuggled against him, raising one hand absently to his sea-roughened cheek. He smiled at Liam over her shoulder.

"Has Rhenford been regaling you with tales of his journeys, my dear?"

"Boring her, I'm afraid," Liam said with a slight bow.

"Nonsense, Rhenford. You're the most interesting man I've met in a long time, and I'm sure Poppae agrees. Don't you, sweet?"

Lady Necquer nodded eagerly. "I was just asking Sir Liam to tell me more of his travels, lord, but he is a fierce keeper of secrets."

"Well, we'll have to change that, eh, Rhenford? Why

not come some night to dinner? You can tell me where to trade next season, and then entertain Poppae. I'm leaving for Warinsford tomorrow, or I'd ask you then, but I'll be back in a few days. You'll dine with us then, eh?"

"Must you leave so soon?" Lady Necquer seemed genuinely upset, but her husband's answer sounded rehearsed, as if they had had the same discussion earlier.

"The snows won't start for another month, and a great deal of what I brought back may spoil, sweet. It must be soon." He kissed her again, and Liam shifted uncomfortably, as though intruding on a private moment.

Lady Necquer returned his kiss absently. "But could not Sir Liam come and entertain me while you are gone? Mayhap just to while away an afternoon?" There was a freight of meaning behind her words, and a plea that Necquer caught, though it flew past Liam.

"Certainly, certainly," Necquer said after a moment's thought. "He shall come tomorrow, then? What do you say, Rhenford? Will you entertain my wife tomorrow afternoon?"

"I . . . of course, of course."

Lady Necquer smiled gratefully at her husband, who admonished Liam to remember his appointment, and whisked her away. Liam stood, confused but strangely happy. He had been in Southwark for over four months, but until then he had spoken—spoken for no purpose other than pleasure—with only one other person.

He smiled to himself and shouldered gently through the throng of celebrating workers to find himself a cup of wine. He drank six more before the end of the evening, eating little, talking no more, and watching a great deal.

Necquer's employees enjoyed themselves thoroughly. They shouted and danced the large group dances favored in the south, encouraging each other with whistles and clapping. The three minstrels kept pace, playing louder and more wildly as the evening wore on. Liam looked on, listening to snatches of conversation about the miracle, and watched Lady Necquer.

As close as they seemed, something was not right between

the merchant and his wife. He recalled a comment he had
not understood. A clerk at the buffet had told a companion
that there might be more than one reason why Necquer had
hurried home, and received a wink and a snicker in return.
Liam guessed now that they were referring to a mistress.
It might explain the strangeness he had detected in the
merchant's manner, but he found it hard to believe anyone
would be disloyal to a woman as young and beautiful as
Poppae Necquer.

Tall as he was, Liam found it easy to keep track of the
diminutive beauty as she moved around her home; and it
was easy to catch Necquer watching her too, with slitted
eyes and an expression that occasionally grew grim. She
seemed aware of it, but not disturbed. It was as if she were
waiting to show him something, but could not find it in the
crowded room.

Towards the bottom of his seventh cup of wine, Liam
realized that the room was stiflingly close, and that the
feeling was gone in the tip of his long nose. Recognizing
an old sign, he prepared himself to go, looking around for
his host. He shoved less gently than before through the
crowd towards the back of the house, his misjudgement
of the gaps in the milling crowd justifying his decision
to leave.

Necquer was not to be found in the rear of the narrow
house, though several drunken sailors were taking turns
walking the length of the rain-slick balustrade that rimmed
the porch, ignoring the long drop to the harbor below. *Someone should stop them*, Liam thought hazily, *but not me*. He
turned and began threading his unsteady way back through
the crowd.

He saw Necquer in the middle of the hall, pressed to
one wall by the thick, rowdy crowd. His face was taut and
grim, and he was staring across the hall at his wife, who
was behind one of the tables that had once been covered
with food and now held crumbs and bones. She was staring,
pale and unhappy, towards the street door, where a young
man stood framed by the lintel. He was brushing rain from
long, ash-blond hair, his handsome face swinging to and fro,

looking for someone. Necquer followed his wife's gaze, and Liam saw him mouth a curse and begin pushing through the crowd towards the door.

Stung by curiosity, Liam followed after, losing sight of Necquer in the crowd. He did, however, see the young man's eyes suddenly widen, and pushed harder against the crowd when the man spun quickly and dashed out into the rain.

The crowd and his own unsteadiness slowed him, and by the time he reached the door and stepped out into the street, the youth was gone. Necquer stood on the cobbles, his fists bunched by his sides, and Liam almost lurched into him. One fist raised, the merchant spun on him, and lowered his arm reluctantly.

"Rhenford," he said, rain trickling down his face into his beard like tears.

"I thought I should thank you before I left," Liam slurred, wiping rain out of his face with a hand that felt unnaturally hot.

"Rhenford, you're drunk!" Necquer gave a laugh, loud and heartily out of proportion, Liam felt, to how drunk he was, but he said nothing. The merchant seemed to need to laugh.

"Who would have thought a few cups of wine could undo a man who'd traveled the world over?" Necquer laughed, immensely amused and immensely relieved by something.

"I thought I should thank you before I left," Liam repeated, very uncomfortable and feeling very serious.

"You're not leaving yet, Rhenford, not in this rain. At least let me send a servant with you. You'll fall in a gutter and catch your death! Wait in the hall, I'll send a servant for you."

Liam let the merchant guide him back into the house, where he leaned against a wall. Necquer started away, then turned back, looking seriously at Liam.

"You will come tomorrow, won't you?" There was an earnestness in Necquer's voice, but Liam was feeling unnaturally hot all over now, and waved the question away.

"Of course, of course," he mumbled.

"Wait here. I'll send a servant."

Necquer strode off into the crowd and almost immediately, Liam pulled himself away from the wall and walked, stumbling slightly, into the rain.

It was a cold, light rain, and went a long way towards sobering Liam up. He wove only slightly back and forth across the narrow streets, turning his face up to the rain to try to clear his head. By the time he had wound his way down out of the rich quarter, further inland to the neighborhood where his rooms were, his head was far clearer, the haze mostly driven out by a piercing headache, like a spike driven into his forehead.

When he had arrived in Southwark during the spring, he had not looked far for lodging, taking directions from the first longshoreman he met. He had been directed to an establishment run by a captain's widow, and she had been glad to offer him her attic garret, the largest room she had.

Climbing the five flights of rickety stairs, he cursed the choice, and when he slammed his head into one of the room's low-hanging beams, he cursed again, loudly. The room ran the whole length of the house, with a low ceiling and one window at the front, where he had placed a cheap table. Apart from a straw pallet and an iron-bound chest, the table and its attendant chair were the only furnishings. Several books and stacks of papers littered the rest of the room, and Liam remembered how impressed his landlady had been.

"A very scholar, aren't you, sir? Never had no scholar here before," she had said, respect like cloying sugar in her voice.

Most of the sheets of paper were blank, but she had not noticed that. He had wondered if Mistress Dorcas could read, and decided that she was probably illiterate.

He managed to light a candle after several attempts, and finally sat down on the chair, which creaked ominously at his weight. He thought of writing, but dismissed the idea almost immediately, the pain in his head a warning against any attempt at serious work. Instead, he stared out the glass-paned window at the rain and offered a blanket prayer to whichever gods kept the attic roof from leaking, and to those who had kept him from throwing up on his way home.

"No more wine," he muttered, scratching with a thumbnail at the spine of one of the books on the table. "Not for a long time."

The candle guttered, disturbed by a crafty draft that had found a chink in the window. Liam shifted slightly and blew the candle out. He undressed in the dark, tossing his soaked breeches, boots and tunic away, and crawled beneath his two soft blankets. It was cold in the garret, and the smell of mold curled lightly into his nose. Rain pattered heavily on the roof for a while, and he thought he might fall asleep to it, but it tapered off, leaving him with a loud silence.

Restless and uncomfortable, thinking of nothing for over an hour, he finally got off the pallet and searched in the dark for his candle. When it was lit, he opened his chest with the key hung around his neck, and dressed anew, in dry clothes. He started for the door and then, as an afterthought, returned to spread his wet clothes on the chair.

The rain had stopped, but water still gurgled in the gutters, and the clouds had not broken. He hesitated in the street, unsure where he wanted to go. He could simply wander the city, but the Guard frowned on that, and there was nothing in Southwark he had not already seen.

He thought of visiting his only friend in Southwark, and then rejected the idea because it was late.

Then again, he thought, *Tarquin's a weird one, and a wizard; perhaps he's still awake. And it's somewhere to go.*

Tarquin Tanaquil was really more of an acquaintance than a friend, but he seemed to tolerate Liam, and the two got along well enough. The wizard lived outside Southwark, beyond a belt of farms and pasturage on a beach to the east of the city, fifteen minutes' ride away.

Liam set off purposefully through the rain-glistening streets, thinking better of whistling.

It took him almost an hour to reach Tarquin's beach on foot, and his headache was gone by the time he arrived. Happily, lights still burned in the house.

The wizard's home occupied a bend in the high seacliffs where sand had gathered, forming a long, secluded beach. A narrow path cut into the cliffs led down to the waterfront, and Liam stood at its bottom for a minute, admiring the view.

Far out over the sea, the clouds had broken, and the moon turned the horizon silver. Closer in, all was dark, the massive breakwater a looming shadow, the sand black. Only the wizard's home was lit, a warm and cheery presence. It was a villa, a rich-looking house: one-storied but long and deep, white plaster and red tile roof with only a slight peak. A broad, stone-paved patio lined the front with steps leading right onto the sand. The wall of the house facing the sea was almost entirely glass, more glass than Liam had ever before seen in one place. Warm yellow light spilled out onto the patio.

Liam sprinted across the sand, packed down with the rain, and sprang up on the breakwater. Broad as a roadway, it led him along the beachfront to a spot directly in front of Tarquin's door.

It was the breakwater and the beach that had led him to meet the wizard. The coastline near Southwark was almost entirely high cliffs; larger, more stolid cousins to the Teeth. In his early explorations, Liam had learned that there were almost no places where one could swim in the sea, except for Tarquin's cove. Mistress Dorcas had told him about the magician, spouting the normal warnings and superstitions, but one day he had gone down the path, strolled up to the door, and asked if he might swim from the wizard's beach.

The white-haired old man grudgingly gave permission, and from there a sort of suspicious acquaintance began. As the summer wore on and the weather grew hotter, Liam's visits to the beach grew more frequent, and the occasions when the busy wizard recognized his presence grew as well. One time he invited Liam to sit on the patio with him, and they had spoken briefly. From there, it had only been a short while before he was invited in, and their conversations had grown longer.

Standing on the breakwater, alternately looking out to sea and back at the villa, Liam thought that he would never have woke the wizard merely to tell how he had gotten drunk and could not sleep. But since the house was lit, he felt it would be no imposition.

He hopped off the breakwater and strolled across the sand to the patio and the glass-fronted house. He rapped once on one of the thick panes, and waited. There was no reply, so he opened the door, more of a window that slid aside in grooved wooden tracks, and stepped inside.

Though it was chilly outside, the house was warm. Sourceless light filled the entrance hall, bringing out soft highlights in the polished wood of the floor. Corridors and more sliding doors, these of solid wood, led off the room.

"Tarquin?" Liam asked softly, and a shudder ran through him. He had never been further than the entrance hall and one small room off it, a sort of parlor overlooking the beach.

"Tarquin?" he called again. The sound of the waves lapping against the breakwater sounded louder inside than out.

Boldly, he strode down one of the corridors leading towards the rear of the house, and found himself in a stone-paved kitchen, with a huge wooden table and a cavernous baker's oven. No wizard. He noticed that the table was unscarred, the sanded planks unmarked by use.

"Tarquin?" he called again, raising his voice. No response.

He left the kitchen and returned to the entrance hall, choosing the second corridor. Two doors opened off it, one open. More of the sourceless light spilled out, and Liam saw the foot of a bed.

Filled with a dread as sourceless as the light, he approached the door slowly. Then he plunged into the room, awaiting a shock, something loud and frightening. Nothing happened, and he breathed a sigh. Tarquin was in his bed, his hands clasped on his chest. His full white beard spread luxuriously over his scrawny chest.

The room was small, meant to hold nothing more than the bed, which was broad and canopied, carved with dancing figures and covered with a red blanket. There was nothing on the walls, no rugs or rushes on the floor. Only the bed, and its solitary occupant.

"I'm sorry, Tarquin, I didn't know you were asleep."

Liam paused, his relief dissipating. Tarquin had not moved, though his eyes, sunken in the mass of wrinkles that served the wizard for a face, were open, and Liam would have sworn they were not when he first came in.

"Tarquin?" He tentatively put a hand to the wizard's shoulder and pushed. Even through the blue cloth of the robe, Liam could feel the chill.

A trance, he hoped, *let it be a trance*.

He pushed again, this time at the wizard's hands. They fell away to either side in what might have been a gesture of supplication. The palms were stained red. The hilt of a small knife jutted from his chest. The blue robe was dark with blood, and the ends of Tarquin's beard were red, like the bristles of a brush barely dipped in paint.

Liam's eyes narrowed and he leaned over the bed, looking at nothing in particular, taking in the whole. Tarquin looked like he had been laid out for burial, legs decorously together, robe smoothed. The red blanket barely registered his presence, neatly hanging over the edge of the bed, unwrinkled.

The sound of waves slapping the breakwater suddenly intruded on Liam's thoughts, brought into focus by another noise closer at hand. A thin, dry coughing whispered from out in the corridor.

"Fanuilh," Liam whispered. He was thinking of Tarquin's familiar, a miniature dragon. Where was it?

Without a thought, he rushed from the bedroom. Another whispered cough came from behind the second door in the corridor. He pushed open the door and stepped in.

He had a glimpse of a workroom, three long tables, a wall lined with books, another lined with jars of murky fluids and dried things. Another cough.

Then there was a sharp pain in his leg, and a jolt that

traveled the length of his body. The pain swelled like blossoming light, flooding to his head. Something within him was being stretched, racked beyond its limits. Pressure built and built, pulling the thing, cracks appearing in its smooth surface. Frozen upright by the pain, he felt the thing in him finally begin to split, torn in two. Absurdly, he thought part of it slipped through him and out the leg where the pain began.

Soul? he thought, and fell.

CHAPTER 2

LIAM WOKE AT sunrise, feeling hung over. His head pounded, and ripples of uneasiness radiated out from his stomach through his whole body. He did not open his eyes for a long while, lying instead on his back on the floor, examining his aches internally.

He noted the dull, throbbing in his ankle, and remembrance flooded in. Slowly, he forced his lids up and stifled a shout. He gasped silently, turning the shout into a long-drawn breath, and did not move.

Tarquin's familiar, Fanuilh, was lying weightlessly on his chest, its wedgelike head curled between its paws. The little creature stirred restlessly in its sleep, dull black scales rippling, leathern wings flaring briefly to settle back against its gently heaving sides.

"Fanuilh," Liam breathed, and the dragon's eyes flicked open. It heaved itself unsteadily up on its forepaws, slipped slightly, recovered its foothold. Liam could see the dragon's neck and belly, covered with yellow scales as dull as the black ones on its back. For a moment, they were both still, Fanuilh's yellow, catlike eyes boring into Liam's blues. A slim tongue flicked out of the sharp-toothed mouth and ran over the dragon's tiny chin, where the scales gave way to a tuft of coarse hair.

We are one.

The thought intruded in Liam's head, like a flash of illumination. It stayed there, his other thoughts revolving around it. For a moment he thought he might have heard it, but it remained, and did not dissipate. It was a thought in his head, but obdurate and unyielding. He tried to think other things, questions, but they could not force it out.

16

We are one.

Just as suddenly as the foreign thought had appeared, it went, and Fanuilh shuddered and collapsed again on his chest.

Liam lay on the floor for long minutes, unwilling to touch the creature on his chest. Finally, when its breathing grew even in sleep, he forced his hands up and gently surrounded the form. Slowly, with fear as much as tenderness, he picked up the sleeping dragon and placed it beside him on the floor. The scales, instead of feeling hard or metallic, were like ridged cloth, moire or corduroy, soft and warm. As he moved it, Fanuilh exhaled, and its breath was rank and foul.

Like a dead man's, Liam thought, and repressed a shudder until he had put the sleeping dragon down. Then he rolled away and up to his knees, feeling his stomach turn over. His hangover was well out of proportion to the amount he had drunk.

'*We are one*,' he remembered and shook his head in denial. He stood shakily, and stumbled for the door of the workroom. On impulse, he stopped in the doorway and turned to look at Fanuilh. Sleeping on the floor below him, and not on his chest above his face, the dragon looked harmless, and Liam suddenly bent and scooped up the creature, cradling it against his chest as he looked for a better place to put it.

The worktable nearest the door was empty, and Liam deposited Fanuilh there. The creature did not stir, and, after a moment staring at it, he turned on his heel and walked out of the room.

He limped blindly for the kitchen, ignoring Tarquin's bedroom, his pounding head and raw throat calling for relief. He could think of nothing but cold water, and perhaps bread, or a hot bun. A type of pastry he had once eaten in Torquay sprang to mind, and his stomach rumbled unpleasantly. The sea, when he saw it through the glass walls of the entrance hall, was shiny pink with the new sun, the clouds of the previous evening gone. Morning filled the hall, streaking the shadows of the window panes across the floor like bars.

In the kitchen, the sourceless light still ruled, banishing shadows. He searched bins and cupboards, hoping only for bread and water. Water he found in a jar by the tiled stove, far colder and sweeter than it had any right to be.

Tarquin's magic, he thought, and grimaced, thinking of the hilt rising from the old man's chest.

He lifted the jar to his lips and drank deeply, washing away bile and roughness, gasping with the intensity of the cold. When he put the jar back next to the stove, he felt heat on the back of his hand and stepped away from the stove suspiciously.

Why not? he thought, and yanked open the metal door on the oven's front. Banked coals lay beneath a metal rack, on which rested four small, round buns, piping hot, just like the ones he remembered from Torquay. Hunger took over from caution, and he snatched one of them, juggling the hot pastry back and forth between his hands until he could drop it on the table.

He picked up the jar and drank again, then put his attention to the bun. It was almost too hot to eat, but his stomach roiled, and he forced a bite down. By the time the taste registered, his stomach was quieter.

It was delicious, exactly like the ones in Torquay, laced with currants and nuts, lightly spiced with cinnamon and something sweet and sticky he could not identify. It was wonderful—and clearly magic. The buns were certainly fresh-baked, not reheated, and the coals were as hot as if they had only been lit for an hour. More magic, he supposed, wolfing down the rest of the bun. He had never connected magic with small things like hot cinnamon buns and ice-cold water. Only things of magnificent proportions—calling forth demons, sinking ships, destroying armies. It made him think differently of Tarquin.

Thinking of Tarquin brought him to the corpse in the bedroom, and he frowned. Snatching two more buns from the oven, he went back to the bedroom.

Tarquin was stiffening; that much he could tell by looking. Dead at least twelve hours, as far as his experience as a surgeon and soldier could tell. He leaned against the doorjamb and stared at the corpse, absently eating some of the delicious bread.

"Murdered," he said aloud, and might have laughed at the obviousness of the conclusion.

By whom? Why? He realized he did not know Tarquin well enough to even hazard a guess, and supposed the only one who might know was Fanuilh, and Fanuilh was only a brute beast.

Or was it?

We are one.

The thought had not been his. And the creature had been staring at him so intently. Liam had heard stories that wizards and their familiars were bound in special ways, but that was the result of complicated spells and dealings with supernatural beings, the sort of thing reserved for those who worked with magic.

Swallowing the rest of his second bun, he left the corpse and went to the workroom. Fanuilh was still asleep, curled up with its snout touching his hind legs.

Like a dog, but scaled and winged and clawed and able to send its thoughts into my head. Liam winced and moved away.

The workroom's large windows looked out onto the narrow stretch of sand separating the villa from the cliffs, and let in a gray, shadowy light to illuminate the room. The first table held only Fanuilh, the second a single empty decanter of glass, but the top of the third was completely covered. Liam had not seen it in his brief glimpse the night before, but the morning light showed the table's display, and he wandered over to it.

It was like the sand-table models he had seen engineers make during sieges, but far more complex. It reproduced, in miniature, the coastline around Southwark; but where a mercenary engineer would have been happy with crude representations, the model in Tarquin's workroom was perfect in every detail. The Teeth lay exactly at the center of the table; water on one side, the harbor and city on the other. The town was the most impressive part, completely detailed, right down to the Necquer's harborside porch, and Liam's own garret window. Tiny ships with full rigging rode at anchor, and Liam saw that they actually *rode*, swaying slightly as if on swells. Acting on a hunch, he put his finger down into the harbor. The ships *were* moving, and the water, when he brought his finger to his mouth, tasted of salt. What he had thought well-sculpted whitecaps proved on closer inspection to be real breakers, flowing constantly against the Teeth. The Teeth themselves were rock, and felt as cold and wet as their larger brethren.

Liam whistled in awed admiration and the dawning of an idea.

At the far end of the table stood a lectern, over the edge of which hung a heavy chain. With his eyes fixed on the model, Liam moved around to the lectern. A massive leatherbound book lay open on it, held down with the chain. Tarquin's spellbook, Liam supposed, and read the first few lines on the page that lay open. Abstract, theoretical language, studded with phrases in some foreign tongue Liam had never met; nonetheless, he understood enough of what was written in Taralonian. It was a spell for removing matter to another plane of existence; "translating substance," the text called it.

"He made the Teeth disappear," he whispered. "Damn!"

As a last act, Liam thought, there could be few better. A final testament to Tarquin's power, grandiose proof of his reputation in Southwark as a truly great wizard. Liam wondered if Tarquin knew that it would be his last spell when he cast it.

A paper-thin piece of wood projected from further on in the book, marking another page. Liam pushed the heavy pages aside and scanned the lines of the second spell. Much of the language was the same, and he recognized some of the foreign phrases, but the point of this one was to cloak matter, to make it invisible.

If Tarquin had been trying to decide which spell to use, he must have chosen the one for transforming matter, or else

Necquer's ships would have been resting quietly beneath the sea, not to mention Necquer himself.

Could someone have killed the wizard for that?

Liam's eyes lost their focus on the page as he thought.

Who would want to kill Tarquin? As far as Liam knew, the old man had no enemies—at least none that he had spoken about. Then again, he did not know much about the wizard. When they had spoken, it had only been in generalities, about faraway places or things long past. Nothing about each other's lives in Southwark, or their present business. But then Tarquin was a wizard, and they made enemies everywhere. They quarreled among themselves, they had disagreements with those who sought their services, they were marked out by power for the fear and suspicions of the masses. It would not have been hard for Tarquin to acquire enemies, but it was strange that a man who could alter the work of nature in such a way could not defend himself.

I am awake.

It was a thought like the first; hard-edged and stony, brazenly pushing other thoughts away to grab his attention. His head snapped over to look at the table where he had put Fanuilh.

You have eaten. I should eat as well.

There was no doubt the thought came from Fanuilh, and Liam remembered the bite. Why had the thing bitten him?

So that we would be one. I must eat, but I am weak.

Liam crossed the room slowly, eyeing the little dragon. Its yellow eyes never left his.

"Are you doing this? Putting thoughts in my head?"

You do not need to speak. Only think. And I am.

"How?"

We are one. May I eat? The serpentine head nudged at the final bun Liam held in his hand. Liam knelt by the edge of the table, so that his eyes were on a level with the dragon's, and held out the food.

Fanuilh's head snaked out and ripped off a large bite, chewing and swallowing in rapid gulps. Liam watched, fascinated, as the dragon ate more, gulping down the whole bun in seconds. When it was done, it began very gently licking its claws, though it continued to stare at him.

You are confused.

"How are we one?"

You know already. You are wiser than you seem.

"Then—you are like a familiar to me? Bound in that way?"

As you are bound to me. We share a soul now; your soul rests partly in me, and partly still in you.

Liam rose, shaking his head in confusion. "Why did you never speak like this before?"

We were never one before. This can only be done between those who are one. Look.

Suddenly, Liam's sight went black. He cried out, and then his vision returned, but his perspective was wrong. He was looking up into an angular, unlined face, framed with close-cropped blond hair. Pale blue eyes rolled sightlessly on either side of a long, thin nose. It was his nose; he was looking at his own face.

You see with my eyes.

"I want to see with *my* eyes!" he said, and there was another sickening jolt of blindness before he returned to his own perspective. The dragon's head was cocked to one side, regarding him curiously. "Never do that again!" he admonished shakily.

You can do it as well.

"I don't want to!"

Perhaps you will.

There was a long silence. Liam wondered, and then stopped wondering, realizing the dragon could read his thoughts.

"I want you out of my head!"

You can keep me out.

"How?" he demanded.

I will show you, but you must do things for me.

"Do things for you? You've stolen my soul, you little beast! I want you out of my head!"

I am sorry. It was necessary. I was dying. We may—
Liam felt the edge of the thought, notched like the blade

of a broken sword, as the dragon paused—*We may make a bargain.*

"A bargain! What have you got in return for my soul?"

We only share it. I would not have taken even a small part, were it not necessary. Master Tanaquil thought my gifts worth a small part of his soul. And it does you no harm. But if you help me only a little more, I can teach you things.

"What things?" Liam demanded.

There are things that must be done, and then I will teach you.

"What things?"

How to keep me out, how to see with my eyes. Other things as well.

Despite himself, Liam was intrigued.

"Magic?"

Not much. You do not have the mind for the complicated kinds. But smaller ones, perhaps, and other things. I can help you write your book.

"My book? How did you know of that?" The dragon cocked its head again, and Liam raised a hand. "No, never mind. I understand."

I shared all these things with Master Tanaquil. I can teach you. If you will do things for me. The dragon still looked directly at him, but there was no expression in the creature's eyes.

Liam heaved himself to his feet, favoring his unbitten leg. "What things?"

First, you must bring me more food. In the kitchen, think of raw meat, desire it, and look in the oven.

"I noticed that. An easy enough condition." He limped to the kitchen, and though it was difficult to make himself desire raw meat, eventually the oven produced an uncooked cut of beef, which he brought back to the dragon.

Fanuilh tore into it, biting and chewing in the same convulsive gulps. It did not stop sending its thoughts, however.

Second, the message appeared in Liam's mind, *you must tell the Duke's man in Southwark of Master Tanaquil's murder. His name is Coeccias. Can you find him?*

"The Duke's man? The Aedile? Yes, I can find him. I would have told him in any case. What else must I do?"

Third, you must nurse me to health. As painful as the sharing was for you, it was much worse for me. I almost died when Master Tanaquil was struck down.

"When he was struck down," Liam echoed, and then asked intently: "Do you know who killed him?"

I do not.

Liam mused over this, disappointed, and the dragon did not interrupt him for a while. Then:

I am weak. It will perhaps take a month for me to recover.

Brought out of his reverie, Liam nodded. "Yes, of course. Simple enough. Is there anything else?"

One other. I will tell you when you return with the Aedile.

Liam balked. "Tell me now."

It will be simple enough for you, and there will be time enough when you return with the Aedile. You must be sure he brings a ghost witch.

"A ghost witch? What's that?"

He will know. Tell him that. Is it a—again, the shorn-off thought, as though the phrase was unfamiliar—*a bargain?*

"Yes," Liam said, after a moment's thought.

Then go.

Stung, he turned abruptly for the door, only to turn back. "Why don't you know who killed Tarquin?"

Master Tanaquil could exclude me from his mind at will. He often did.

"You can teach me to do that?"

I can. I will, when you fulfill the last thing I will ask. Now go.

Still Liam paused, wondering to himself. It was strange to talk and receive the response directly in his head; it was strange to take orders from a tiny, weak dragon; it was strange not to argue—but what, he asked himself, could he do?

It is as strange for me to give orders as it is for you to take them. When you have fulfilled my last request, I will teach you how to be my master.

With that in his head, Liam limped out of the house and onto the beach.

Between Liam's limp and his distracted thoughts, it took far longer to return to Southwark than it had to come out the night before.

Fanuilh had taken part of his soul, but for some reason he felt neither violated nor angry. Liam knew himself to be accepting by nature, taking what was given and making the best of it. There was, really, nothing he could do: he had heard enough about wizards and their familiars to know that the link could only be broken through the death of one of the sharers. He had no idea what would happen to his soul if Fanuilh died, and he had no intention of finding out.

As he thought of it, he reasoned that the experience must indeed have been worse for the dragon. He still had his soul; part of it was simply resting in Fanuilh. The dragon, for a time, had not had a soul. Liam tried, but could not imagine what that would be like.

On the whole, he thought he should pity the little creature, but he could not manage it. It was, perhaps, the nature of the thoughts Fanuilh sent into his head. They were just that—thoughts, without any emotional content. He had never realized just how important the voice was in conveying feeling. Fanuilh's thoughts could not reveal pain or humor or sadness, only information.

Did the little dragon feel emotion?

The tasks it had set out for Liam were relatively simple and, apart from nursing the dragon back to health, would take very little time. It seemed a small thing to do, and when the nursing was over it would teach Liam to close off his mind, and maybe other things of greater value. It seemed a fair bargain, if the dragon could be trusted.

He reasoned all this out on the long walk back to Southwark, through the still-damp pasturage and stubbled fields. The sun was two hours above the horizon before he reached the city, hanging weak and watery in the fall sky, lending no warmth. It was chilly, and he felt dirty and hungry again. He decided to return to his garret before searching out the Aedile.

Walking up the steep hill to his lodgings, he realized that the pain in his ankle was lessening, and he could place more weight on it. He stopped in the street and examined his boot. There were two punctures the size of large nails in the tough leather. He scowled, wondering what sort of holes had been left in his flesh.

Once in his rooms, he called the landlady for hot water. She brought it up to him in a bucket, with an indulgent expression.

"Overmuch wine, Master Rhenford?" she asked, arching an eyebrow and grinning. "I thought scholars never indulged."

He exaggerated a frown and shooed her away. Sitting in the chair, he tenderly tugged off the punctured boot and checked his ankle, prepared to wash away a crust of blood and bandage a wound.

His ankle was clean, and only two small, circular scars indicated where Fanuilh had bitten him. He gave a short whistle, shook his head, and stripped to wash.

Refreshed by the hot water and feeling much less sick, he dressed in clean tunic and long breeches and felt ready to find the Aedile. He snatched a warm cloak from a peg on the wall and went out.

The Duke in whose lands Southwark lay was a great believer in the very old ways of Taralon. The title Aedile was taken from the language the Seventeen Houses brought with them to the land; so all titles used to be, before the last king of House Quintus died childless and the throne fell to lesser lines.

Even in Liam's Midlands, where they prided themselves on maintaining the old customs, such a man would have been titled colloquially, called Sheriff, or Constable. But Southwark's Duke held to the old ways, and the man was called Aedile.

It impressed Liam, this respect for the days when Taralon was strong under the Seventeen Houses.

He found the Aedile at home, directed there by a member of the Guard who was hurrying home from his shift. It was a small house on the fringes of the rich quarter, neat and well maintained, though somehow out of place beside the larger houses of merchants and rich tradesmen.

A bald servant reluctantly let him in, and bade him wait in a spartan parlor.

A bachelor, Liam thought, noting the decorations— swords and armor, a few hand-drawn maps of the city, the worn but comfortable-looking furniture. He knew little of the Aedile except his name, and a reputation for tough but fair dealing. He had heard that Coeccias would rather break up a tavern brawl with his own fists than take the brawlers into the Duke's court.

Nothing in the Aedile's appearance contradicted his reputation. He was short and broad, heavily muscled, with a thick mane of tangled black hair hanging down below his shoulders. Water beaded in his untrimmed beard, annoyance in his small eyes. Veins and scars ridged the hand with which he curtly waved Liam to a seat.

"Your name, sirrah? And what business," he grated, "that needs must break my breaking fast?"

The Aedile held a buttered piece of bread in his hand, and crumbs dotted his simple black tunic.

"Rhenford, Aedile Coeccias, Liam Rhenford. And there has been a death."

Coeccias laughed loudly. "Come, Liam Rhenford, death is commoner than cheap bawds, and those are very common in Southwark. Surely my breakfast is worth more than mere death!"

"Not mere death, Aedile," Liam contradicted politely, still standing, "but murder. The wizard Tarquin Tanaquil has been murdered."

"Has he? In truth? Now that—*that* might be worth more than my breakfast. That might, in truth."

Liam explained the circumstances, avoiding any mention of Fanuilh, and watched Coeccias take it all in, suitably sober, nodding. When he had finished his brief account, the Aedile nodded firmly once more.

"Well, it seems there's more in it than in my breakfast. I must see the body. Y'have a horse?" Liam nodded. "Good. Collect it, and meet me at the city gate."

"Wait a moment, Aedile. Shouldn't we have a ghost witch present?"

"Aye, that we should." Coeccias paused and regarded him strangely. "It'll little like Mother Japh to be dragged out of her house this early, but we should. I'll fetch her."

The burly man bustled him out of the house into the street, and strode off towards the heart of the city. Liam turned towards the stable where he kept his horse.

It was only a few moments before Diamond was saddled and ready, and Liam was mounted before he thought of his appointment with Lady Necquer. He called the stable lad over and offered him a small sum to take his regrets to the merchant's wife. The dirty boy grinned hugely at the amount and dashed off without a word.

Shaking his head, Liam spurred his mount towards the city gate.

He had a suspicion that Coeccias was not the man to find Tarquin's murderer, unless it could be done easily. And he feared it would not be easy. Honest and competent as the Aedile might be when it came to keeping sailors in line and patrolling the streets at night, Liam did not think he could pry secrets out of Tarquin's corpse.

Which, he further thought, was a shame, since there was no one else in authority to pursue the matter, and he already liked the blunt Aedile.

Southwark had no wall; the steep inland sides of the rise on which the city sat and the jagged Teeth seaward had always been considered protection enough. So it had no gates to speak of, but the beginning of the track to the east that led past Tarquin's cove was marked by two standing columns of worn gray stone, and this was called the city gate.

Liam arrived there before Coeccias and waited on his mount beside one of the pitted stone columns, watching the traffic of farmers' carts and horsemen that straggled along the muddy track.

He had waited far longer than he thought necessary, and for the tenth time was about to go back into the city to look for Coeccias when the Aedile's voice called to him.

"Liam Rhenford! Hark, man!"

Coeccias now wore a tabard over his black tunic, gray linen emblazoned with the Duke's three red foxes, and he rode a mare that looked worn down beside Liam's snorting roan. Two mounted Guardsmen carrying upright spears flanked him, the Duke's foxes on gray badges sewn to the shoulders of their boiled leather cuirasses. Behind them, astride a wall-eyed pony, was an ancient woman bundled in shapeless, faded robes, her face wrinkled as an old apple.

"The ghost witch," Coeccias said, when he noticed Liam's glance. "Mother Japh. This is the man who found the corpse, Mother."

The old woman snorted and mumbled.

"More like the fool saw the master in a trance; he *is* a wizard, all said." Her voice was no more than a whisper, but Liam caught it.

"It may well have been a trance, Mother," he said politely, "but I was not aware wizards cast spells with daggers in their chests."

The woman sniffed indignantly, and Liam arched an eyebrow at the Aedile, who, it seemed, could not decide whether to laugh or frown. He settled for taking charge.

"We'd best to't, then."

He booted his mare into a walk, and the Guardsmen followed suit.

CHAPTER 3

"NO SPIRITS," THE wrinkled old woman announced in a soft voice, returning to the entrance hall, where Liam and the Aedile waited.

They had waited for her judgement for over an hour while she wandered around the house, humming a little tune to herself, her bright, birdlike gaze darting here and there. She passed through the entrance hall several times, each time favoring Liam with an unpleasant look.

After Liam had satisfied Coeccias that Tarquin was indeed dead, the Aedile had drawn him out into the entrance hall and nodded to Mother Japh, who began her work.

"We mustn't disturb the witch while she searches for spirits," he whispered.

"How does she do it?" Liam whispered back, wondering.

The Aedile shrugged and spoke nonchalantly, his hand resting lightly on the hilt of his shortsword. "Truth, I don't know. But if Tarquin's sprite's here, angered or hot on revenge, she'll feel it, and it may be she can learn something from him."

Liam had never heard of a ghost witch, and the idea interested him. If she could speak with Tarquin's ghost, she might be able to find his killer. He studied the witch closely whenever she appeared.

The two Guardsmen stayed on the stone veranda despite the chill wind off the sea, which the watery sun did nothing to relieve. Coeccias had grumbled irritably when they silently took up their posts, but he did not argue with them.

"And as no ghosts haunt the pile," the witch went on, "and no sprites linger, angry or the like, it follows that the killer's not here."

When the witch had rendered her judgement, she suddenly offered Liam a warm smile, and Coeccias scowled. Liam started and flushed red. He turned on the Aedile.

"You thought *I* did it? You thought *I* killed him?"

Coeccias scowled fiercely at the old woman, who offered him a placid smile. "I suspected, but——"

Liam cut him off angrily. "Then why would I fetch you? Why would I tell you, if I did it?"

"Easy, man, don't rate me. Many's the man's covered his deed thus, and I was only making sure. And y'are Liam Rhenford, are you not?"

"So?" He could not believe the man had suspected him. He prepared to revise the friendly opinion he had devised of the Aedile.

"Truth, it's known that you had traffic with the wizard, more traffic than anyone in Southwark ever had, and who else was there to suspect? And you'd never've known what I thought, if this foolish old woman had kept a still tongue!" He scowled again at the witch, and Liam stalked away, fuming.

A touch on his arm brought him around, and he glared down into Mother Japh's wrinkled, beaming face.

"Take no affront, boy. I thought you'd done it, too. You've an innocent visage," she said, "and that's the worst mark against a man that I know."

Liam did not reply; Tarquin had once said something like that to him. They had been discussing a question of history; Liam had made a point he felt was particularly telling, and the old wizard had begun to laugh. "Get you a beard, Rhenford," he had said. "None'll believe so innocent a face."

"And now, Aedile Coeccias, it likes me to go home, if you can spare one of your frightened soldiers to take me there."

Coeccias shook his head and dispatched one of the Guardsmen to escort the ghost witch back to Southwark. When he returned to the entrance hall, Liam was still thinking over what Mother Japh had said, and how it echoed Tarquin's words.

"She hit the mark, Liam Rhenford. Y'are too innocent for your good."

"Perhaps if I got a hideous scar, or lost an eye and wore a patch I'd be better off, eh?" he asked sarcastically.

Coeccias laughed and clapped Liam on the shoulder, and his anger slowly dissolved. He gave a small smile.

"A scar, a patch! Aye, those'd serve!" The Aedile laughed a little more and went on, still amused. "Unfortunately, Mother Japh's rare wrong, and I can't clap you in for the murder. Which means there's nothing for it but to try and find the killer. We'll search the house."

He led the way with Liam trailing curiously in his wake, eager to explore more of the house. The Aedile questioned him as they went, gleaning details of his relationship with the wizard.

"And you've no idea who might have wanted him dead?"

"None. I didn't really know him well—only from swimming off his breakwater, and the occasional talk. No clues there, I'm afraid."

They stood in Tarquin's library, just beyond the parlor. Books lined every wall; there were no windows in the walls, though a small glass cupola in the roof let in a dim light. Coeccias gave Liam an incredulous look when he mentioned swimming.

"You swam? In the sea?"

"Yes," Liam said.

"No one swims in the sea!"

"I do," Liam said simply, offering no explanation, and the Aedile shrugged in disbelief.

For a moment they stood quietly and marveled at the innumerable books, each impressed in his own way. Liam paced along the shelves, running a finger down leatherbound spines, checking the titles inscribed or painted there. Coeccias stood directly beneath the cupola, turning around in a circle and taking it all in.

"And when did you say you found him?"

"Last night. I—"

"Last night?" the Aedile snapped. "Why didn't you fetch me then?"

Liam goggled for a moment and started to tell about
Fanuilh. A thought stopped him.

I was drunk . . .

"I was drunk, you see," he finally said, embarrassed.
"And when I saw him, I, well, I fell, and hit my head."

Show him the bump.

"I have a bump, you see." He fingered the back of his
head, and noticed for the first time a distinct swelling at
the back of his head. "I didn't wake up until early this
morning."

"Cupped, eh?" The Aedile smiled and Liam relaxed,
though his face was still red with embarrassment. "I suspect
that's the only thing that'd make a man bother a wizard in
the night."

He left the library, and went across the hall and down the
corridor to the bedroom. Liam followed, angry, wondering
if the dragon had known they would suspect him.

I thought they might, came the response, hard in his mind.
He stopped in the corridor. *That is why I told you to bring
the ghost witch.*

Coeccias paused before the door to the workroom, looking back at Liam.

"Will y'attend me?"

Liam shook himself and hurried down the hall. The Aedile
was looking at the table where Fanuilh lay, its slitted yellow
eyes staring balefully back at him.

"Now whatever's this? The wizard's pet?"

He stepped lightly over to the table and slowly extended
his hand towards the dragon's neck, trying to appear open
and friendly. Fanuilh followed the Aedile's hand, swiveling
its head as Coeccias reached for its neck, fingers bent to
scratch. At the last moment the dragon snapped weakly,
and Coeccias withdrew in shock.

"Little beast!" he exclaimed, rubbing his hand as if the
dragon had bitten him, though Liam knew it had missed.

"It's a shame the little creature can't speak. He might tell
us everything."

"Aye," Coeccias muttered, then threw a cursory glance
around the room. "Naught disturbed here," he said, and

left abruptly. Liam stayed a moment, looking at the dragon. Slowly, as the Aedile had, he extended his hand; Fanuilh let him scratch, arching its back in pleasure against Liam's nails. The softness of the scales was still strange to him, and he rubbed them curiously for a moment. No thoughts came, so he patted it once more and left.

There was only one other room, with a cupola like the library but wide windows as well. Motes danced in the weak beams pouring in.

"Anything missing?" Coeccias asked.

"I don't know. I've never been in here before."

Strange objects filled the white-plastered room, hanging from the walls and arranged in free-standing cases of dark, polished wood with glass tops. A collection of thin, elaborately carved wands on a bed of felt in one case; coins with inscriptions Liam could not read in another; jewelry of strange design—rings, bracelets, phylacteries—in another. On the walls, a small tapestry the size of a hearthrug, depicting a stylized eagle soaring powerfully over purple mountains; a stringless, round-bodied lute hung by its neck; a sword and shield, simple and battered, beside a horn chased in silver.

"Truth," the Aedile said, turning to go, "it seems there's naught stolen, so I needn't bother the fences."

Liam reluctantly followed him. "Eh?"

"I needn't bother the fences." Liam's questioning look remained, so Coeccias went on. "Naught stolen, Liam Rhenford. So checking the fences won't discover the murderer."

"Oh, yes, yes. I see." His mind was still on the strange objects on the walls and in the cases, and he wished the Aedile had stayed there longer.

"So, with no thievery, we've only personality. Did anyone hate him? Hate him enough to stick him, that is?"

Liam shook his head. "I wouldn't know. I don't think he knew many people in Southwark—except me, that is."

"Oh, I think many people knew of him, if you see, and there's tales enough of some having dealings with him. I'll see about that, and see if he has a testament."

"A testament?"

"A will." Coeccias instantly supplied the synonym, interpreting his hesitation as confusion over the southern dialect. "He might have left one, registered with the Duke's clerk. Some do, you know."

Liam said nothing; he did not think Tarquin was the kind to leave a will.

"And then there's the interring. Someone'll have to bury him." The Aedile looked expectantly at him.

I will take care of it.

"I'll take care of it," Liam said suddenly, paling at the intrusion. "We spoke of how he'd want it once. Theoretically, of course. I never thought . . ."

The Aedile's expectation turned to puzzlement, and Liam fidgeted. The dragon was arranging things in a way he did not understand, prompting him along paths he couldn't follow. But Coeccias misunderstood his reaction.

"How old are you, Liam Rhenford?"

"Thirty," he responded.

"Thirty," the Aedile mused. He was easily ten years older than Liam, and the harsh lines around his eyes softened. "And never seen a corpse ere this?"

Liam frowned. He had, many times. More times, he guessed, and deaths far worse, than the Aedile had.

Go along.

"No," he said shakily.

"Shall I leave my man to help you?"

No.

"No, I think . . ." He paused, with a convincing gulp. "I think I can manage."

"Well enough," Coeccias said at last. "I'll be about my business, then, if y'are sure."

Liam nodded briefly.

The Aedile nodded as well and went for the door, stopping to ask where Liam was lodging.

"In case I hear anything, or need to speak with you, if you see."

When Liam told him, the Aedile took his leave, collecting the other Guardsman. Liam went out onto the veranda and watched them wend their way up the narrow path. When they had topped the cliff, he went back in.

Fanuilh still lay on the table in the workroom, looking up at him serenely.

The scratching was good.

"And I suppose you'd like some more?" Liam asked sarcastically, but he put out his hand and scratched the clothlike scales. "How much of that did you know would happen?"

I anticipated a great deal of it. The dragon stretched pleasurably, if stiffly, underneath his hand, the simple, happy motion at odds with the cold thoughts.

"Why did you make me lie about hitting my head?"

You know.

Liam was surprised to find he did know. Coeccias had called the dragon Tarquin's pet; he did not understand about familiars, and if Liam had tried to explain he would have presumed that—

"You didn't want him thinking we'd killed him together, you and I."

It would undoubtedly have occurred to him, and it would have made things difficult.

"So now he thinks I'm a weak fop, a man who turns squeamish at the sight of blood. One who's never seen a corpse before."

Do you really care?

Wordlessly, Liam shook his head, and pulled his hand away from the dragon, struck by a thought. He imagined Fanuilh, a dagger stuck in his claws, hovering over Tarquin's sleeping body.

A thought crashed down on the image, blotting it out.

That is foolishness. I could do no such thing.

"Of course not," Liam said hastily, stepping away from the table. It was foolishness, after all. The dragon could not have known he would come along, that there would be another soul for it to share.

There are things to do. You must fulfill our bargain.

"Yes." He shook his head, scattering the shards of his image. "You'll teach me how to keep you out?"

Yes, and more.

"And all I have to do is nurse you to health?"

And the other.

"The other," Liam repeated blankly, then remembered: "The one you said you'd tell me when they'd gone?"

Yes.

"What is it?"

You must find whoever killed Master Tanaquil.

"Find the killer? That's what Coeccias is for," he said doubtfully.

You do not think the Duke's man can do it.

"I don't think he can, no. But if he can't do it, how could I? That's foolishness." He straightened and walked over to the model, his back to the dragon.

You knew Master Tanaquil better than the Duke's man. I knew him better. Between us, we can imagine who might have done it, and find the person. Besides . . . you have done this before.

"Only a few times, and . . ." Liam whirled. "How did you know that?"

We are one. Your memories are mine, and mine would be yours, if you knew how. I know your thoughts everywhere.

There was no special emphasis on the last, but Liam imagined it, and blushed.

"You know what I was thinking, in the city?"

Of course.

He shook his head, trying to drive the thought out. "No matter. Those were a long time ago, and the circumstances were different. I was very lucky."

Nonetheless, you have searched out murderers before. And you think you carry Luck with you.

That much was true, and that was how he thought of it—Luck, personified, like a deity who watched over him. And he had, once or twice, unraveled mysteries.

"Even granting that I thought I could find the killer, why? Why do you want me to? Why bargain for that?"

For the first time, Fanuilh's thought swirled, shapeless. It took what seemed a long time to form.

I do not know.

"What would we do when we found out?"

Again, the thought coalesced slowly.

I do not know.

"Give the murderer to the Aedile?"

I suppose so.

Liam wondered if the dragon was harboring dreams of vengeance, and blushed again when Fanuilh responded.

I do not think so. It is simply something I feel must be done. Master Tanaquil was good to me.

Liam sighed, turning back to the model of Southwark, losing his gaze in the intricate details. He thought of Tarquin, and their all too few conversations. The man had been interesting, if somewhat reserved. Pleasant in his way, seemingly harmless, an eccentric recluse claiming wizardry. But he had made the Teeth disappear, and he had a room filled with strange artifacts that Liam wanted to explore.

I can show you how they all work. They can be yours. Is it a bargain?

He sighed again, leaning forward, resting his hands carefully on the edge of the model.

"See if you can't stay out of my head for a few moments, will you?"

He had already decided to do it, he realized. If for no other reason than that the old man had let him swim off his breakwater. And if the dragon was lying, in any way, about anything, well, then . . .

But he did not finish the thought. He simply let it swirl away, broken off, unsure of what he would do.

"Very well, it's a bargain. I'll need to know everything you can remember about Tarquin."

Four hours later, as the pale sun sank down towards the horizon, Liam rode the muddy track back to Southwark. His stomach was queasy again, and though the ache in his ankle had not returned, he found the lump on the back of his head throbbing.

He had questioned the dragon closely for a long time, dredging up every detail of anyone who visited Tarquin. He was surprised at how many people besides himself had made the trip out from the city and down the cliff path, and, at the same time, how little Fanuilh knew about his master's business. The dragon could remember some names and most faces, and snatches of conversation, but apparently Tarquin had made a practice of excluding his familiar from his thoughts and his dealings. It seemed strange to Liam, to hide yourself from one you had voluntarily chosen to share your soul, but Fanuilh had not thought it out of the ordinary.

It had taken very little time to bury the wizard. He and Tarquin had never discussed their preferences for interment, but Fanuilh assured him that the old man had had no preference, and that simple burial would be enough.

Liam had gone up the beach and found a spot close by the cliffs where the sand was heavier and more like dirt. Using a board, he scooped a deep narrow hole, cursing as the sand ran back into the grave. Finally, sweating through his tunic despite the cold wind off the sea, he decided it was deep enough and returned to the house for the body.

He wrapped it in the scarlet blanket and gingerly put his hands beneath it. Though the old man had been scrawny, his corpse was far heavier than Liam expected, but the stiffness was familiar from several battlefields. He managed to get the body to the grave, cursing his stupidity in choosing a site so far from the house.

When he finally had Tarquin in his resting place, he stood for a moment, looking down at the red-wrapped bundle. It looked pitifully small at the bottom of the sandy trench, like a bright toy lost or forgotten by a careless child. The smell of brine and rotting seaweed filled his nostrils, stinging and cold.

Liam had spent so long among strangers, peoples with strange gods and alien rites, that he could not think of whom to pray to, or how to pray. Undecided, he thought of nothing, listening instead to the slap of waves against the breakwater, and the rumble of the sea beyond.

"I suppose I can only . . ." he finally said, and left the sentence unfinished.

It did not take as long to shovel the sand back in.

He went back to the house only long enough to take his leave of the dragon.

You do not have to go back to the city, the dragon thought as he stood in the doorway of the workroom.

"I can't stay here," he muttered.

It would be easier.

"The answers you want are in Southwark. It'll be easier if I stay there."

There is that. But you will eventually stay here.

Something in the thought—something imagined, Liam said to himself, though he felt it had been there—implied certainty.

"It's not mine," he said. "I'll be back tomorrow morning." With that, he walked away, and the dragon thought nothing more at him.

It was cold, as the year crept into its old age, and Liam folded his cloak closely about him. A procession barred his way briefly as he entered the city; he sat his horse patiently, waiting for it to pass. There was a small number of shaven-headed acolytes in pure white robes, carrying blank wax tablets and chanting sonorously. A gaggle of lay worshippers followed, heads bowed, and behind them came a crowd of solemn children. Liam wondered what it was all about, and then vaguely remembered that a number of processions in honor of the Goddess were supposed to be performed before Uris-tide. He noted that the omnipresent beggars were silent as the procession went past, and that the one-armed man who squatted in the gutter by him only rose to grasp his stirrup and moan when the marchers were out of sight. Tossing the wretch a coin, Liam spurred Diamond away.

He stopped at a stall that sold hot foods after he had stabled Diamond, and bought sausages and steaming bread, thinking of the magic oven in Tarquin's villa. He pushed the thought away. He hoped the sausages would stay hot until he got home, and hurried to his garret.

They did, and the grease had soaked into the bread. He thought they tasted wonderful, after he had carefully cleared all the papers and books off his table. He savored every spiced bite, and sucked his fingers when he was done.

Outside his window, lights showed in some of the darkened streets, flickering torches and lanterns marking inns or temples; orange flames marched purposefully up and down lanes, and he thought of the Guard making their dusk patrol, checking doors and shooing beggars off the streets.

Sighing wearily, he washed his hands in the cold water left from the morning and set about sharpening his quill and preparing ink. Then, with several blank sheets of paper before him, he set to work outlining what Fanuilh had told him.

In the week before Tarquin had died, four people had visited him. It seemed like a large number, but when Liam thought of him as a wizard and not as an eccentric recluse, the visits did not seem so strange. An apothecary Tarquin had known well; a handsome young man who might have been a minstrel; a merchant of high standing with a bodyguard of toughs; a woman heavily cloaked. He dutifully wrote them down along with all that the familiar could recall about them, filling a sheet with his neat, cramped handwriting. All might have an innocent reason for seeking the help of a wizard, dangerous as that was held to be.

"Ask a wizard's help to find silver," ran an old saying that his landlady had sententiously quoted him, "and be prepared to pay him gold."

Liam wondered who made up those sayings, and whether he might be the one who had put a dagger in Tarquin's chest.

Shaking his head fiercely to clear away the thought, he turned his attention to the list he had made, and chose the apothecary to begin with. Fanuilh said the two had had a fight, or at least a very loud discussion, and that the druggist had stalked away grumbling darkly.

It seemed the best lead, not only because of the argument, but because the apothecary was the only person of whose name Fanuilh was sure. Ton Viyescu.

Tomorrow, Liam thought, *I'll go see Ton Viyescu. And what will I say to him? 'Pardon, Master Druggist, but did you murder Tarquin Tanaquil? Or perhaps I should put it this way: are you missing any daggers?'*

He pursed his lips sourly. Fanuilh had read his mind correctly—he *had* searched out a mystery or two, but on those few occasions he had had authority. He had been allowed to ask questions, and piece together facts, and there had been armed men to back him up.

Cursing, he suddenly recalled the dagger. He had not looked at it closely, and it had not been there when he buried Tarquin. Coeccias must have taken it, though Liam had not seen him do it. His respect for the Aedile went up a notch.

I'll have to see it, to know if it's important. And how do I do that? 'Excuse me, Aedile, but could I look at that knife? You see, I've lost mine, and I was wondering if the murderer might have picked it up . . . '

He thought of telling the dragon he could not do it, simply could not search out the murderer, but then he remembered its cold eyes and hard-edged thoughts. Fanuilh would never let him out of the bargain.

A knock interrupted his mental wanderings, and he strode slowly over to the door. It was his landlady.

"Your leave, Master Liam. I knew not you were in, or I'd have brought this sooner. A message from a lady, Master," she added. With a meaningful look and a knowing smile, she held out a folded, sealed piece of paper. He snatched it, almost but not quite rudely, his mouth narrowing at her insinuations.

"Thank you," he growled, and began to shut the door. She would have stopped him, but he stopped himself. "Mistress Dorcas," he began, thinking to ask her what she knew of Ton Viyescu.

"Aye?" Her very eagerness dissuaded him. She was a decent woman, he knew, but entirely too given to gossip.

"No, nothing. Thank you." He smiled warmly and firmly shut the door over her protests.

The letter, when he had finally stopped peering curiously at the intricate wax seal, was from Lady Necquer, forgiving his absence and asking him to come the next day. There was a note of pleading to it, he thought, as though she desperately wanted him to come. She even named the hour, and the comment she added about being deeply insulted if he failed to arrive might have been light, but hinted to him at something more serious. Not that she'd be insulted, but . . .

"Perhaps she's fallen in love with you, you handsome rogue," he said aloud. "Liam Rhenford, breaker of hearts."

He laughed harshly at himself, and felt better for it.

Still, there was something about the letter that made him decide to keep the appointment. The hour she had set was in the afternoon, and he could speak to Viyescu and make whatever other cautious inquiries he needed to in the morning.

As Liam lay in his bed later, trying to sleep, faces circled in his head, their clamoring keeping him awake.

Coeccias, Mother Japh, the merchant Necquer and his wife, his landlady, Tarquin and Fanuilh. In the four months since he had arrived in Southwark, he had counted a day eventful if he had gone to Tarquin's to swim. And suddenly he was drunk at parties, receiving invitations from rich women, investigating murders and losing part of his soul.

It was a great deal for him to think about, after four months of isolation. The faces pressed around him, a rabble of voices and new memories. And above them all, for some reason, loomed the diminutive dragon, and its slitted cat's eyes, and solid thoughts like bricks in his head.

Liam was a long time getting to sleep.

CHAPTER 4

EVEN AS LONG as Liam was getting to sleep, he woke shortly after sunrise, the noise of the stirring day rising up through his window. Carters shouted, it seemed, directly below, wagons creaking and oxen bellowing for the sole purpose of waking him. Children had gathered as well, their high-pitched games designed with his ruined sleep in mind.

Grumbling, he pulled himself from his pallet and used the slight dampness at the bottom of his water bucket to wash the film from his eyes. When he felt he could see sufficiently, he searched for and lit a candle.

There was little light in the garret; the window was small and the sky clouded over, filled to bursting with big-bellied rain clouds.

"Rain," he muttered miserably. "And I had such hopes of a ride in the countryside." The joke made him smile a little, though, and he picked up the bucket and went down the stairs two at a time, whistling by the time he reached the bottom.

His landlady was not up, as he knew she would not be, but there was a kettle heating in the huge kitchen hearth. A thin, gray-looking girl, the landlady's only servant, froze when he came down, whistling a sea chantey. Her eyes bulged, and he realized he had not put on his tunic.

Liam let his whistling slide off and grinned wolfishly at her; she took one look at his scarred torso and his whipcord muscles before fleeing wordlessly into another room.

What would Lady Necquer say if I arrived shirtless?

His grin widened, so wolfish the poor drudge would

undoubtedly have fainted, and he filled his bucket with hot water from the kettle.

Back in his room, he scrubbed himself thoroughly. While he dried, he scraped away the thin growth of stubble on his face with a pumice stone, wincing at the abrasion. He thought of Tarquin's comment on his beardlessness, and Mother Japh's.

"Hang them," he growled, and tried his wolfish grin again, liking it. Dressing in his best, a forest green tunic with white piping and matching breeches, he felt better than he had in a long while.

Since he had come to Southwark, he realized, and swiped at the dirt on his high boots, managing to bring a shine to a small circle of leather. He looked at the rest of the muddy, stained bootleather, and shook his head.

Not good enough to shine my boots, but better than in a long while.

His hangover was gone, the lump on the back of his head much smaller than the day before. And he had something to do. Not since long before he came to Southwark had he had something worth doing, and the thing he had come to do—his book—had simply not happened. Now he was in the middle of something. He had little idea how to go about it, but it was good to wake with a purpose.

Filled with the wonder of this small discovery, he belted up his tunic and took money from his seachest to fill his purse. As he put the money away, he saw a small knife in a plain sheath and hesitated only a moment before picking it up. The last time he had tried to solve a mystery, a dagger had proven useful.

Liam closed the chest, locked it, and hung the knife on his belt. He put his hand on the hilt and tried the wolf's grin again, laughed at himself, and went downstairs.

This time he did not startle the drudge, who looked at him with relief, as though in his fine tunic he fit the mold of a respectable scholar much better than he had when half-naked and whistling dirty sailors' songs. He did not smile at all when he asked her if she knew where the druggist Viyescu's shop could be found.

She did not, but timidly suggested he try Northfield or Auric's Park, two sections of the artisans' quarter. He smiled very gently at the poor girl and thanked her politely before leaving. He switched over to the wolf's grin as soon as he was out the door, and chuckled to himself as he walked the few blocks to the stables.

The lad he had sent with his message the day before was not there, but a boy who might have been his brother was more than willing to carry a message for him.

"Tell the Lady Necquer I'll be glad to wait on her at the hour she suggested," he said, and then when the boy dashed off down the street, "Hey, boy! The message can wait until you've fetched my horse!"

When the shamefaced boy had retrieved his mount and repeated the message to his satisfaction, he sent him running again, and set off himself for the city gate.

The fat, slate-gray clouds put him in mind of winter, though the breeze from the sea was not very chilly. He remembered his previous winter, spent in a land where the sun shone hot and full all the time, and even the rains had seemed dazzlingly bright. He rode past pastures of cold, colorless grass and fields shorn clean, stripped naked for the coming winter, and smiled. It would be his first winter in Taralon in a long time.

Fanuilh was waiting for him, still on the table in the workroom. The villa was warm, though no fires burned. Liam noticed for the first time that there were no fireplaces where they could burn. This was more of Tarquin's magic, he realized, still working even after the wizard's death. Liam had not known magic could work that way.

The spells are powerful, as was Master Tanaquil.

The dragon was looking at him, and again he found it difficult to connect the placid serpentine face with the stone-block thought in his head.

"You're up early," he said cheerily, trying to dispel some of the silence that echoed loudly along the gleaming wood and clean white walls.

I need little sleep. Would you get me food?

"Raw meat it is, little master. By your leave," Liam said,

bowing deeply before the dragon. It stared up at him with what Liam guessed passed for curiosity, and he hurried off to the kitchen, thinking hard of uncooked steak.

As he watched Fanuilh neatly snap up mouthfuls of meat, he paced eagerly around the room, stopping and starting as one thing and another struck his imagination.

"What are all these things in the jars?" He was looking at one in particular that might have been the preserved head of a dog. He shuddered and moved on, not waiting for an answer.

You are very light today.

"Well, my little master, if you could read my mind, you would know why."

Yes. You have accepted the bargain fully. You are eager to begin. I thought you would be.

"Did you?" This sobered Liam slightly, and he paused before the tiny model of Southwark.

You carry Luck with you, and are checking to make sure you have not lost it.

He laughed out loud.

"True enough! I'm like a man come from the market, patting his purse to see if it still holds his gold. Only I can't feel for my Luck—I have to prove it the hard way."

Fanuilh chewed placidly while Liam chuckled over its judgement. When the last of the meat was gone, it rolled slowly over on its back and exposed the dull gold of its belly.

Scratch? it thought. Liam could almost see the question mark, like black ink in his head. He hastened over and rubbed the dragon's stomach with his knuckles. The feeling like ridged cloth fascinated him.

You will see the druggist today?

"Viyescu? Yes, he seemed the proper place to begin."

What will you say to him?

Liam frowned, concentrating on evening out the area of his scratching, switching to his fingernails. "I don't know," he said at last, flashing his wolf's grin. "I'll find out when I get there, I suppose."

Do not smile like that at him.

He laughed again, and the dragon squirmed impatiently beneath his hand, indicating that it had had enough scratching.

"If Your Highness has had enough, I'll be on my way," he said.

Do not smile like that at him, the dragon thought again, and Liam threw a groan at the ceiling and left quickly.

He frightened his roan by leaping heavily into the saddle and kicking hard with his heels, urging the horse up the narrow cliff path at a fast trot.

He frightened himself with his own high spirits. With the cold and the shorn fields and the lowering gray clouds, with a dragon holding part of his soul and his only acquaintance dead, he should have been depressed.

Instead, he was eager to begin his search.

Viyescu's shop was on the landward side of the city, in a quiet section of the artisans' quarter called Northfield. The rise on which Southwark sat was steep on the south, so that the houses of the rich quarter rose above each other on streets like mountain paths; but the slope was far gentler to the north, and the streets of the artisans' quarter were broader and less steeply inclined. Cobblestoned in the same black stone as the rest of the city, they nonetheless seemed brighter because the houses had fewer stories and more of the gray vault of sky showed beyond the peaked gables.

A helpful washerwoman and a colorful sign directed him to the apothecary. Above the scrubbed doorstep hung a yellow board on which a skillful hand had painted a wreath of ivy over a steaming thurible. The brand was heated by a stooping woman whose breath was flames.

Uris, Liam remembered. Though Uris-tide was not celebrated in the Midlands, he knew enough of her from the sea, where she was honored as the Giver of Direction, the inspirator of navigators and charters. He also remembered her as the patron of alchemists, herbalists, and druggists, though most of those that he knew gave her only lip service.

Ton Viyescu, it seemed, gave her more credit than that.

"A religious man," Liam said to himself and, assuming a grave expression, walked into the shop.

Viyescu looked almost exactly as he had expected, almost familiar in a tantalizing way Liam could not put his finger on, but the state of the shop was unexpectedly different. The druggist was short and gnarled like the roots he sold, with a magnificently tangled expanse of bushy black beard flecked with gray creeping up his cheeks and endangering his tiny, gleaming eyes. He wore a stained leather apron tied over equally stained fustian that might once have been white but was now an ugly yellow-gray. His hands, composed almost entirely of huge knuckles, rested impatiently on the wooden counter. He stood behind it like it was a wall and Liam a spear-shaking raider.

The shop, however, was not the musty, disordered mess he had expected from his other experiences with apothecaries. It was crowded, but each thing seemed to occupy its proper place. Herbs hung in bunches from dowel racks, the spacing between each leafy bundle exact; roots in open boxes filled shelves, their names carefully painted in clear letters on the shelf beneath them. Flasks, pottery jars and heavy glass decanters lined the higher shelves, ranked like soldiers and labeled like the roots. The druggist's protective counter was bare and clean; behind him ran another counter, on which were neatly arranged the tools of his trade. Several mortars with pestles in attendance, a tiny brazier with glowing coals, a thick-bottomed glass beaker for boiling, and a rack of glass and copper tubes of different lengths, jointed and beveled so they could be attached one to the other.

A precise man, Liam thought, as well as religious. It came to him where he had seen Viyescu before: he had been in the procession the day before, at the front of the lay worshippers.

"You are the apothecary?" He managed to achieve a decent Torquay accent, thick and musical.

"I am Ton Viyescu," the druggist growled, eyeing him rudely, and Liam assumed it was his normal manner. His accent marked him from the far northwest, a harsh land by any standards, and not likely to breed politeness.

"I only ask because I have, well, I have important business, and I wish only to deal with a, well, with someone
who really knows."

Viyescu squinted suspiciously at him, his beady eyes
almost lost in wrinkles. "I know what there is to know
about herbs, Master . . . ?"

The question was so pointed that Liam could not ignore it.
"Cance," he answered. "Hierarch Cance, from Torquay." He
chose a religious title, and it seemed to affect the druggist.

"Ah, well, Hierarch, what can I do for you?" There were
no protests of humility, but the hunched man's attitude loos-
ened a little, and he stopped squinting and shifted his hands
slightly on the counter, indicating a willingness to serve, if
not an eagerness.

"You see, I came to Southwark to meet a man, a *wizard*"—he whispered the word, as though it were dangerous
in itself—"and now I find he is dead. Murdered." He nodded
somberly, but inwardly he cursed. The druggist was nodding
also, not the least surprised, although he seemed a little
puzzled.

"And who would this wizard be, Hierarch?"

"One Tarquin Tanaquil," Liam responded cautiously.
"Perhaps you knew him?"

"Oh, I knew him. I knew him well enough." His tone
indicated that the acquaintance had not been pleasant, and
there was something else, a change in his eyes, like the
shutting of a door.

"You sound as though you did not like him," Liam said,
but continued before the druggist could respond. "I ask, you
see, because he was engaged on, well, on certain works for
us that are of some importance. Uris-tide is almost upon
us, you know." He filled the last sentence with as much
importance as it could hold, and let it hang in the air of
the shop, competing for preeminence with the musty smell
of dried herbs.

"Hm. So it is," the druggist finally said, nodding himself.
"He did not seem the sort of man who would care much for
Uris-tide. A nonbeliever, he seemed to me, Hierarch."

"Ah, well, the ends of the gods are often served by those who do not know them," Liam said hastily.

"Still . . . Tanaquil was a strange tool for the gods, if you ask me. A filthy man, of filthy habits."

"How filthy? Evil? Did he serve the Darker Gods?"

"No, no, not that," the druggist said quickly, his hands finally leaving the counter to protest the accusation. "Simply not a godly man. A worldly man, like so many, given to his pleasures, and not much bound by the heavens' laws," he continued bitterly. "And proud, very proud. He would not listen to others. I meant nothing else."

"You knew him well, then?"

"Better than most, I suppose. We had reasons for dealings—I sold him certain roots he had difficulty attaining."

Liam gave a sigh of relief. "Then you knew of his business. Tell me, did he—" He got no further, stopped by Viyescu's dark scowl.

"I did not know his business, Hierarch," he said flatly.

"Oh." He did not need to fake disappointment, only a reason. "I had hoped . . . you see, the work he was engaged in was very important, and when I heard he was dead, I thought he might have confided in a colleague."

"We were not colleagues. He was a wizard; I am an apothecary. The two are not the same." Viyescu spoke coldly, crossing his arms firmly on his chest, but Liam sensed something beyond the distinctions of professional pride.

"I know, but there are no other wizards in this benighted city, and I thought, 'Who else would a wizard have dealings with?' and thus came to you. And when I saw Uris on your sign, I allowed myself to hope." He also allowed himself a small sigh.

Viyescu relented a little, letting his hands drop to the counter. "I am sorry, Hierarch, but my business with the wizard extended only to selling him certain roots, and occasionally procuring the rarer types for him. No more, Hierarch, no more."

"Yes, I see, I see." His head dropped, deep in troubled thought. "You wouldn't by any chance have sold him any Percin's Bane, would you?" Percin's Bane was very rare,

Liam knew, and only grew in the King's Range; he chose it because it was uncommon.

"No," Viyescu responded immediately. "There is no Percin's Bane in the south."

Liam waited, hoping the druggist would go on, but Viyescu showed no sign of continuing, so he shook his head resignedly and walked to the door. As he was opening it, the druggist's voice stopped him.

"May I ask, Hierarch, how you know Tanaquil was murdered?"

"I was there," Liam answered, and then hurried on: "At his house, yesterday. The morning, actually, after he had been killed. One of the Sheriff's men told me about it. I was quite shaken. The enchantment was so important to us." He let the door close and turned back, trying to inject innocence into his question. "Is the death not common knowledge? I would think the death of a wizard as powerful as Master Tanaquil would be instantly known."

"Tarquin was very reclusive. I doubt if half the town even knew he was alive."

"May I ask how you know of his death?" He arched an eyebrow politely, but Viyescu still stiffened.

"The Aedile—the Sheriff—told me of it when he came to question me. He apparently had the same thought as you."

Liam gnawed a knuckle worriedly. "I can only hope he was not killed by those who would stop our work. Tell me, had he any enemies? Perhaps among the foes of religion?"

Viyescu laughed harshly, like crunching gravel. "The foes of religion were least likely to be his enemies, Hierarch." He stopped and thought, weighing something, and then went on firmly. "Though I cannot imagine any others who would be. He was very jealous of his privacy, as I've said."

Considering this for a moment, Liam gnawed more. "Tell me, if you would, when did you see him last?"

"Only a week or so ago, Hierarch. I went to see him on an unimportant matter."

"I thought you only had business dealings with him?"

"Well," Viyescu said slowly, "yes, only business dealings. Yes." He tugged at his bushy beard, chewing a little at the end of his mustache. He was considering something of even greater importance than before, and finally spoke uneasily, choosing each word with care, measuring the effect on Liam. "There was a woman, really a girl only, who was in trouble." Liam assumed a questioning air, and the druggist went on reluctantly. "Caught in sin, Hierarch. Pregnant." He spit the distasteful word out.

"And so you went to see Master Tanaquil? I don't understand."

"The girl came to me, trying to buy an herb called santhract. It can destroy a pregnancy, Hierarch."

Liam meant only to show curiosity, but Viyescu seemed to misread his expression, and his cheeks burned red with anger beneath his upward-creeping beard.

"I do not sell this herb, Hierarch, and so I told her! I told her only to pray, but she cursed me, and said something about Tarquin, so I went to him to warn him of her sin." He spoke thickly, indignation and righteous anger and something else, maybe desperation, making him slightly frightening.

"You did right, Master Apothecary," Liam said softly.

"Thank you, Hierarch," Viyescu said, still angry, and Liam detected more disappointment than gratitude in the words. He murmured some thanks of his own and headed for the door.

In the street, with the thick door between him and the angry apothecary, he breathed a deep sigh of relief, and offered up an apology to Uris on her sign for impersonating one of her priests. Then he apologized to his fluttering stomach. Though his face felt cool and there was no sweat on his forehead, the back of his neck was flushed, and heat gathered in his armpits and at the small of his back.

His roan was skittish, smelling his disquiet as he swung up into the saddle, and he soothed the horse with a steady hand and a gentle, "Easy, Diamond, easy."

Damned horse is more upset than I am, and he didn't even pretend he was a priest. Which I'll never do again, he thought, urging the horse to a trot through the uncrowded streets.

Viyescu had not been particularly threatening, for all his gruffness and angry talk of sin, and the weird edge of desperation that had hung like smoke around him. But it was dangerous to pretend to be someone he was not, he decided. Though he was a relative stranger to the town, the possible complications were enormous.

Still, for his first attempt, the interview had yielded some results. A cursing girl, deep in sin, who muttered things about Tarquin. She was not on his list, and perhaps she should be.

After all, who might have gotten her pregnant?

He remembered an afternoon early in the summer, drying in the warm sun on the breakwater. The sound of laughter had roused him from his heat-induced torpor, and he had swiveled his head around to look at the stone veranda. Tarquin had been hugging a young woman, who was struggling with him and giggling. She pulled away finally with an embarrassed glance at Liam, and scurried up the path, holding her skirts high. And the old wizard had rubbed his hands briskly together, tipping Liam a lecherous wink before going inside again. It was before he and Tarquin had ever really spoken, and Liam had gone back to the sun thinking only that it was amazing for such an old man. But then, he was a wizard after all, and he had heard of spells. . . .

Who would risk killing a wizard?

An angry husband or father, or even the kind of woman who would try to buy santhract from a worshipper of Uris. Or a druggist who detested sin, and perhaps had a more personal relationship with the young woman than he wished to reveal.

It was not much more than speculation, Liam knew, a kind of daydreaming; but it might lead to something more, and it was the only clue he had.

Another thought struck him as he rode south out of Northfield, into the narrower, steeper streets of the poorer quarters, where his lodgings were. The Aedile had been there before him. He felt sure he knew far more than Coeccias did about Tarquin's doings, but the idea of having the blunt man precede him around town did little to quiet his stomach. And it was entirely possible that his name might be raised in the course of the Aedile's questioning, which would make his own investigation more difficult.

Being little known in Southwark might have meant he could continue to pretend to be someone he was not, though his own inclination was against it; but if someone caught him out because of something Coeccias had said, it could be dangerous. On the other hand, being little known also meant he knew little. If he had had more information about Viyescu, he might have gotten more out of him.

He tried to think who might supply that kind of information. Barkeeps and the like, of course, though they were often unreliable. His landlady was certainly a great gossip, but he *knew* she was unreliable, and gossip often ran both ways.

His stomach grumbled, and he realized it must be long past noon. There would be time to eat, he hoped, before his appointment with Lady Necquer.

Suddenly, the wolf's grin spread over his face. Lady Necquer very much wished to hear about all the places he had been, and he very much wished to hear about the place they were.

Perhaps they could help each other.

Liam had misjudged the time; it was only a little after midday when he stabled his horse, and he had almost two hours before he had to be at Necquer's home. He ate lightly at a tavern near his garret, taking his time, thinking of polite ways to question the merchant's wife about Southwark.

When he was done, he went back to his room and gathered up a few maps and some books. Then he set out on foot for the Point, climbing the steep streets with his papers tucked under his arm. Bells clanged faintly over the Duke's court, the sound muffled by the heavy storm clouds. A ragged bootblack squatted by the side of the road beside the ironbound door of a merchant, and Liam had the boy shine his boots, tossing him a coin far larger than the job deserved. The boy peered up at him for a moment with what seemed like scorn; Liam shrugged and strode away, up the hill towards Necquer's.

An elderly servant in a simple smock opened the door for him before he could knock, and led him through the house towards the stone porch at the rear. Without its crowd of celebrating commoners, the house seemed hallowed, almost templelike: delicate furniture lightly carven, gilt-framed mirrors and tasseled tapestries from far lands, crystal and silver, rich, dark woods. Traces of Necquer's occupation showed in the distant origins of some of the crystal and the foreign landscapes in the tapestries, but on the whole it was quietly Taralonian, restrainedly opulent. A hush hung over everything.

Lady Necquer was on the porch, looking out at the rough sea. Wrapped in a heavy cloak of dark wool, she huddled in a high-backed cushioned chair; her fine dark hair whipped wildly around her face, which was pointed anxiously westward, at the Teeth. The wind, blocked out of the street by the high, densely packed houses, clawed fiercely at the exposed porch, howling off the whitecapped ocean. The cold had brought crimson spots to her cheeks, and she frowned pensively.

He came level with her chair and bowed politely. The servant coughed.

"Sir Liam, madam."

The concern that had wrinkled her brow lessened, and she started up, a hesitant smile on her lips.

"Sir Liam! I thought you would not come! Lares, hot wine for us, when we go in." The servant bowed and retreated. Lady Necquer returned her gaze to the sea, and Liam looked at her.

"Hard and cruel to look on," she murmured, stepping away from her chair to the stone balustrade. The wind tugged at her heavy cloak. Liam pressed his books and maps firmly beneath his arm, and felt compelled to speak, as though she had invited comment.

"Yes, it is, but at peace the sea can be the most beautiful thing in the world."

She shifted her gaze to look curiously at him.

"I spoke not of the sea, Sir Liam. Those—" She gestured vaguely towards the Teeth, and then suddenly shivered. "It grows cold. Come, let's in." She led the way, shuddering, into the house. Liam followed.

In a parlor on the second floor, with coals glowing in the small grate, the same servant brought them mulled wine. Lady Necquer removed her wool cloak, showing a high-necked gown with full skirts, completely unrevealing in the fullness of its dyed purple pleats and folds. Her moodiness was gone, and she smiled at him.

"You must forgive my distraction, Sir Liam. The cold days like me not. I grow foolish, and I sorely doubted your coming. You wronged me not to come yesterday. I placed much on it." She faltered, and then went on in a different tone. "But I see you've brought books and charts; come, begin your discourse, and I'll attend with a ready ear."

Liam took a sip of the mulled wine, and began unfolding his maps.

Rain was pattering against the thick-paned windows long before he thought of the wine again. Charmed by her interest and attentiveness, he spoke for a long while, finding more to tell than he thought he would. He had been a great number of places that were only rumors to her, and many more she had never heard of, and he detailed strange customs and foreign peoples for her, drawn on by her obvious interest. With the maps and the books, he traced some of the long pattern of his wanderings, and barely scratched the surface of what he had seen.

Fascinated as she was, she leaned towards him, and her eyes sparkled as he described wonders from far away. Sometimes he caught the hint of a sweet scent and remembered her beauty, but she maintained a detachment, a sort of sexual neutrality in the way she pored over the maps with him. He could not tell if she was being wise or merely innocent.

He did not speak of half he had seen, and almost none of what he had done. He left out the wars he had fought in; the crimes he had, on occasion, had to commit; the worst of the horrors he had seen were glossed over without comment; but she asked shrewd questions, drawing inferences and connections he had never considered.

The lecture became a conversation, and though her eyes darted fairly often to a sandclock on the sideboard, her interest never flagged. In fact, it seemed that the more the afternoon wore on, the more questions she asked, the harder she tried to prolong their talk.

Finally there came a pause, and Liam relaxed in his chair, giving his attention to his now-cold wine and the sky outside. It was full dark, the drops of rain trickling down the panes, silver and gold with reflected candlelight.

"I think I must go now, madam. It is dark, and I'm sure you must be tired." He did not move, waiting for her response.

She did not speak for a long minute, and when she did, it was not to excuse him.

"Tell me, Sir Liam, in your travels, have you ever seen a mirror of the Teeth?" The question came from far away, and she seemed to have relapsed into her earlier depression.

"A mirror of the Teeth?" It was the question that put him off, but she presumed it was her dialect.

"Their semblance, I mean. Anything like them."

"Well, I have seen shoals and reefs of great size, and some coastlines almost as rocky as Southwark's, but nothing as impressive as the Teeth, no."

"Impressive?" she echoed, and it was almost a hiss. "Say rather murderous, or Dark—anything but impressive!"

Her eyes were wide and deep with anger, and her cheeks flushed. Liam stood up hastily.

"It is late. I believe I should go, madam."

Lady Necquer's anger disappeared, and she sank back in her chair, deflated.

"It would be well, I suppose, Sir Liam." She stood wearily, as though it were an effort. "I should invite you to dine, but with my lord gone, it would not be seemly." She ventured a wan smile.

"Will he be long in Warinsford?" Liam inquired politely.

"He returns in two days, ere Uris-tide. I anticipate his return eagerly." The smile grew more natural.

"As do we all, I'm sure. Goodnight, madam."

She followed him to the stairs, thanking him for entertaining her.

"A most gentle discourse, Sir Liam, and one I would gladly repeat. Perhaps—" She stopped high on the steps, her smile draining away. From the hall came the sound of voices, the servant's polite husk and another, smooth and refined, but angry:

"I tell you, man, I've an appointment with the lady!"

Lady Necquer clutched Liam's arm.

"Relay to Lares that I am sudden sick, if you would," she whispered, and then continued, more fiercely. "And please, Sir Liam, return tomorrow!" He began to equivocate, but she pressed his arm. "Please!"

He took a deep breath and nodded once. She turned and fled back into her parlor. With another breath and a bemused shake of his head, Liam descended to the hall.

The handsome young man who had fled Necquer's party stood in the doorway, glaring down at the servant. A rainstained cloak mantled his broad shoulders, dripping water on the wooden boards. With an arrogant flip of his head he looked Liam over, and dismissed him by raking a hand through his sodden mane. He returned his attention to the servant.

"I'll repeat it once more, churl: this is the appointed hour of my meeting, and I mean to have it!"

Liam's eyes narrowed, examining the angry man in detail. A perfectly drawn face, strong chin, nose just sharp enough, widely set, flashing eyes; broad chest, tall, well muscled. His voice echoed magnificently, eloquent and musical. A golden, leonine hero to Necquer's dark tradesman.

Now why would a woman like Poppae Necquer spend an afternoon with the likes of me, and then flee such a one as this? Liam wondered.

"Lares," he said, "the lady asked me to inform you that she is indisposed."

Both the servant and the handsome man turned to him.

"Aye, Sir Liam," the servant said gratefully, but the young man glared at him with deep hatred. Liam returned the stare impassively, and suddenly the other spun on his heel and marched out of the house, slamming the door loudly behind him.

In the moment of silence that followed, the two men shared a look—indifferent surprise for Liam, immense relief for the servant. Liam broke it first.

"I wonder, Lares, if you could find me a piece of oilcloth. I'm afraid the rain would do little good for my papers."

He indicated his books and maps with a small smile, and the old servant scurried off willingly to look.

CHAPTER 5

LIAM HURRIED HOME through the dark, slippery streets, and found his landlady waiting for him, wringing her hands anxiously. He was soaked to the skin and tried to ignore her, wanting nothing more than to go to his room and dry off.

"Oh, Master Liam," she exclaimed as he brushed past her, "the Aedile was here only an hour gone, conning about for you!"

"Was he," Liam said politely, heading for the stairs with a bright, empty smile.

"Think you it was about the wizard's death?"

That ground him to a halt, and he turned slowly.

"What?"

"I thought, you having passed more than the odd hour with him, that the Aedile might suspect you!" She mispronounced "Aedile" to rhyme with "ladle," but he did not correct her.

"Did he say that? And how did you know Tarquin was dead?"

The stern edge in his voice unnerved her, as though it had confirmed her fears. "No, not so I recall. He mere said he'd have words with you, but I thought that you knowing the wizard—" Liam cut her off.

"How did you hear that Tarquin was dead?"

"Well," she fretted, "I didn't exactly know to be certain until the Aedile came, but's being bruited around the town by some. I heard from one who knows a member of the Guard."

Liam smiled grimly and started up the steps.

"But, Master Liam, what should I do if the Aedile comes again?" she called after him, and he laughed at her worry.

"Show him up," he called back, "and pronounce his title correctly!"

In his room he unwrapped his papers from the sheet of oilskin Lares had given him, and checked them carefully to see if they had gotten wet. When he was satisfied they had not been harmed, he changed to dry clothes, a far simpler tunic and long trousers of gray flannel. He draped his wet tunic over his chair and eyed his boots with displeasure. The punctures from Fanuilh's teeth had let water in, soaking his feet, and he put them aside, hoping they could be repaired. He slipped on a pair of low felt shoes and lay down on his pallet to think.

Coeccias had come looking for him, and if it wasn't already, the news of Tarquin's death would soon be common knowledge to those who cared to know.

The first could mean any of several things. Possibly there were some simple questions the Aedile had forgotten to ask him. More likely something had come up that had caused the man to suspect him anew, despite Mother Japh's judgement. Least likely, of course, was that the Aedile had decided to share whatever information he had. Liam frowned at the thought.

The fact that the death would soon be common knowledge meant he had been right to presume his investigation would become vastly more difficult. It also made Lady Necquer's uselessness more disappointing.

There was something desperate going on with her, concentrating her so completely on herself that she would have little interest in helping him. It revolved around the handsome young man, obviously, and Liam's visit and her insistence on it had been along the lines of a distraction from her greater problem. Or perhaps, he realized, as protection.

Whatever the reason, she was in no state of mind to involve herself seriously in the affairs of a dead wizard. Nonetheless, he found himself curious about her problem. What danger the young man presented Liam could not guess. If he was a lover, she had no reason to fear him. He could not threaten exposure, as Liam had known lovers to do, because it was clear from his behavior at the party that Master Necquer suspected something. It was equally clear that he did not blame his wife.

What, then, could be the problem?

Although he was partly aware that he had a more important riddle to unravel, he gave himself over for a while to considering the distraught young woman.

The heavy tread of boots on the stairs and Mistress Dorcas's voice interrupted him after a while. She spoke loudly, repeating "Aedile Coeccias" several times, and it was painfully obvious that she was trying to warn him. He got up quickly and surprised the Aedile by opening the door before Coeccias could knock.

"Rhenford!" he said, blinking his eyes. "It's well y'are in. I've been conning for you."

"So I've heard, Aedile. Please come in." He smiled over Coeccias's shoulder at his landlady, who was hovering nervously on the stairs and rolling her eyes. "Thank you for showing the Aedile up, Mistress Dorcas." He deliberately stressed the proper pronunciation.

"I'm afraid you've frightened my landlady, Aedile," he continued when he had shut the door firmly in her face. "She thinks you mean to arrest me for Master Tanaquil's murder."

Coeccias ran a scarred hand through his now-trimmed beard and looked around the garret with mild curiosity. "Truth, Rhenford, I may well do that ere long. I've seen some rare parchments this day." He stood by Liam's table, idly shuffling the papers there, occasionally sparing a glance out the window. Liam leaned casually against the door.

"Oh?" he said, with as much indifference as he could muster.

"Oh? Oh, indeed. Rare parchments, I say, rarer than rare. The wizard's testament, booked and noted in the Duke's own court, by the Duke's own clerks, and waxed with the Duke's own seal. A rare testament, that."

"How rare, Aedile Coeccias?"

The burly officer found something that interested him in the papers on the table, and Liam thought belatedly of his list of suspects.

"Y'are a scholar, Rhenford?" Coeccias asked suddenly.

"I have studied," Liam began, wincing over the list.

"Tarquin must've liked scholars, Rhenford. He left you all."

"What?" He could not hide his astonishment, and forgot the list. "Left me all?"

"Seat, fortune, goods—all. Y'are amazed?"

"Of course," Liam stammered. "I hardly knew him!"

"Better than anyone else, it seems. It'd be a strong stroke against you, in the Duke's court."

The return of Coeccias's suspicion hit Liam hard on the heels of the news of Tarquin's will. "You know, in the days when your title was coined, if a man were falsely accused, his accuser was held guilty for the crime," he said coldly.

Coeccias chuckled. "I'd expect a scholar to know that—but I'd also expect him to know that the Aedile's office exempted him from the same statute. How else to uphold the law?"

Stung, Liam flushed. He had not thought the rough-looking Aedile would know the law's qualifier. His hands bunched at his sides, but he said nothing. Coeccias dropped his eyes to the paper that had interested him.

"I'll admit, Rhenford, I came intent on clapping you in. I thought the testament would unnerve you, and if pressed hard, you'd break. But now I think I've erred. Y'are a poor actor, Rhenford, too poor for a killer. And I uncover this scribbling." He held a piece of paper up, nothing but mild curiosity in his voice. "Now, it strikes me strange that a scholar should have a list of a dead man's acquaintances, with notes of arguments and visits all within the last sevennight. Truth, very strange. I'd almost say that scholar was idly scribbling a list of who might have taken off the dead man. Wouldn't you?"

He gave a small smile, and Liam frowned but said nothing.

"Can you think of a reason why a scholar should make such a list?"

"Perhaps," Liam said slowly, trying to control the anger he knew should be directed at himself for leaving the list out, "perhaps he thought the Aedile was too much of a fool to find the murderer, and decided to do the job himself."

Coeccias roared with laughter, filling the garret with the surprising sound. He slapped his knee with the list.

"Truth, perhaps he did! Perhaps he did! Oh, y'are a rare murderer, Rhenford, a rare murderer!" Fresh laughter exploded out of him as he folded the list carefully in quarters and stowed it in his black tunic. Liam had no idea what to do, and simply waited while the Aedile finished his laughter.

"Come," Coeccias said finally. "I'd have you eat with me, Rhenford."

It was drizzling still, but Coeccias chose a tavern nearby, and ducked quickly through the cold shower without a word. Liam sat across the plank table, looking at the Aedile with distrust only half-concealed as the larger man called across the almost empty common room to order beer and food. When the keeper had recognized his order, he turned to Liam with a serious look.

"So, the eyes that scan tomes now con a murderer."

Liam nodded, wondering what the Aedile was thinking.

"Truth, Rhenford, that likes me not. I'm not sure I need you murking the waters with ill-advised questions. Now, I know you think me a clown"—he held up a hand to forestall Liam's denial—"and you may have the right of it. The eagle's eyes are not mine, and I don't see into shadowed hearts. I'm certainly simpler than a scholar, no matter how innocent his face. Yet I'm still Aedile."

"Which means?" Liam had begun frowning deeply at the mention of his innocent face. He found it difficult to contain his uneasiness, and drummed his fingers on the table, looking around the tavern through the smoky rushlight.

"Which means I can't very well allow you to search out an assassin on your own. Yet you have a list of possibles that I'd never have had, and you knew the wizard best. Not well, perhaps, but better than any else. And I can't tell you not to search."

"So?" He was on the brink of being rude when a serving girl came by and placed beer in clay steins on the table, along with a basket of bread, salt and boiled eggs. The Aedile dug in, salting a torn piece of bread and an egg and eating them in big bites. He left Liam waiting impatiently until he had washed down his first egg with a gulp of beer, and then spoke as he set about preparing a second egg.

"So, Rhenford, I'll find you running about the town, as I said, murking the waters and making my work harder. And," he said, gesturing significantly with his egg before biting into it, "you'll find me doing the same to you."

Liam took an egg and nibbled at it unsalted, some of his irritation dissipating as he guessed where the Aedile was headed.

"So we are in each other's way, Aedile. That will be inconvenient if either of us is to resolve this."

"Truth, inconvenient is too small a word for such a large stumbling block."

"What will we do about it?"

Coeccias once again paused as the girl put down two steaming pies on wooden platters.

"I could ask you not to involve yourself," he said, steepling his fingers over the pie and examining Liam's face, and then waved away the suggestion with a laugh. "But I've enough sense to know you'd not. Y'are serious about it? Not merely dabbling to satisfy a scholar's curiosity?"

"Very serious." Liam began eating, cutting into the meat and vegetable pie, highly spiced as most food was in Southwark. He waited for the Aedile this time, who only spoke after he had gone through several bites of his own pie, and then only around a large mouthful.

"I know not why, but I'll warrant you mean it. Then if you'll not keep out of it, and are serious, and my position means I can't keep out of it, and must be serious, then sense says we work together."

It was what Liam had guessed, but he kept his satisfaction from his voice.

"That would seem to be a good idea."

"Good. Then lay out what you know, Rhenford."

Liam eyed him with a half-smile. "How do I know you won't simply listen and then arrest me to keep me out of your way?"

"Truth, you don't," Coeccias said with a wolf's grin that looked far more natural than Liam's earlier one. He must have blanched, because the Aedile snorted and held out his hand, after wiping it on his black tunic. "Would my word suffice?"

"No, no, I'll trust you," Liam said hastily, and Coeccias withdrew his hand with another snort.

Without mentioning Fanuilh, he elaborated on the list the dragon had given him. He had thought it would be difficult to explain knowing so much about Tarquin's visitors, but the Aedile asked no questions, simply nodding as Liam ticked off each visitor and what he knew of them. Finally he came around to his interview with the druggist Viyescu, his imposture of a Hierarch, and what he had learned from it.

Coeccias listened in silence, working his way through his entire pie before Liam was finished. When he was done with the meal, he pushed the platter away and leaned back from the table with a sigh.

"Well, I'll admit you've a great deal more information than I. I did ill not to clap you in yesterday and examine you closer."

"So what do you know? Apart from the will, that is?"

"Only what you've told me, Rhenford. Truth, I knew little enough about the wizard."

"Nothing!" Liam exclaimed. "You know nothing? It looks like I've made a poor deal!"

"I, on the other hand, have made off surpassing well, wouldn't you say?"

Liam massaged his brow roughly, but he had to chuckle at the Aedile's sated-cat grin. "Well, then," he finally said, "the least you could do is try to live up to the bargain."

"It would seem fair," Coeccias grinned.

"What about the knife? You took it, I assume. Was there anything special about it?"

"Only that it was of the sort used by rude players, jugglers and the like. They come in pairs, and have uncommon broad hilts; in one of the pair, the blade retracts harmlessly. For death scenes and the like in entertainments."

"Well, then, that would point to the minstrel—" Liam began eagerly, but caught himself when Coeccias started to interrupt. "Or a clever man who wished to put the blame elsewhere."

"Y'are quick enough. A clever man who wished to point as far away from himself as possible. If he chose a player's knife, that would make him high-born, or at least rich. That would indicate the merchant you saw. And 'less I miss the mark, he would be Ancus Marcius. Oft he travels with the sort of rough boys you described, and is given to the sort of blustering you heard. When did you say he came to the beach?"

Fanuilh's memory had been good, but his sense of time was inexact; the only way to place the date of the merchant's visit was by the weather.

"A day or two after the last of the really fierce storms. I don't remember the day exactly; it was gray and overcast, but didn't rain all day."

Coeccias grumbled thoughtfully. "That would be just after Marcius lost his richest ship on the Teeth."

"The Teeth? You're thinking of Tarquin's model?"

"Truth, it struck me as an interesting plaything for a wizard. Perhaps he failed in some business of Marcius's. The merchant's not very forgiving, I've been told."

"Then maybe you ought to question him."

Frowning, the Aedile poked at the remains of his pie. "Better ask the wind to stand still, or summon the stars to court, than question Marcius. He's high-placed and high-handed, and the offense he'd take would be worth my post. I'd rather you did it."

"Me? If you can't question him, how can I?"

"Make out you're a Hierarch again, or better yet, play the King of Taralon. He'd answer quick enough." Liam grimaced at this reminder of his play-acting with Viyescu, and Coeccias snorted a laugh before going on more seriously. "Best of all, Rhenford, go to him as a scholar seeking employment. Give him your various qualifications, and tell him your previous master, a certain wizard of much power, has been murdered. You seek a new master of sufficient position to protect you from your former's enemies."

"And shock him with Tarquin's name so that he slips up?"

"That'd do."

"And then he has one of his guards knock me out and the next thing I know I find myself a galley slave on one of his ships."

"That'd not do, but if y'are careful, it shouldn't happen. Be meek and mild, innocent as a babe. If he's clever enough to've planted the player's blade, he'll never think a mere pen-nibbler could've found him out. Cleverness and pride go hand in hand."

"Your opinions on human nature pale before the thought of several years chained to a galley seat."

"If you don't return from his offices, I swear I'll personally search every one of his galleys before it leaves Southwark," Coeccias answered cheerfully.

Liam laughed ruefully. "And offer me your best wishes for a pleasant journey, I'm sure. But that'll have to do, I suppose. I'll go see him tomorrow. What will you do?"

"Since you can't go after Viyescu anymore without full religious vestments, I'll search him out again, and maybe trail him with one of my men. Mayhap we'll see if he has any pretty, sinful women in his life."

They left it at that, and Liam let Coeccias pay for the meal, arguing that since he would be facing a possibly murderous merchant the next day, he was doing far more than his share of the bargain. While Coeccias laughed over that, he left the quiet inn and hurried home through the rain.

Sleep was not as long in coming as the day before; in fact, it was all he could do not to drop off as soon as he stretched out on his pallet. There were, however, some

things he wanted to think through, and he stayed awake for
a few minutes, hands laced behind his head, staring at the
pitted wooden beams over his head.

Taken together, the day could not in any way be considered a failure. His visit to Viyescu had provided him
with an interesting possibility, and a line of investigation
he had not imagined. That a woman of any kind could be
involved fascinated him, though he found it hard to imagine
Tarquin begetting children at his age. The vague memory of
the flushed young thing on the beach that summer morning
came back to him, and he turned it over in his head for
a while.

He let it go with a sigh, thinking that however interesting it
was, as a motive for murder it was less than adequate. More
important was his new partnership with the Aedile, which
promised him far more of a chance at discovering Tarquin's
killer than anything he could have imagined. However simple the burly man looked, he was much shrewder than Liam
had guessed, and he knew that Coeccias would make a better source of information on Southwark's inhabitants than
Lady Necquer, who had enough distractions of her own to
worry about.

In a sense, it was more important that he liked the Aedile.
He felt at ease with him, able to joke and talk naturally,
unconstrained by the notions and proprieties that kept him
almost formal around Lady Necquer.

My luck again, he thought.

Pleased with the alliance, he considered the merchant,
Ancus Marcius. From Coeccias's description of his high-
handed and often brutal dealings, both in business and in
private, Liam thought Marcius considered himself more of
a trading prince than a mere merchant. The ship he had
lost on the Teeth had been only one of many, but rumor
had it that he was taking the wreck almost personally, and
had even gone so far as to send threatening notes to several
of the local temples, demanding more vigilant prayers and
services on behalf of commerce.

Liam smiled in the dark at the man's arrogance, and
thought that Marcius's own high self-opinion would make

it easy to play the meek scholar in search of a position.

Nonetheless, he was not at all sure that anything of worth would come out of the interview he would have to arrange the next day, unless he could somehow persuade Marcius to take a more than passing interest in him.

Fanuilh, he thought, might be able to help him there. Perhaps there was a spell of some sort. . . .

With a great and sudden yawn, he turned over and began to let sleep claim him, thinking about the dragon. He wondered why it wanted Tarquin's killer found so much. It would have been natural if the creature were enraged, or wildly vengeful, or showing anything approaching emotion, but it betrayed no feelings of any kind. In fact, Fanuilh never seemed angry or amused or depressed or anything at all; it was just there, and following its own obscure purpose.

That night Liam had a dream he had not had in a long time, in which he stood helplessly by and watched his father's keep burned to the ground by the host of another lord. The building that was burning, however, was his landlady's, though the logic of the nightmare insisted it was his father's keep, and the miniature dragon flew crazily about through the smoke and flames, suddenly as huge as one of its larger cousins.

When he woke up to the leaden knocking of rain on his window, he dismissed the dream, which had recurred on and off for most of his adult life, along with its strange new additions.

"I thought I'd left *that* one far behind," he muttered, dragging himself from his warm bed to face the wet and dreary day.

CHAPTER 6

IT WAS NOT wise of you to tell the Aedile, Fanuilh thought at Liam, after he had brought meat from the kitchen. Soaked to the skin despite his heavy cloak and unhappy at having had to make the ride all the way out to Tarquin's house in the early morning rain, Liam snapped back.

"Well, there wasn't much I could do otherwise! He could have made it very difficult to go on! He's not as stupid as I thought, you know."

Yes, I know.

Irritably shaking out his cloak, Liam went on. "Besides, I would have had to tell him once I found out, wouldn't I? Unless you were thinking of having me search out Tarquin's murderer just for the personal pleasure of knowing. Justice would have to be served, right?"

The dragon's thought formed slowly. *I suppose . . . perhaps I did not think it out completely.*

"Well, I did, and I think I didn't have any choice about telling him, and I think I have a much better chance of finishing this business with his help. And it's done, so there's no use arguing about it."

The dragon did not reply, lying on the table and giving its full attention to the meat Liam had brought. He tried to wring some of the wetness from his cloak but gave up finally, hooking it over one of the shelf uprights.

"Since you're so interested in giving advice," he said, "I don't suppose you have any idea how I can interest Marcius enough to gain a little of his time."

The thought that came back was interrogatory, like a question mark stamped down on his thoughts.

72

"I don't know, maybe some spell that will make me irresistibly fascinating, so that he can't tear himself away from me. Maybe a love potion, so he'll confess all his soul's secrets to me. . . ."

I know very few spells, and none like that.

"I was joking," Liam explained. "Have you any practical ideas on the subject?"

I am not sure if Marcius is the proper suspect.

"I'm not sure either, Fanuilh, but there has to be some sort of order to my investigation, or I might as well just send out criers asking the killer to show himself in the town square at noon."

I understand. I simply do not believe it is worth spending the time.

"Well, then," Liam said with an exasperated sigh, "it's a good thing it's not you who'll have to spend the time, isn't it? Besides, he may lead elsewhere, like Viyescu. I'd never thought a druggist could kill, and still am not inclined that way, but he told me about this mysterious girl. I presume you know what I'm talking about?"

The dragon cocked its head and looked at him, as though the question were strange.

Of course. I can—

"Pluck the thoughts right out of my head?" he said ruefully. Another thought began slowly to form, but he tensed and hurried on. It faded away. "Do you remember what she looked like?"

I did not see her. I only heard a voice.

"How did she sound? Young? Old? Angry? Sad? What?"

Seductive.

Fanuilh replied with such certainty that Liam was momentarily taken aback. By the dragon's recollection, the woman had visited Tarquin on the afternoon Viyescu's sinner had stormed out of his shop, but if she had been angry with the wizard for getting her pregnant, would she have sounded seductive? Perhaps Fanuilh had misunderstood her tone.

She cooed.

"All right," he said aloud, "I believe you. She was seductive. But why? Viyescu implied that someone, perhaps

Tarquin, had gotten her pregnant, and that she was angry about it. So why coo?"

I do not know. I only heard her coo before Master Tanaquil sent me away.

Liam began pacing thoughtfully around the room, idly picking up glass jars and books and strange tools without paying them much attention. He leaned against the middle worktable, where a single lonely glass decanter stood. Picking it up, he tossed it from hand to hand as he thought. The label, a small square of white paper pasted to the smooth surface, read VIRGIN'S BLOOD, though the beaker was empty and a thick black X lay over the words. Liam grimaced and put the decanter down.

The dragon did not interrupt him, but he found it annoying to know that all his mental processes were constantly open to observation. He itched to be able to keep his head to himself. Despite the irritation, however, he came around to an idea.

"Fanuilh, do you remember a woman who was here during the summer? Sort of pretty, dark-haired, a girl, really?"

Donoé. Master Tarquil called her his 'little barmaid.'

Pleasantly surprised, Liam smiled. "His 'little barmaid', eh? Did she come often?"

Perhaps three or four times, but she was not the one who cooed.

"I didn't think so. Do you know where she was a barmaid?"

You think she might help you find the cooer.

"It's a possibility, you have to admit."

I do not know where she worked.

"Then perhaps Coeccias can scour all the taverns in the city, eh?" He only half-meant it.

Not all the taverns. Only the ones Master Tanaquil was likely to frequent. There should not be so many of those.

Likely to frequent, Liam wondered. "Did he go to the city often?"

Once or twice a week; more often during the summer. I do not know what he did there.

The model of Southwark caught his eye, and he went to it. "Fanuilh, this model—do you know why he made it?"

For a spell. I do not know for whom the spell was intended. He rarely included me in that aspect of his business.

He could think of no other questions, but stayed in the workroom, dipping a finger in the miniature waves with a distracted air. The pattering of the rain on the windows lulled him, and his thoughts wandered and grew unfocused. The Teeth of the model, small though they were, duplicated the grandeur of the original, inspiring a sort of awe and no small amount of fear. With an effort, he eventually shook himself and tore his gaze from the tiny rocks. He took his cloak from the shelf and frowned to find it still damp.

"I have to go," he said, putting the clammy cloth around his shoulders. "Unless you can think of anything else to tell me."

There is nothing.

Liam shrugged irritably. "Fine. If you think of anything . . ."

I will let you know.

"Are you sure there are no spells that would help? Or maybe one of those things in the other room? The one with the cases?"

No. The thought was firm, and brooked no questioning.

Pursing his lips in consternation, Liam left.

From Coeccias's and Fanuilh's description of his manner, Liam had expected Ancus Marcius to be a big man, but the figure on the docks was small, pretentious only in dress.

Ignoring the light drizzle into which the morning's downpour had resolved itself, the merchant stood among a group of stevedores, shouting instructions about the unloading of a battered carrack. Though the rest of the waterfront was empty, Marcius's men bustled along as though there were nothing unusual, stepping briskly in accordance with the merchant's commands. They brought bales and chests down the gangplank and loaded them onto a line of carts drawn by mules waiting miserably in the icy drops. The harbor was quiet except for the slap of bare feet on gangplank and wet stones, and the water was a still and metallic gray, pocked with rain and curtained by a bank of mist rising off the sea. The Teeth hovered across the harbor, vague black shadows.

Marcius was short and slight of build, and his clean-shaven face bore what seemed a perpetually sour look. His clothes, though sodden, were magnificent: doublet and hose of silk dyed a delicate blue, with a heavy cloak of deep purple and low boots of shining leather. Liam thought of his own boots, and the water that was even now soaking his feet through the holes left by the dragon's teeth.

For a few minutes, Liam watched the merchant and the activities he was directing. Then, keying himself up, he crossed the slick stone of the waterfront to where Marcius stood.

"Speed, you knaves, speed! Do you think this wetting likes me?" the merchant shouted. Liam stopped a few respectful paces away and coughed politely. Marcius did not turn, but the man by his side did, showing an ugly face made worse by a long, jagged scar running across his face from ear to ear, bisecting his mouth. A bodyguard, Liam knew, and he made himself quail slightly beneath the man's contemptuous look.

"What do you want?" the guard lazily sneered, dropping a hand to the small cudgel at his belt. Drops of rain gathered on the puckered edges of his scar.

"A word or two with your master, if I might."

"Your name?"

"Liam Rhenford, a scholar."

"Well, Liam-Rhenford-a-scholar, Master Marcius has no time for you now. Be off." The guard scowled and jerked his head to indicate the quickest path of retreat.

Liam cringed and begged. "Please, sir, I've something he might find valuable, if only he'd give me a moment. It's very valuable, on my life."

"Heard you what I—"

Marcius, who, though only a few feet away, had not given any hint that he was paying attention, suddenly spoke without turning to them. "If the fool took a wetting to speak, it'd only be right to hear his piece. Speak, scholar."

The guard scowled again and moved aside, letting Liam move up to the merchant's side.

"Many thanks, Master Marcius, many thanks. You'll not regret it, I swear." The fawning sounded ridiculous to Liam, but Marcius seemed to expect it, and he kept it up. "I've come off a bad time, Master, and my situation is not very sound. I'm in a bad way, and I need money somewhat desperately."

"This smacks of a loan, scholar. Where's the value for me?" Marcius still did not look at him, but spoke impatiently. He was much shorter than Liam, who hunched himself abjectly and allowed his hands to grab each other in supplication.

"I'm coming to that, Master, soon enough. I only want to show you my position. My former master, you see, has died," he lowered his voice confidingly, "has been *murdered*, you see, and I am left to a hard lot."

"Murdered?" the merchant said in a normal tone, and Liam bobbed anxiously, imploring quiet.

"Yes, Master, and I'm afraid I may be marked."

"Marked, you say? Who was your master?" He still did not look at Liam, but his voice registered interest.

"Tarquin Tanaquil, Master, but—"

"Tanaquil, you say?" The merchant gave him a hard glance. "The wizard?"

"Yes, Master."

"I did not know Tanaquil had any apprentices." Marcius's eyes narrowed with interest. "How far were you in the art?"

"I was not his apprentice," Liam said regretfully, "just a scholar he employed for certain correspondences."

Marcius lost his interest with a grunt, turning back to the ship and irritably flicking an errant lock of his stylishly long black hair back into its damp place.

"If y'are no mage, what use can you be to me?"

The guard took this as a hint, and laid a rough hand on Liam's sleeve, but he spoke up quickly.

"Before I came into the wizard's employment, Master, I traveled a great deal. I have maps to many places."

Marcius turned slowly to him, his curiosity back, and nodded imperceptibly at the guard, who removed his hand reluctantly.

"Your name again, scholar?"

"Liam Rhenford, Master."

"Rhenford," the merchant mused, looking up at Liam with as cold an appraisal as he might have given a shipment of goods. Perhaps colder, Liam thought, wiping cold streamers of rain off his narrow nose; he would at least know how much the goods were worth.

"Rhenford," Marcius repeated. "I've heard of a scholar who sold Freihett Necquer a set of charts. Could you be that scholar?"

"I am, Master," Liam said nervously.

"Those charts brought him a bulky fortune this season. And now you say you worked for Tanaquil?"

"I was in his employ, sir, yes."

"Have you the charts here?"

"Yes, sir," Liam responded eagerly, and began digging into the satchel at his side.

"No, no, no," Marcius said with evident disgust, "don't be more of a fool than the gods made you, Rhenford. I don't want to peer at maps in the rain. Bring them to my offices, early tomorrow. You know where those are?"

"Certainly, certainly. I'll be—"

"Early, Rhenford. And bring your mappery."

The merchant walked away without another word, ignoring the stevedores, who continued their work. The guard trailed along behind, offering Liam a sarcastic half-bow and a menacing grin, horribly distorted by his scar.

As soon as the merchant was out of earshot, Liam muttered an insult. *I'm no dog, to cringe and cower*, he thought, and let his posture settle back to normal with a relieved grin. It was more fun to be a mysterious, self-important hierarch than a cowardly clerk, he decided, and set off in the opposite direction.

Liam climbed the steep streets that led up from the harbor to his lodgings. Dirty rainwater rushed whispering through the gutters down to the harbor. He stopped when he was high up in the city and looked back.

The work that still went on around Marcius's carrack might have been performed by ants, and the other ships riding at anchor might have been those of Tarquin's model, the forest of naked masts and spars mere twigs in the distance. He felt as though he might reach out and brush the leaden waters of the roadstead, or pick up one of the ships with his hand. Or, if the mist had not hidden them, take hold of the Teeth and tear them out of the sea, roots and all.

Had Tarquin felt like that when he cast his spell? Like a god on a high mountain with a storm raging unnoticed around him, reaching down a massive hand and rearranging the world to suit his whims? It was a strange idea, and Liam shook rain out of his face and cursed his soaking feet before resuming the climb to his garret.

He smiled gently at the kitchen drudge and greeted her politely. She shuddered and hid her face, remembering his wolfish grin. Shrugging ruefully, he beat a retreat up to his room.

There was nothing more for him to do before his afternoon visit to Lady Necquer. When he had changed into his third and last set of clothing, and spread that morning's wet ones out to dry, he realized he had time to kill, and sat himself with a sigh at his table by the window. His papers were still there, and some of his books. So many blank pages.

When Liam had arrived in Southwark, he had fully intended on filling those pages; had, in fact, bought particularly expensive paper for the task. Hundreds of sheets of it, and in four months he had covered exactly three of them with writing. All he had to show for his intentions were three pages of notes and outlines and, of course, the maps of his travels. He wondered where the time had gone.

Wandering the town, exploring it without noticing the sights. Daydreaming at his window, staring out at the harbor and ignoring the view. Swimming off Tarquin's breakwater.

He shuffled the pages of notes around, debating trying
to do something with them. His list of suspects no longer
lay beneath them, stowed safely now in Coeccias's pouch,
but he remembered it clearly. He now had faces to attach
to some of the names.

The druggist, the merchant, the cooing woman, the minstrel. He thought he might as well add the barmaid, Donoé.
The last three he had not seen, and he wondered how he
could ever possibly find them on Fanuilh's sketchy remembrance. He was getting places, he knew, but if he had to
continue running around the town in punctured boots and
a perpetually sodden cloak, he thought he might confess to
the murder himself.

With an explosive sigh he pushed the papers away and
went to his trunk. Beneath a layer of small clothes and
trinkets lay a bulging sack made of sailcloth. He snatched
it out and upended it on his blanket.

Silver and gold coins clinked together with the happy
sound of large amounts, and two or three gems winked dul-
ly, their vibrant color only a memory in the shadowy garret.

A fortune by Southwark standards, where a single silver
coin was his monthly rent. He had over fifty, and a like
number of gold coins, and he knew it little mattered that
the faces and inscriptions on them were of kings and in
languages that had never been heard of in Southwark. Gold
was gold and silver was silver, no matter whose head was
on the coin.

He picked out two of the gold coins, and hesitated before
picking out a third and dropping them into his belt pouch.
When the sack was back in his trunk with its contents
replaced, he left his room and walked briskly out into
the street.

Liam bought himself a new, heavier cloak that was supposed to be weatherproof, and ordered several suits of warm
winter clothes from a tailor in the rich quarter. The man
bustled and fawned nicely when shown the gold coin, and
promised "eminently satisfactory results" in a few days.
Liam left feeling slightly better, and warmer already in his
new cloak.

A cobbler repaired his holed boot while he waited, and took an order for two new pairs with gape-mouthed pleasure. A leatherworker yielded up a beautifully tooled belt and a proper scholar's writing case, made to hang from the belt, with pockets for pens, paper and ink, blotter and seals.

His maps rattling around in the roomy writing case, snug in his waterproof cloak and dry toes wriggling in his fixed boots, Liam felt good despite the rain and the blank pages in his room. He bought himself a large lunch in the inn Coeccias had led him to the night before and enjoyed it thoroughly.

When he was done, tolling bells announced that it was time to visit Lady Necquer, and he set out for the merchant's home. The rain still poured steadily down, now gurgling in the overflowing gutters, and the afternoon sky might well have been night, but he whistled, and felt well.

"Master Rhenford," Lares said with unaffected pleasure when he opened the door. "The lady was not sure you'd come."

Liam merely smiled and allowed himself to be let in and led up to the second floor.

Lady Necquer looked pale, but delighted to see him, as though he were a reprieve.

"Sir Liam! I doubted your coming!"

"I could not stay away, madam. It is a great pleasure to enjoy your company." He spoke blandly, the statement only a pleasantry, but her breath caught.

"I . . ." She faltered, and a silence yawned in which Liam fidgeted uncomfortably. He wondered what he could possibly have said, and thought of the handsome, angry young man at the door the other day.

Lady Necquer smiled weakly and fixed her eyes on her lap, spots of color reddening her pale cheeks.

"I beg your pardon if I am skittish, Sir Liam. I thought you were . . . an echo, perhaps." She forced herself to look at him and the smile grew more assured as she gestured him to a seat across from her. "Please, sit, and tell me more of your travels."

He took the offered seat, peering curiously at her. "I'm sorry to be a mere echo, madam. I don't think your husband asked me to come to bore you with repetition."

Something in his tone, or perhaps his mention of her husband, relaxed her, and the unnatural blush faded. Glad of it, he went on.

"If there is anything you need to discuss, madam, or if you'd rather be alone, I would gladly . . ." He let the sentence hang, expressing his readiness to help with open hands. She shifted in her seat, allowing the smile to drop. The look of unhappiness that wrinkled her forehead and pursed her lips seemed very pretty to Liam, and the openness with which she shared her feeling made him feel somewhat special. It had been a long while since anyone had taken him into their confidence.

"Your tendered help is as salve to my troubles, Sir Liam, and I thank you. Yet I am beset by troubles that I may not share with you, much as I'd like. For the time, it is good of you to keep me company. Now," she said briskly, trying to banish the tension with a bright smile, "we'll only have light talk. Tell me such things as you remember made you laugh."

Having set the subject, she sat back and waited, her brow clear and her eyes bright. His mind was blank for a few moments. Nothing particularly funny had ever happened to him, and he found that all he could remember were the faces of other women, one and all in attitudes of sorrow or depression.

Liam did not tell her this, but his look of consternation led her to prompt him a little, and presently he recalled a puppet show he had seen in a caravanserai in a desert country.

Before long, he had a string of stories to tell, half-remembered snatches of the highly stylized comedies popular in his student days in Torquay, the antics of acrobats and clowns from the courts of distant kingdoms, folk tales told by wizened men in a hundred markets, and songs heard in taverns around the world. He even brought out an entire verse of "The Lipless Flutist," a fairly clean one, and half-sang, half-recited it for her in an embarrassed way.

She laughed and clapped her hands when he was done, and he was struck anew by her youth and prettiness. He wondered again what could have upset her so, and thought angrily of the youth. Her unhappiness was obviously connected with him, and Liam cursed the man mildly.

A comfortable silence followed her good-natured laughter at his poor rendition of "The Lipless Flutist," and he only spoke after a while because the question popped into his head.

"When did you say your husband was returning?"

"Your pardon?" she asked, starting from some daydream. "Oh, he returns tomorrow, I hope. He is so often away."

He regretted the question, but she went on, sighing sadly. "So often I sit here alone, and feel his absence strongly. I wonder if he is wracked at sea, or taken by pirates, or bandits—they say there are bandits much abroad this year. On land, bandits wait for him; at sea, giant beasts, storms, the Teeth . . . oh, the Teeth are far the worst."

Shuddering, she dropped her eyes to her lap again, and Liam berated himself for upsetting her, though her returning to the Teeth interested him. So many lives in Southwark seemed to revolve around the grim rocks—Lady Necquer with her morbid fear, Marcius with his sunken ship, Tarquin with his spells. The only teeth in Southwark that had harmed him were Fanuilh's, and a cobbler had fixed that. He almost chuckled, but did not.

"I'm sure he'll return in perfect health."

She drew a deep breath and caught a smile. "Oh, I'm even surer than you, Sir Liam. But you'll grant me the right to worry, I hope." He offered her a small bow from his seat, and she continued lightly. "Now tell me, have you ever left anyone to wait for you? I'd wager you must have left weeping women in a hundred ports."

"No," he said seriously, "I don't think so. I am very easy not to miss."

She scoffed. "I can scarcely credit it, Sir Liam. Surely there is some love who drew you here to Southwark, a beauty who was planted on the docks, awaiting your return with weepy eyes and a kerchief soaked with tears."

Lady Necquer was not flirting, he decided, but teasing. He shook his head, and noticed how dark it was outside. Raindrops still trailed gold and silver on the panes. He would have to go soon.

"Then if it was no woman, what drew you, who've seen the world over, to so remote a corner of it as Southwark?"

"I had been shipwrecked for some months, madam," he lied, "on a desert isle far east and south of the Freeports. The ship that rescued me was bound here, and I was in no position to argue about its destination." He had indeed been stranded on an uncharted island, but the conditions were somewhat different from a shipwreck, and the things he had seen there would have unduly upset her, he was sure.

Even the mention of a shipwreck dampened her spirits more than he would have wished.

"I had no idea, Sir Liam. It must have been horrible." It was clear from her veiled eyes that she was imagining her own husband in such a position, and he frowned.

"Oh, by no means. Very comfortable, really. It did not rain half so much as it does in Southwark, and was warm as summer the year round. I left it with some regret. Of course, I had none such as you to return to, madam. If I had, I probably would have swum the ocean to return."

Lady Necquer smiled gratefully, and he rose reluctantly.

"I'm afraid I must leave you now."

She rose as well, and though she protested that he must not leave, she led the way to the stairs. There she made him promise to return the next day.

"My husband is due to return in the evening. I am sure it'd like him if you waited with me, and dined with us."

She seemed to mean it, and he assented with pleasure.

At the bottom of the stairs, Lares waited with his cloak. With a smile he took it, ignoring the man's attempt to put it on his shoulders, knowing either he would have to stoop or the short old man stretch to accomplish the feat.

"Tell me, goodman," he asked while he tied on the cloak,

"who was the young fellow that was here yesterday?"

The servant grimaced with disgust, and probably would have spat if he were outdoors.

"That one! A common player, from the Golden Orb Company, rabble all! Lons is his name, sir, and he plagues the lady unmercifully, all because she let him sing a few songs for her once. Most disgraceful, he is. He fits the old list, good sir, you know: 'vagrants and sturdy beggars, rogues, knaves and common players.' A very rogue, he is!"

Liam smiled at Lares's vehemence, but the old man did not notice.

"He was lurking about earlier, sir, but I happened to mention in a carrying tone that you were visiting the lady, and he skulked off in high dudgeon, I can tell you! A right rogue, that one!"

His cloak secured to his satisfaction, Liam shook his head in proper disapproval at Lons's knavery, and left before he laughed.

Once again he felt good in the rain, daring it to penetrate his snug cloak and patched boots. Even though it was a fair walk from the Point to his garret, he arrived with little more than a few drops on his face and hands, and decided that he had never spent money so well.

Mistress Dorcas was waiting for him in the kitchen, a folded piece of paper clutched in her hands. She handed it to him, apprehension clear on her face.

"It bears the Aedile's mark," she whispered fearfully, still mispronouncing the word.

Annoyed, he tore the paper open and read the note quickly. Coeccias's unruly scrawl invited him to the same tavern they had visited the evening before, the White Grape, and suggested a time.

"Is all well, Master Liam?"

"No," he said grimly, "I'm to be executed tomorrow at dawn." He went up the stairs without another word.

The hour Coeccias had set was only a little while off,

but he took the time to put away his writing case, taking out the maps and placing them on the table. When he went downstairs, his landlady was still holding a hand to her chest, breathing heavily.

"Y'ought not to say suchlike," she scolded. "I thought my heart would leap from its seat, to hear of such, even in jest."

"Well, why else would the Aedile summon me if not to execute me?"

"Faith, I know not, Master Liam, but y'are very wicked." He was almost at the door when she regained enough composure to be nosy. "What was his discourse?"

"He wanted to dine with me," Liam called over his shoulder as he left. "The condemned's last meal, he called it."

He shut the door on her leaping heart.

Coeccias was not at the tavern yet, but the White Grape was almost full and Liam was glad to catch the last open table. The girl who brought him the wine he asked for looked at him strangely, recognizing him from the night before and that afternoon.

Sipping the vinegary wine, he rested his elbows on the table and surveyed the customers of the inn. They were quiet, respectable types, not so rich as to belong in the quarter further up the hill, but not given to the noisy dens lower down by the harbor. They sat close to their tables and talked in low voices that suggested sobriety and mildly serious talk, not secrecy. He thought he and Coeccias had probably looked that way the night before and would look that way tonight, and wondered how many more nights they would look so before they had found Tarquin's murderer.

Or before we give up, he mused over a particularly sour mouthful. *If the dragon will let us give up*.

He did not want to think about Tarquin, or Fanuilh, and cast back to his afternoon with Lady Necquer. She was a pretty, refined young innocent, such as he had forgotten existed. Years at sea and in foreign lands had left him unused to dealing with Taralon's well-bred, though he had once been counted high in their ranks. Her problems interested him. They were different from his own, problems of the living, not the dead, and he turned to considering them.

This Lons, a mere player, hounded her, undoubtedly out of passion, because of her pale beauty. A part of him did not blame the man, but mostly he disliked Lons's arrogant voice and handsome face, as well as his rude presumption.

The man was an actor, traditionally one of the lower classes. The list Lares had quoted was from an old law, naming players and the others as undesirables who might be subjected to various fines and punishments just for being what they were. The law no longer stood, but the old prejudices still survived. Though Liam did not share them, he understood them, and knew it must be painful for Lady Necquer to be plagued by one she must consider beneath her.

She must unwittingly have led the boy on, asking him to sing for her and probably showing the same warm approval as she had shown his stories.

Of course, she doesn't think I'm likely to pester her like Lons, because I've such an innocent face.

Liam grinned ruefully into his cup, and looked up to see Coeccias.

"Now what brings such sunny summer to your visage, Rhenford? Have you flushed our quarry?"

Shaking his head, Liam gestured the Aedile to a seat, which he took with a wry smile.

"No, just enjoying a joke at my own expense."

"Then the day has not gone well for you?"

"No worse than yesterday."

Coeccias eyed him curiously and gave his order to the serving girl.

"You should not drink the wine here, Rhenford. The best they have in the house graces the wooden board over the door."

"I'd noticed."

The girl brought Coeccias a mug of beer, and he sipped from it before speaking in a low tone that seemed to fit the quiet tavern.

"Had you no luck with Marcius?"

"I have an appointment with him tomorrow. Very early.

I told him I had served Tarquin, and that seemed to give him a start. He asked me if I knew any magic, and was very disappointed when I did not. I'll try to sound him out a little more tomorrow."

"You think he killed the wizard for a failure of magic?" The theory clearly attracted the Aedile; he leaned even further forward with an almost laughably serious expression.

"Well, it was one of his ships that crashed on the Teeth. If he'd had some contract with Tarquin, then it would seem Tarquin did not live up to it." Coeccias leaned back with a small smile of satisfaction, and Liam qualified his statement. "I would not be in too much of a hurry to arrest him, though. He didn't exactly go white and confess when I mentioned Tarquin's name."

"Shrewd ones never do, Rhenford. But I'll grant your doubts. And as it seems you've done your work, I'll report on mine."

He had gone to see Viyescu early in the day, and hinted about a girl who was known to have been an acquaintance of the druggist, and who had bragged in her cups of knowing a certain powerful wizard.

"Though by straight and true I'm not supposed to do such, it was wondrous effective, a great spur to him. There were no bloody confessions, true, but just a few hours later he barred his shop early and found his way to a suite of rented rooms in the lower quarters. A man of mine followed him, and when our druggist left, sore disappointed, he made some discreet inquiries."

The Aedile paused, it seemed, for effect, and leaned back, waiting smugly to be asked the outcome of the questions. Liam waited too, and looked around the common room with an ostentatiously apathetic air. For a few moments, both were silent, before Coeccias's desire to tell overcame his desire to make Liam ask, and he resumed his report with a sour grunt.

The rooms, the owner of the house reported, were rented by a young lady who always arrived masked and cloaked, though the rent was brought to him by a common messenger. The lady was only there a few nights out of every month, but had, on occasion in the past, received a robed and hooded visitor, presumably male. Neither had been there recently, but the rent was still brought by the messenger every month.

"So, what make you of that?"

"Viyescu keeps a mistress."

"No," the burly officer said scornfully. "A hooded, robed visitor? Rented rooms and great secrecy? It's clear we've found the wizard's bawd!"

Liam frowned and shook his head. "Wizards aren't the only people who wear robes, Master Aedile. Priests do too, and some officials, and I've known rich men who affect them to seem sophisticated. What's more, men who value their appearance of virtue have been known to wear disguises when indulging their vices. You think Viyescu went there to warn the girl about your investigation. What I think is far more likely is that Viyescu went there so that his mistress could soothe his fears and worries. You must have startled him a great deal, and he felt the need of her comfort."

It was Coeccias's turn to frown, and Liam pressed on.

"Next month's rent will be due in two days. I'll wager if we wait until then, we'll find that the messenger brings it, which'll prove the girl wasn't Tarquin's. And I'll wager even more that if we trace the messenger, we'll find he gets his money from a man in a neat little apothecary's shop."

The Aedile scowled unhappily, recognizing the validity of Liam's argument.

"Still, it bears searching out," he said stubbornly.

Liam agreed, but only on the principle that they should make the best of what they had.

"There's something else I'd like you to check on. I remember a girl Tarquin once mentioned, a barmaid named Donoé. I think it might be worth our while to talk with her. Can you have your men find her?"

"Seek out a single barmaid? In all of Southwark? Better ask us to find a pearl dropped in the harbor! Have you any idea how many taverns and inns and bars there are in this city?"

"Not that many that Tarquin would have gone into, let alone struck up an acquaintance with a barmaid there. I bet you won't even have to look beyond the rich quarter, and there are none too many bars there."

"All right, all right, I'll send someone round to con for this barmaid. Donoé is her name?" At Liam's nod, the Aedile repeated it with a *humph* of displeasure. "Barmaids! I offer you th' assassin complete in this rented girl and her monthly rooms, and you throw it away on barmaids!"

"Not just on barmaids. There's still Marcius, and the minstrel we haven't met yet." An idea struck him, left over from his thoughts of Lady Necquer. "Say, Master Aedile, what's the Golden Orb Company?"

Confused by the sudden change of subject, Coeccias replied slowly, trying as he spoke to figure out the connection.

"A troupe of players here; they put on a series of entertainments and performances the year round. They've two theaters in the city, a summer amphitheater and a covered one for winter. Often in the winter I close them out, and send them packing to the heath, to perform for the villagers and keep the pest at bay. A close theater in the winter breeds the plague like a she-rabbit coneys." Enlightenment suddenly dawned around the neatly trimmed beard. "You recall the knife, if I guess aright, and think to find your minstrel there! Shrewd, very shrewd, Rhenford! I hadn't thought to comb that rabble for him!"

"No, no, that's not what I meant," Liam said hurriedly. "That's not what I was thinking at all." He began to explain his afternoon with Lady Necquer, but thought better of it. "I just heard the name earlier from my landlady, and I hadn't heard of it before. I thought I might go see a performance."

"Truth, a passing excellent idea! I'll wait upon you, and if you espy the minstrel, that'll be one more way for us to look."

Coeccias smiled happily and dug hungrily into the food

the girl put before him. Liam felt a flutter of discomfort. He could not identify the minstrel, because he had not seen him; Fanuilh had, but he couldn't explain that to the Aedile. They might sit through a hundred performances with the minstrel in every one, and Liam would never know it.

He ate his own meal with much less interest.

CHAPTER 7

THE COVERED THEATER the Golden Orb Company used in the winter was in the Auric's Park section of the artisans' quarter, far from both the sea and Liam's lodgings. Half-timbered, it towered windowless over the surrounding homes and shops, cut off from them by narrow lanes on two sides and wide streets on the others. High above the street a giant gilt ball hung from a projecting hook, rain sparkling on its surface; the places where the golden paint was peeling were barely visible in the light leaking from the entrance. With only its bottom hemisphere visible, it looked impressive, like a strange moon.

A sizable crowd stood outside the theater's three sets of wide wooden doors, waiting to get in, and more jammed into the small lobby. They were mostly rough-looking men and women, apprentices and seamen, clerks and workers, inured to the rain and cold. With no obvious resentment they allowed the occasional better-dressed patron to move through their ranks directly to the entrance, shoving aside to create a path for the rich or well-to-do that closed up immediately behind them. Liam and Coeccias were allowed to pass this way, like ships cutting a wake through the sea, and came up to a man seated behind a barrel, wearing a tunic of motley, the squares of brightly colored cloth marking him out from the plainer clothes of the audience.

"Good even, Master Aedile. Come to close us out?" His eyes sparkled and his lips twisted with a combination of humor and good-natured malice.

"No, Master Player, only to watch the process. If the play likes me not, belike then I'll send you packing to

92

the countryside." Coeccias smiled as well, and gestured to Liam. "He'll quit us, for a box."

Liam frowned and dug out a silver coin. The Aedile had seen the coin he used to pay for his dinner and, deciding that Liam had done the least work of the day, told him off to pay for the evening. Liam dropped the coin on the barrelhead; the player in motley bowed dramatically over the money and waved them inside.

The small lobby was even more closely packed than the street, but the crowd parted for them again. Before him, between heavy, crudely squared wooden pillars, Liam could see the stage, raised above the heads of the people jostling in the pit, but Coeccias led him away to the left and up a narrow flight of steps. The second floor of the theater was a gallery, segmented into booths by the heavy pillars continuing up from below. The Aedile took one of these booths, and motioned Liam to sit beside him on the cushioned bench.

Inside, the Golden Orb's theater was hexagonal, with the raised stage a disproportionately large edge. Two stories of boothed galleries made up the other edges, while the floor was open and seatless. The poor massed there, a sea of heads talking noisily and gaping impatiently at the stage, while the rich who had cut their way through the crowd filled the galleries; each booth framed expensive clothes and well-fed faces.

Looking around at the others in the galleries, Liam whispered to Coeccias, "I don't think we're appropriately dressed for the boxes." He indicated the Aedile's crumb-strewn shirt of unrelieved black and his own simple cloak and tunic. Coeccias nodded absently, his own attention fixed on the empty stage.

"I suppose not. But those're guildmasters and merchants and high tradesmen in the other boxes, who needs must impress with their wealth their apprentices and drudges below. Y'have neither employees nor servants in the pit, and I hope none of my Guard is down there, or I'll have their heads. And what's more," he added after a thoughtful pause, "they have to impress each other. I think neither you nor I need to do that."

Liam digested this, inspecting the theater with idle curiosity. The huge wrought-iron chandelier reminded him of the great theaters in Torquay, as did the layout of the stage, with its curtained recess and small balcony. He remembered the few plays he had gone to see when he was a student in the capital, and was surprised that Southwark boasted a theater so much like Torquay's. Of course, the roof was thatched, not stone-arched and groined, and the proscenium, balcony and recess were made of plain, undecorated wood, not elaborately carved marble; still, the basic design was the same. And what the Golden Orb lacked in sumptuous decoration and formal sophistication, it made up for in excitement.

The theaters in Torquay had seemed strangely joyless, dark rituals of culture and sobriety; in Southwark, the crowd buzzed and chattered eagerly, excited and impatient for the show to begin. He wondered what the play would be like. He had not bothered to ask Coeccias about it, and as he was about to speak, a sudden wind gusted throughout the theater, cold and foreboding. It rushed outward from the stage with a roar, over the heads of the groundlings, and circled the galleries, rising upward, almost visible in its loud progress, before plunging at the chandelier. Hundreds of candles flickered and guttered wildly, dispersing monstrous shadows before they died. Then the wind died as well, leaving the audience suddenly silent in complete darkness.

"Watch," the Aedile whispered, lightly touching Liam's arm. Liam jumped at the touch in the dark, and peered intently towards where he thought the stage was.

A clean, white light like that in Tarquin's house slowly grew over the stage, evenly illuminating the acting space and limning the expectant faces of the audience, drawing just their features out of deep black shadow. A rowdy groundling called out, "Knave Fitch!" and the cry was taken up with happy applause and whistles from the pit as the growing light revealed a fat man in motley poised in an attitude of thoughtfulness.

With overly dramatic gestures he announced himself to be the Knave Fitch the groundlings had called for, and their loud shouts of approval clearly showed that he was a great favorite. He gave a prologue describing the action of the play, garbling the lines for comic effect, and the groundlings responded with hoots of laughter. Coeccias laughed as well, and Liam smiled at the clown's posturing.

When he was done with the prologue, Fitch bowed grandly, tripping on his cloak in the process, and exited to general applause.

The sourceless light dimmed and then swelled to the quality of a summer day, and a troop of women dressed as princesses skipped on stage, primly gathering flowers in an imaginary forest. After a few lines of introduction, the lead princess called for her ladies to provide music, and a tune suddenly invaded the theater. The lead princess, dressed in a diaphanous dress cut startlingly short, stepped forward and began a graceful dance in time with the music. The lesser princesses ranged themselves around the stage, watching the princess dance respectfully.

She looks like Lons, Liam thought with some amazement. She did indeed resemble the actor Liam had come to see. If anything, she was more attractive than the young man, with shining golden hair hanging below her shoulders and strong, bold features that hinted at sultriness despite her regal attire and almost prurient dance.

Even as he thought how pretty she was, however, the music shifted slightly, the beat faster and the tune wilder. One by one the lesser princesses rose and began dancing as well, keeping behind the leader. She, in turn, changed the style of her dancing, gradually losing all pretense of prudishness. The pure, pastoral aura that had hung around the scene disappeared, and she danced wantonly, the high cut of her dress revealing tantalizing stretches of well-formed thigh. Her dress clung strategically to her breasts and certain other points of interest, blousing over her stomach to pull in around her thighs. She danced with wild abandon across the stage, following the music as it swelled, rising through a series of crescendos to a peak that was clearly meant to be sexual.

Liam watched, fascinated and, he had to admit, aroused

by the intentional sexuality of the dance, and blew out an astonished breath when it was over, and the lead princess dropped to her knees, flushed and panting, her hair disarrayed like a golden nimbus around her head.

"Small wonder the guildmasters say the theater is a degenerate influence on their apprentices," Coeccias whispered, as impressed as Liam.

He was going to respond when a figure entered who caught his attention. He hissed in a breath at the sight of Lons striding over to the breathless dancer, and leaned towards the rim of the booth.

"What?" Coeccias asked immediately. "Is that our minstrel?"

Liam waved the question away, focusing his attention on the actor, who walked across the stage to the breathless dancer and helped her to her feet. At first he thought they were supposed to be lovers, but as the scene progressed it became clear that they were brother and sister. When it was over, and the sourceless light dimmed again, he settled back on the bench and frowned. Coeccias poked him impatiently.

"Truth, Rhenford, speak! Is that our minstrel or no?"

"I'm not sure. I'll have to see him again."

The Aedile snorted impatiently, and settled back to watch.

The princess's face and form swam before Liam's eyes, and he compared her to Lons, surer now that he had seen them together that they were related. He thought with displeasure of Lons's haughty bearing and his arrogant handsomeness. Just the sort to plague the poor lady, he thought, a self-involved rake, presumptuous and crude. Liam found he disliked the actor intensely. The sister-princess, on the other hand, drew him powerfully as, he realized, she probably drew every other man in the audience. She was stunning, attractive in an inviting way that was completely foreign to the beauty of Lady Necquer. He compared the two women, and pictured Lons between them.

Scene followed scene, and the play progressed. It concerned the various misadventures of the prince and princess, with the ridiculous antics of Knave Fitch as their court jester thrown in for comic relief. The princess only danced once more, but with the same breath-stopping effect. The sourceless light dimmed often, rising again to reveal different scenes. Several magical creatures made appearances, startlingly real on the stage. Liam thought the makeup and scenery remarkably well done, until a dragon entered to menace the prince and princess, and breathed a gout of fire across the audience.

Coeccias leaned over. "There's a wonderful illusion-maker in those wings," he said, as if he were letting Liam in on a secret with which he was familiar.

Liam smiled faintly, because he had seen the big Aedile flinch at the dragon's appearance. The mention of the illusion-maker who was projecting the marvels that crossed the stage, however, brought Tarquin into his mind. He should have been looking for his murderer, not enjoying himself at provincial theatricals.

Still, Lons's well-shaped and already well-hated face kept revolving through his thoughts, along with that of his enchanting play-sister. She spoke little, but her movements held his attention, and he watched her more than any of the other actors, including Lons, who, as the hero, had by far the most lines.

There was no intermission, and the play lasted for over two and a half hours. The audience, however, never lost interest. Between Lons's heroics, Fitch's obscene jokes, the illusion-maker's phantasms and the princess's sultry beauty, it was a tremendous spectacle, and the eventual denouement was breathlessly awaited.

Lons and his sister confronted the evil duke who had hounded them throughout the play, beating off his minions until they faced the villain himself. There was a long, tense display of swordplay between Lons and the duke, filled with flourishes and narrow escapes, and the crowd gasped and shouted over each pass.

Duel or no, Liam could not take his eyes off the princess, who spent the scene pressed against the proscenium arch, watching in palpable anxiety. Her sheer dress disarrayed to display just enough, her breast heaving with intense fear, she was perfect—or so she seemed to Liam. He believed her completely, and was only vaguely aware of it when Lons finally triumphed. Blood spurted high, more magical illusion, and the hero let fly with a well-chosen epithet on his evil foe, but Liam was watching the princess.

The crowd shouted and cheered madly, but the victory was only conveyed to Liam by the princess, by the delicate way she turned her head at the death blow, and the noble way she forced herself to look on the bloody corpse.

How often he had seen people look on the dead like that! While the rest of the audience noisily celebrated the conclusion, he sat enthralled and deeply impressed. She was magnificent; looks and figure aside, she was amazing, an artist such as he had never suspected the theater to hold. He doubted Lons had carried off his reaction to the death nearly as well.

She was—

Vision died, the theater went black, and for a split moment he thought the illusion-maker must have failed. Then he knew he was blind. His hands bunched convulsively, fiercely gripping the cloth of his breeches. He strangled a scream, and groaned instead.

His breath came in quick hisses, and he knotted the cloth above his knees over and over again.

Calm.

The thought crashed down on his fear, but the terror of blindness rose up again and he groaned a second time . . .

The hero is the minstrel.

. . . and then a third, as the blackness swirled and resolved itself into the stage and the theater, and Coeccias's face. The beard and the reflected illusion-maker's light hid his concerned look in a diabolical mask, but Liam barely noticed.

"Truth, Rhenford! What's amiss?"

"The minstrel," he grated, lurching to his feet in the haze of anger that washed away his paralyzing fear. "The hero is the minstrel," he finished, and bolted out of the box towards the stairs, brushing off Coeccias's hand.

In the street he marched grimly towards his quarter, oblivious to the rain.

"Bastard," he muttered. "Damned bastard in my head."
He ground the curses and worse between his teeth, bringing
them in and flinging them silently at the dragon.

Blinded me! The bastard!

Fanuilh did not respond, but Coeccias's heavy hand on
his shoulder brought him to a stop.

"Truth," he said, honestly confused, "I knew not whether
to stay or follow. What's possessed you, Rhenford? Is that
minstrel Tarquin's assassin?"

"No, no, I don't know," Liam scowled fiercely, unable
to explain. "I'm not sure."

"Is he or no? What know you?" The Aedile's voice sank
into suspicion, and he cocked his head to look at Liam from
the side. "What aren't you telling?"

"Nothing," Liam hastened to assure him, trying to hold
onto his anger. "There's just something I've remembered.
I don't know whether it'll mean anything. You'd think it
ridiculous." Coeccias started in heatedly, but Liam cut him
off. "I've just got to check on it. Look, have one of your
constables find out where Lons lodges, and meet me tomorrow at the White Grape at noon. We'll go over and see
him."

He winced when he realized he had said Lons's name,
because there was no way he could have known it. Coeccias
must have caught it too, but Liam did not give him a chance.
He swung around and ran off into the rain.

"Rhenford!" He heard the Aedile bellow behind him, and
then: "Damn!" But the curse sounded resigned, and he kept
on, trotting through the rain.

In the hopes of dredging up his dying anger, he deliberately recalled the sight, or lack thereof, of complete blindness.
He had been hung over and ill the first time, in no condition
to appreciate the experience. It had been different in the
theater. The complete absence of visual input—even the
normal phosphorescence of closed eyes—had been terrify-
ing, and the damned beast had inflicted it on him without
a moment's hesitation.

By the time Liam reached the stable, the bells were tolling
midnight, and he had given up on rebuilding his anger to

its first flaming height. Still, he pounded on the door until the night lad woke and grudgingly let him in. A silver coin wiped the sleep from the boy's eyes, and by saddling Diamond himself Liam improved the lad's mood tenfold.

Driven by the last of his ire, he made the cold, wet trip out to Tarquin's, and shuddered as he led his mount down the narrow path in the cliff, imagining the belltowers in Southwark ringing one o'clock.

The sea was an indistinct mass to east and west, though a pier of golden light stretched out from the wizard's home, spilling warm and golden from the glass front over the sand and across the water in a spike to the horizon. The beach was firmer underfoot than usual, condensed by rain. He felt a stab of anger rise up as he stamped into the quiet, well-lit house, tearing off his clinging, damp cloak.

Fanuilh lay in the same position on the table in the workroom, calmly gazing at the door through which Liam stalked.

I will not do it again without asking, the little dragon thought at him, and though the block in his head was as empty of tone as ever, he imagined how it would sound if spoken. As if they had discussed the matter, calmly, and reasonably come to the conclusion the dragon thought to him.

Liam was not pleased by his imagination, and his anger briefly and pleasantly flared.

"You're damned right you won't do it again, you bastard! Because if you do, I swear I'll leave you alone here to starve to death, do you hear!"

He felt better when he had shouted, and though he would have preferred it if the dragon had showed any reaction other than stony calm, it was enough. The last dregs of his anger swirled away.

"Don't the lights in here ever go out?" he asked after a while.

It was important to know. The hero was the minstrel.

"Really? They don't ever go out? How interesting!" He chuckled wryly to himself, since Fanuilh would not do it for him.

I will tell you about the house when you live here. When

you have fulfilled your bargain, you will be master.

"And you'll stay out of my head and show me many things I never dreamed of and all will be well with the world," he said wearily. "Let's not go into that again."

You will have to stay here tonight. It is too late to return to Southwark. You should go to sleep now, so that you can meet the merchant in the morning.

"It's not my house."

It is, but for the moment that is not important. You should sleep.

He suddenly felt wide awake. The icy cold was leaving his bones, his numbed fingers and ears were thawing, and he felt more awake than he had in the theater.

"I'll sleep here, but first . . ."

He left the room briskly and went to the kitchen. The house felt strange, full where he had expected it to be empty. There were none of the flat echoes one finds in abandoned rooms. As though it were waiting, he imagined, and drove the idea away with the image of a jug of chilled red wine, beads of moisture trickling down its sides. He was careful not to look at the jug by the stove for a moment, but when he did its sides were slick, and an exploratory finger came up wet with wine. And excellent wine, by the taste of the drops sucked off his finger. Shaking his head, he dispelled the wine and conjured a raw haunch of meat, feeling a little ridiculous as he closed his eyes and bunched his face with effort.

With the haunch on a wooden platter thoughtfully provided by the magic oven and his own imagination, the jug under his arm, Liam returned to the workroom. He dropped the platter in front of Fanuilh and sat crosslegged on the floor by the table.

"Eat up, familiar of mine. I need you to clear up some points for me, and you'll need your strength." He started to go on in the same vein, but stopped and changed tracks. "How is your strength? How are you?" The thought blocked immediately.

Better, but not completely well. I cannot fly yet, though I can move a little. Perhaps a week more.

An image of the tiny dragon skimming over the sand and looping up to dart out over the sea entered his head, and he remembered seeing it fly during the summer, silhouetted by the sun. He had been greatly impressed when he first saw it, but over the course of the summer had come to take Fanuilh for granted, another possession of Tarquin's, like the wizard's fantastic beach house.

Liam nodded as though something important had been decided.

"Well, I think I'll stay here for a week then, and nurse you lovingly back to health."

That would be good. The house is yours. Now you wish to clear some things up.

Toneless though the thought was, it nonetheless conveyed to Liam that the dragon knew exactly what he wanted to discuss. How could it not, when it could read his mind?

"I certainly do. Your memory's far from perfect, familiar of mine, and things are moving a little quickly for me to be wandering around with an incomplete schedule of events. Let's begin from the beginning, shall we?"

There were two events around which to arrange Fanuilh's imperfect sense of time: the death of Tarquin and the disappearance of the Teeth. It had apparently flown over the Teeth the day before, and, returning the next day, noticed their absence.

Between Liam's coaxing and puzzling and the dragon's willing answers and descriptions of the weather, they formed a sketchy timeline, to which Liam added his own observations.

Three days before the Teeth disappeared, Ancus Marcius had appeared at the door of the beach house with his thugs, rude and demanding. He had left after a short time, and his feelings about the interview were not apparent to Fanuilh, though Liam added that only a day before a rich ship of his had been smashed to splinters on the Teeth.

On the same day in the afternoon, Lons sought the wizard out, and remained closeted with him for some time. Fanuilh, told off and bored with waiting, had flown down the beach, and did not see him leave.

Two days later the most violent of a season of violent
storms raged all day long, from early in the morning until
just after dark. That evening, the woman with the seductive
voice had come, and Fanuilh had been shut out again. And
she was hooded and cloaked, it explained, so it had not seen
her face.

"Even if she had been naked," Liam said consolingly,
though nothing in the thought had conveyed regret or a
sense of guilt on the dragon's part, "you probably wouldn't
have seen her anyway. It was pitch dark all day, and the
night was worse." He himself had endured most of the storm
wrapped in a blanket in his garret, watching quietly as the
Storm King howled and spat his defiance at the world.

Tarquin spoke with her at some length, and Fanuilh was
only allowed in the house several hours later. Liam coughed
over this, wondering if they had done much talking, but he
let it pass. The wizard had been preparing something since
the day Ancus and Lons had visited him, and that night he
set Fanuilh to watching the house for spirits.

"Spirits?"

*They can ruin a great magic. The power draws them from
the Gray Lands, like moths. They flutter about it, and get in
the way. Master Tanaquil drew them often.*

"And you can drive them away?"

I have a form of power that can decoy them away.

"Well," Liam said, impressed by any subject he did not
understand. "Well."

They went back to the timeline.

Tarquin remained in the workroom all night, casting the
spell. He went to bed at dawn, exhausted, releasing Fanuilh
from his watch almost as an afterthought. As a welcome
break, the dragon had flown over the Teeth, and found them
missing.

"Or rather, didn't find them missing," Liam mused, running a long-fingered hand through his fine blond hair. The
dragon snapped down the last of the meat and gazed at him
incuriously. He took another gulp of wine, which was still
wonderfully cold.

The wizard received no visitors for the next three days,

as far as Fanuilh knew. He remained in the house, mostly in his bedroom, ordering his familiar to bring him food.

Removing the Teeth from this world took a great deal out of him.

"So you're sure it was him?"

Who else?

"And he removed them? He used the spell the book was opened to, not the illusion spell?"

I flew down to where they should have been. They were not there. And a mere illusion spell would not have cost him three days of rest.

Chastened, Liam went on.

On the second day of Tarquin's rest, a messenger had arrived from town, bearing a folded, sealed letter. The wizard had read the paper, laughed and mentioned Marcius's name with a chuckle. Then he burned it. That was the day Freihett Necquer made his miraculous return, Liam remembered.

The next day—surprised, Liam realized it was only four days ago—Tarquin stayed in his room till early evening. At dusk he called for Fanuilh to heat water for bathing, and cleaned himself thoroughly. Then he dressed in his most impressive, wizardly robes, the blue ones Liam had found him in, and shut the dragon out for the evening. He had rubbed his hands in the peculiar way that meant he was happy about something, and mentioned extra payments in a deliberately cryptic manner. That was the last time Fanuilh had seen him alive.

He was murdered at approximately midnight. Fanuilh knew this because it had felt Tarquin's death, felt the soul leaving its master, and had collapsed to the sand outside the house. From there it crawled inside, and Liam arrived only an hour after that.

Liam knew the rest. He sat against the wall, sipping at the wine, which was still cool, though he had to hoist the jug high and angle his head uncomfortably to get at it.

Tarquin died at midnight. That would allow Lons enough time to finish whatever performance he was in and get out to the beach. Marcius's whereabouts he did not know, but if the merchant were involved, he probably would have sent one of his hired swords. Viyescu's movements were a mystery as well, and he did not even know who the woman with the seductive voice was. It did not look encouraging when he pieced it all together, and he realized that he had done little more than scratch the surface.

You had not visited Master Tanaquil for a long while. He mentioned your name often. The block erased his own thoughts, and he looked dazedly up from the jug.

"He did?"

Try as he might, he could not understand the portrait Fanuilh had painted. At one moment, Tarquin dismissed the dragon like a mere servant, simply sent the bearer of half his soul away like an inconvenience. Then, apparently, he took the time to wonder about a man less than half his age whom he only saw rarely.

Tanaquil was a good master.

As usual, there were no hidden overtones to Fanuilh's communication, but Liam felt he had offended, and fumbled an apology.

"I meant to come, but the rains had set in . . . and the ride is long. It is a rather out-of-the-way place."

It will not seem that way when you live here.

Did that mean his apology was accepted? That whatever spirit he had offended could rest?

The wine suddenly affected him all at once. His head felt thick but weightless, detached from the rest of his body. He eyed the long legs that now stretched out in front of him as if they were not his.

"I'd better get some sleep."

With an effort, he managed to gain his feet, and the dragon's eyes followed him, the sinuous neck angling up as he rose.

Where will you sleep?

"I'll find a place. Goodnight." Deliberately watching each step, he made his way out of the workroom and around to the kitchen, where he deposited the jug with elaborate care. He even patted it once, to reassure himself that he had put it there.

No more thoughts came from the dragon, and his own were pleasantly unable to form, skipping from one to the other without being able to settle anywhere. With the same measured tread, he sought out the low divan in the library. It did not occur to him to sleep in the bedroom where Tarquin had died.

Curled up on the couch, blinking blearily at the rows of book spines on the shelves, he cursed himself tiredly for not finding a blanket. He knew, however, that he would not need it. The library was warm, just warm enough to sleep in without a blanket. He was perfectly comfortable in his clothes. Only the light was annoying, bright and intrusive, but even as he thought this, it began to dim, dying evenly to a dull glow that was strangely peaceful.

Wrapped in the warmth and dimness of the wine and the magical house, he fell softly into sleep.

CHAPTER 8

WAKE.

Liam was not dreaming until a few seconds before he woke, when suddenly he was walking through an ancient ruin that subtly reminded him of one he had seen years before. There, however, the giant sandstone pillars had been inscribed in a sinuous script he could not read; in his dream they were covered with the word *wake* in huge letters, like a command.

WAKE. WAKE.

The stones were in better shape than he remembered, as though they had just been carved, and the message took on an urgency the old ruins had not possessed.

WAKE. WAKE. WAKE.

He snapped away from the desolate city of his dreams, and knew he was in his library.

Tarquin's library, he reminded himself.

You are fully awake?

"Yes," he muttered, then raised his voice. "Yes, Fanuilh, I'm fully awake."

He got up quickly from the couch to forestall any further questions, and scrubbed at his eyes. Then he went to the kitchen and pictured warm water and spiced buns. Mists of steam rose from the jug after a moment, and he found hot rolls in the oven like those he had eaten the first day. He slicked back his unruly hair and washed his face, fingering the stubble. Then he had the stove conjure up another platter of uncooked meat and went to the workroom to present it to Fanuilh.

"In case you get hungry while I'm gone," he said. "At least it won't get cold." He laughed at his joke, but the little dragon just cocked its head. Liam rolled his eyes, and the empty decanter on the second table caught his attention.

"Why did Tarquin leave that out?"

I don't know.

The lack of expression in Fanuilh's thoughts maddened him; he felt as if the creature was hiding something from him, using a sort of mental poker-face. "I don't know," when spoken, could mean a hundred different things, or a thousand. It could carry any significance, different by shades, determined by tone and pitch, the speed with which the words were spoken. A wealth of information could hide in the quavering of a syllable, the length of a vowel.

I am not hiding anything. I simply do not know why he left it out.

"I know, I know. It's just . . . frustrating." It was not fair to blame the dragon.

It is strange, though. Master Tanaquil was very neat. He did not usually leave things lying about unless he intended to use them.

"Time to go," Liam said abruptly after a moment. "I'll be back later." He walked quickly outside to his horse, munching on a bun as he went.

Yesterday's rain had stopped, but the skies were still overcast, and everything was wet. The trees along the road back to Southwark were a sodden, lifeless black, stripped of their leaves by the winds of the past two weeks. Rich, musty smells rose off the muddy fields. The fields and the sky, and Southwark when he finally came in view of it, looked colorless and leeched out, a painting composed only in varying shades of gray.

Nonetheless, he had slept well in the magic house, and the sweet taste of the buns lingered in his mouth like a pleasant memory. He felt good, and he smiled at his landlady's worried chattering over his being away the whole night. He did not even tease her, stopping only to reassure her and pick up his writing case before stabling his horse.

Marcius's offices were in a warehouse a few streets back from the waterfront. They were not difficult to find, but Liam walked back and forth on the cobbles for a few min-

utes before going in, thinking of how to handle the interview. His hand dropped to the writing case at his belt,
where his maps were securely settled. Then he slumped
his shoulders meekly and knocked.

The warehouse fronted directly on the wide street, built
of salt-stained gray boards, blank and featureless except for
the huge wooden doors. His knocking sounded feeble, and
he raised his knuckles again when a smaller door, cleverly
set into its larger brothers, opened, and a ratlike head was
thrust out and snarled lazily.

"What would you?"

"Please, I have an appointment with Master Marcius. My
name is Liam Rhenford."

The ratty man looked him up and down disdainfully and
then withdrew. A few seconds later the man from the waterfront the day before appeared and gave Liam a mean smile
constricted by his puckered scar.

"The scholar comes to serve his time! Enter, good scholar!" He stood aside, motioning for Liam to enter, but when
Liam stepped forward he suddenly put himself in the way,
so that Liam had to stop short. The rat squealed a laugh,
and Scar's eyes gleamed.

"Well, come in, scholar! Why hem? Why haw? Do you
wish to see Master Marcius or no?"

"Please, I have an appointment," the Rat mocked in fal-
setto.

Liam studied Scar, noting the cudgel at his belt and his
heavy build. A regular thug, though the scar was from a
sword and not a knife. A soldier, maybe? Liam was taller,
with a longer reach, and thought he could probably have
taken the guard; but he had more important business.

"I swear, sir, I have business with Master Marcius," he
whined. "You were there when the appointment was made."

Scar dropped his restricted smile and heaved a bored sigh,
letting Liam pass. "Aye, I was there. Come in, you womanly
scholar. Marcius cannot see you yet; you'll have to wait his
leisure."

Nodding gratefully, Liam eased past him and into the
warehouse. It was long and lofty, empty space rising unin-

terrupted to the raftered ceilings. Crates, boxes, bales, barrels and jugs filled little more than a third of the floor space, clearly the result of a poor year's trading. The cargo of one big carrack might have filled the rest of the room. But that carrack, Liam thought, was just then rotting sixty feet below the sea at the base of the Teeth.

The two guards took seats around a barrel on which a stub of candle flickered. Scar ignored him, settling himself comfortably with his treelike legs stretched out. He ran a dirty-nailed finger along the trench that bisected his face. The Rat kept glancing in Liam's direction and chuckling. Liam chose a barrel several feet away from them and took a seat, focusing his attention on the stairway that ran along one wall of the warehouse.

It was exposed, made of the same weathered gray boards as the building, and ran the length of the wall to a closed-in loft at the rear of the room, illuminated along its way by torches placed in irregularly spaced sconces.

Liam waited for almost an hour. Scar and the Rat carried on a desultory conversation, almost but not quite oblivious to his presence. He did not listen to them, but looked around the room, particularly at the staircase, or at his maps. Impatience grew, and he wanted to get it over with, afraid he would lose all his carefully prepared meekness if he were angry. He prepared himself a dozen times to tell Scar or the Rat to ask if the merchant would see him yet, but always decided against it.

When he was going over the advantages and disadvantages of pressing his appointment for the thirteenth time, the door to the closed-in loft was flung open and he stood up as Marcius called out angrily.

"Is the scholar here yet?"

"Aye, he's just arrived, Master Marcius," Scar called loudly, with an evil grin at Liam. "Just this moment!"

"Send him up immediately!"

The door slammed shut and Scar came over and shooed him to the stairs, trying hard to keep his ruined face straight.

"Heard you the master, scholar? Immediately! Go to, go to!" He fluttered his hands towards the stairway, and Liam hurried over to the accompaniment of the Rat's squealing laughter.

The stairs were dilapidated, creaking ominously beneath his weight, and Liam skipped over them as lightly as he could. The door of the loft had no latch, and swung open beneath his knuckles. He peered into the room as owlishly as he could and inquired politely:

"Master Marcius?"

"In, in! Stand not by the doorway, sirrah! Y'are late enough as it is!"

Liam inched into the room, anxiously rubbing his hands together.

The merchant sat on a high stool beside an expansive secretary laden with papers and account books bound in gold-stamped leather. Open braziers filled with glowing coals flanked him, shelves and pigeonholes stacked with ledgers and scrolls spread around the walls. Wrought iron candelabra bore clusters of candles, reflected as tiny constellations in Marcius's sourly appraising eyes. Dry and perched high on the stool, he was impressive: his oiled, ringleted hair hung perfectly to his shoulders, his clothes hung beautifully from his spare frame, and the height he gained from the stool allowed him to look down his aristocratic nose at Liam.

"Well and well, scholar," the merchant said after peering at him coldly for a minute. "Report says you've a whole store of goods to vent—maps, charts, directions, soundings—the rounded whole wanting for a rich voyage. Report has it you've made Necquer far richer than he's any right to be."

"I gather he has done well," Liam said guardedly, unsure where the merchant's elaborately casual conversation was heading.

"I wonder then, why you come to me to vent this mappery? Why not sell them to Necquer?"

"Master Necquer does not appreciate my services, Master. He won't even pay me what he owes me, and I must leave Southwark soon enough, so I need ready money. The whole city speaks well of you, lord, and I thought to try my luck here."

Marcius considered this for a moment, apparently indifferent.

"Necquer won't pay you, eh?" He smiled dreamily, contemplating something that pleased him. "Your fault of course, sirrah scholar. 'A Freeporter's purse is drawn tighter than a crossbow,' they say. Your fault entirely."

Liam's agenda was not being followed to his satisfaction, and he tried to turn the talk away from Necquer with a fresh spate of whining.

"Oh, please, Master Marcius, I am in a desperate position. Now that Master Tanaquil has been murdered, I have no protection in Southwark. If you'll only buy these charts, I can leave—"

"Why?" Marcius interrupted without heat." Why should I buy your charts, when it were just as easy to follow Necquer's ships next season? Can you tell me that, scholar?" He smiled to himself, as though he had just made a telling point, but Liam was prepared.

"Ah, now, a shrewd, a very shrewd question, Master," he said in a flattering tone, "but I've an answer. You see, Master Necquer was impatient. He bought only a single set of my charts in the middle of the summer, after most of his ships were gone. He only wanted the maps to those ports he could easily reach. And those are the poorest of the ones I can guide you to. If he had bought other charts earlier, he might have reached far richer ports, but as it was he barely made it back by the close of the season, and only the miracle kept him safe. . . ." He let the silence draw out, but Marcius did not react to the hint about the Teeth. Instead, the merchant seemed to consider his words for a moment, then spat out a question suddenly.

"How do I know you won't sell me your charts and then go speak with Necquer? Twice as much for you, eh?"

"Oh, no, Master, I'd never deal with Master Necquer again. Why, he has not paid me for the first set of charts! Besides, I must leave Southwark soon."

"Your harping on that theme is most tiresome. Why are you so anxious to part our city?"

"I've explained, Master. I fear I'm in some danger from

those who killed my former master, the wizard Tanaquil."

"Know you who took him off?"

"I . . . no, Master Marcius, I don't."

"Then how do you know y'are in danger? You, a mere cowering scholar?"

"I don't know, Master. I'm simply afraid. It was *murder*, after all."

Marcius considered this as well, and Liam wondered if he had gone too far. The merchant had shown no reaction that was clearly incriminating, and Liam felt frustrated. How much of Marcius's suspicion was due to business shrewdness, and how much to guilt, he could not tell, and the uncertainty tempted him to further baiting.

"Well and well, Scholar Rhenford, for all y'are a low time-serving wretch, let's see your maps."

Opening his writing case, Liam burst into exclamations of joy. "Then you'll buy! Oh, Master, you will not regret this at all! You'll be rich, I promise, and I can flee Southwark!"

"I said nothing of buying, fool, only looking. Spread them out."

Chastened, Liam tried to be meek as he laid a few of his maps on the secretary in front of Marcius.

For over an hour, the merchant studied the various papers intently, asking clever questions at every turn. At first, Liam stood by his shoulder, explaining different points, but then Marcius loudly complained of a stench. Liam, remembering that he had slept in his clothes, took the hint and went to the far side of the secretary, though he could detect no odor. More of the merchant's snobbery, he guessed.

Whenever he could, he brought Tarquin into the conversation, using him as a reference and a source of information, bemoaning his death and extolling his virtues. Marcius made no comment, focusing his attention entirely on the maps, and the details Liam supplied about the customs and goods of different ports and cities.

At the end of the hour, Marcius decided to buy three of the maps, with a show of reluctance that Liam knew was feigned. The merchant prince was eager to get his hands on them, but did not want to seem so.

"I suppose I could purchase a few of these, scholar. They'd best be true, or I'll see you suffer for it."

"Oh, Master Marcius, they're true, I'll answer for it! And Master Necquer's riches will answer for it as well. He's made a huge pile this season, I assure you."

Despite the dig implicit in comparing Necquer's fortune with Marcius's own sunken one, the merchant prince did not rise to the bait, and Liam grimaced inside. He could raise no reaction in the man, which made him think the merchant dangerous, which reinforced his earlier suspicions. A hard, clever, vain man, who would stop at little, Liam judged.

Reaching into the depths of one of the drawers of the secretary, Marcius brought forth a flat metal chest with a key already in the lock. He turned the key and, keeping the lid between him and Liam, opened it.

"We've not discussed the cost."

A price was arranged, far higher than Liam would have asked, confirming that Marcius's reluctance was feigned. The merchant prince counted it out in silver coins, a tidy stack of them. Liam reached for the money, but Marcius slapped his hand away and covered the coins with a protective hand.

"Here's more to our deal, scholar. You'll straight leave Southwark?"

"Of course! I cannot stay, not if Master Tanaquil's killers are after me!"

"And you'll not stop long enough, perhaps, to resell your charts to good Master Necquer?"

"Why, no, Master Marcius! I swear—"

The merchant stopped him with an upraised palm.

"Don't forswear yourself, scholar," he said, pitching his voice low and stern. "It'd not like me to find you'd given me the lie and dealt with Necquer. It'd like you to part Southwark, and escape your master's murderers. So take the money, and make short work of your leavetaking. Am I clear?"

"Very clear, Master Marcius," Liam responded, licking his lips nervously. "It will only take me a day or so to arrange my departure."

"Then see to it immediately."

He nodded, and Liam scooped up the money and the maps Marcius had not bought, bowing anxiously. As he was pulling open the latchless door, Marcius spoke again.

"One last, scholar. Where are you lodging now?"

Thinking of the peaceful night he had just spent, he almost said Tarquin's, but a second thought intervened, and he mentioned his landlady's. The merchant prince nodded with a frown of disgust, as though the knowledge were important and the address distasteful but not unexpected.

Liam bowed again and scurried out onto the stairs, shutting the door quietly behind him. Sweat beaded his forehead, and his face was twitching with honest nervousness as he hurried down the staircase, but Scar and the Rat let him pass with no more harassment than their scornful smiles. The high squeal of the Rat's laughter followed him into the gray street, mocking.

Once outside he hurried a few blocks away, not thinking, and then stopped to breathe deep lungfuls of the cold sea air. He almost wished it were raining, to cool down his heated face, and wash away the trickles of hot moisture running down his back and under his arms.

I completely botched that, he thought, though he could not exactly say why he felt that way. His dissatisfaction with the whole interview, he guessed, stemmed from the fact that nothing had come of it. Frustrated with Marcius's nonchalance, he had mentioned Tarquin too many times, trying to get a rise out of the merchant.

His conduct, even the veiled threat about Liam's wanting to avoid Tarquin's killers, was ambiguous. He might have been hiding guilt beneath a facade of snobbery and indifference, or the facade was real, and he was innocent. Liam could not come to any conclusion.

The interview had produced nothing but silver coins he did not need.

It was not until he was within a few blocks of his lodgings that he realized with a jolt what really bothered him about the conversation. He had agreed to leave Southwark.

The idea loomed enormously before him, presenting

untold complications. But he would not consider them, ignoring the problems in favor of a second idea that came fast on their heels.

Why was Marcius so anxious to have him out of Southwark? He could not imagine it was solely to keep him from selling the same charts to Necquer. It must mean something more, and there was only one thing it could mean, he supposed.

Feeling suddenly better about the morning's work, he turned away from the narrow streets where his garret was, and headed up to the rich quarter and the tailor he had seen two days earlier.

His clothes were ready, and he spent a few moments admiring them before he had the tailor bundle them up. He paid, and retraced his steps to his garret. There was almost an hour before noon, when he would have to meet Coeccias at the White Grape, so he had the drudge heat water, and washed himself in his room, shaving as well. Then he put on one of his new sets of clothes, a deep blue tunic with soft breeches of owl gray. His good boots and new cloak completed the outfit, and he wished for a mirror to admire himself. There was none, so he went downstairs.

The drudge was the only person in the kitchen, and she stared at his new clothes fearfully. When asked, she stammered that she did not know where his landlady was.

"Well, then, could you tell her that I probably won't be in this evening, so she should not worry. Will you tell her?"

He wanted to laugh at her eager, wide-eyed nodding, and went to the White Grape.

As usual, the tavern seemed empty, though the common room was more than half full. The lunchtime conversations were quiet, and the tables were placed well apart so that sound did not carry. The serving girl recognized Liam, and gave his clothes a second, approving look before coming to his table.

"I doubted you'd come," Coeccias said when he arrived, standing behind his chair for a moment before sitting. "You've tricked yourself up nicely, Rhenford."

"New clothes," he responded, waving a hand in dismissal.

"Well, then, what news?"

"I met with Ancus Marcius this morning."

Coeccias seemed to be waiting for something, edging around a question.

"Anything come of it?"

"Enough to buy lunch, but not much else."

While they ate, he described his conversation with the merchant, and the Aedile listened with occasional murmurs of comprehension.

"I think the warning is genuine," Liam finished. "I think he killed Tarquin over the Teeth, and wants me off the scene because he thinks I may have some information."

"Or he took you for the fool you presented, and played you out your own fears, so you wouldn't deal with Necquer. Your suspicion wilts under that complexion."

It did indeed. Once again he swung back to thinking he had wasted the morning, and his only interview with the proud merchant prince.

"And Marcius expects me to leave Southwark," Liam added gloomily.

"Aye, he does. Naught bettered, Rhenford, and maybe much made worse." The blandness with which the Aedile announced his failure stung him, and he hung his head over his untasted food.

"Well, there's nothing to be done about it," he muttered.

"Truth, nothing. So we'll not nag at it. Let's consider something else, such as where you flew off to last night, eh?" Frank disapproval rode the Aedile's heavy brow, and Liam winced.

"I . . . I was not feeling well."

"The play was not so poor as to be sickening, Rhenford. No excuse. Have you a better?"

"No."

Liam raised his gaze to Coeccias's, and held it against the Aedile's probing stare. After a long moment of tension, the heavy man sighed and relaxed.

"I trust y'are feeling better," he said with heavy sarcasm.

"Much, thank you," Liam replied in the same manner.

There was another tension, but it broke when both smiled tentatively. Coeccias spoke first.

"If y'are feeling well enough, we've other business."

He began to describe what he had found out. His men had not discovered the barmaid Donoé, but they had not been searching the rich quarter. He had reserved the best taverns there for himself, and expected to go the rounds the next morning.

"They're good men all," he explained, "but I'd rather they not fright the poor girl. I'll handle it, and assure the outcome. You may want to attend me."

It was agreed that Liam would go with him, as he knew what he wanted to ask the girl, and might think of more questions when he saw her.

The Aedile had also arranged to be informed if the rent on the mysterious hooded woman's lodgings was paid.

"We'll know by tomorrow noon whether Tarquin was keeping her or no. But more than all this," he went on, growing brisk, "is the player. When we thought him a minstrel, and did not know his face, I was not so hot to clap him in. Now we have his face and his station, and as an actor, he'd've had access to the sort of knife as killed the wizard. He seems most likely to me."

"Then you want to arrest him?"

Frowning, Coeccias tugged at his beard and spoke thoughtfully. "No, truth, I don't. See him, yes, clap him in, no. Strikes me, all proposed to the killing were clever enough to fix the blame elsewhere. And of the choices, the player would be first in my mind to sacrifice—he's the basest. Viyescu's respected, the woman unknown, Marcius nigh untouchable without good cause." He stopped, as though there was more.

"And . . ." Liam prompted.

"And . . . he doesn't look the sort. Truth, did you see him stab that villain in the piece? Now, certain it is that duke earned his death more than Tarquin did his, but the pretty boy winced at it—and that only in a play! Did see?"

"I was watching the girl."

"Aye," Coeccias laughed. "Aye. Well, I think he couldn't have done the real deed, if he blanched at its counterfeit."

"I agree. I've seen him elsewhere, and he doesn't seem the type to fight." At the rise of the Aedile's eyebrows, Liam briefly outlined his sight of Lons at the Necquer's party.

"All Necquer had to do was start for the door, and Lons was off like lightning. He wouldn't fight unless he was pushed, I guess. Too afraid his handsome face'd get hurt. And Tarquin wasn't the kind to push too hard."

"Still and all, it'd like me to see him, and maybe fright him a little. If he is our man, he's been cool enough till now, staying the time in town, and acting his plays. We'll talk with him, and set a man to watch him. He may try to take his leave after our little discourse. If he does, we'll have him."

"And if not, we may still scare him enough to make a mistake."

"Agreed. We'll to the theater. The players practice their performances in the morning, and sup just at noon. If we're quick, we'll catch him before his afternoon's work. Attend me."

Liam dropped one of Marcius's silver coins on the table and they hurried out of the White Grape.

A dullness clung to the theater, like a midnight lover in the morning. The golden orb looked gaudy and the doors had a desolate air, as if the building had been abandoned. They opened, however, and Liam and Coeccias went into the lobby, which felt cold and unused. Though there was a broom in one corner, and the plank floors had obviously just been swept clean, Liam imagined they would feel dusty, or perhaps moldy, if he knelt and touched them.

He did not.

In the theater itself a number of actors sat or stood around the pit, eating their meals and talking in low voices. A few candles flickered weakly in the windowless building, and despite the voices and people, it was gloomy.

The man who had greeted Coeccias at the door the night before detached himself from a whispered conversation and came to stand before them, dressed now in a commoner's smock instead of his colorful motley. He executed a grand, mocking bow.

"Your servant, milord Aedile. Have you come to close us out?"

Coeccias frowned, ignoring the actor's bantering tone. "Nay, player. I'd have words with one of your company. Where is Lons?"

The actor widened his eyes in girlish admiration, and spoke with ironic reverence. "Lons? Our great hero? Lons the Magnificent? I fear me his lordship is not here, milord Aedile, but if you stay a moment, I'm sure he'll grace us."

"When?"

"Soon." The actor dropped his joking. "He's gone to sup elsewhere, and'll be back soon. You may await him here." With another grand bow, he twisted away and clapped his hands loudly, calling for the beginning of the afternoon's rehearsal.

Coeccias frowned sourly at the actor's back.

"I'll not be sad to pack *him* off to the heath."

"Who is he?" Liam asked, watching the actor marshall his company on the stage.

"Kansallus. He pens their sorry scripts, gives them their readings. Owns a share of the theater as well, if rumor's to be credited. A very rogue, but with some excellent parts: wit, voice, good sense. He never fusses when I close him out."

There was a small tinge of admiration in the Aedile's voice.

"If you like him so much, why do you shut up his theater?"

"The Duke'd have it so. He doesn't take with the stage, and especially so when they allow women on it. So, a few days after Uris-tide, it's off to the country with them."

Coeccias sighed ruefully, and they fell silent, watching

the actors rehearse. It was a pastoral comedy complete with
shepherdesses and faeries, in which Knave Fitch played a
large role as a drunken farmer. Even with little practice,
the clown brought humor to the part, and both men in the
lobby chuckled.

Hearing them, Kansallus backed out to the lobby, stopping beside them but leaving his eyes on the stage.

"It pleases you?" he asked, trying and failing to mask his
eagerness.

"Truth, it's a goodly thing."

"Yes, very much. It's funny."

Kansallus drank in the praise, bobbing his head happily
at the stage, as if to encourage the actors.

"But why," Liam asked during a pause while the scene
shifted, "don't you have that girl play the lead shepherd-
ess? The one who played the princess last night? She'd be
spectacular."

"That one," Kansallus said, rolling his eyes. "It'd be worth
my life and my jewels at once to suggest it. She only plays
tragedy, look you, tragedy only. She esteems herself a great
actress, a *lofty* actress. No low comedy for her. Mug? Wink?
Trip and pratfall? Never! Her feet would rot off before she'd
play comedy!"

"A shrew, eh?" Coeccias asked with a wicked grin. "Pity.
She's a fair leg."

Liam nodded in agreement.

"Oh, in faith, I cannot deny it. A fair leg, and a fair ankle,
bosom and face to keep the leg company. Enjoy what you
see on the stage, good sirs, because you'll never see more
of Rora anywhere else, least of all warming your bed."

"Rora?" Liam thought he would have done well to find
Kansallus long before, when he was searching for someone
who knew Southwark and would tell what he knew.

"Rora," the actor confirmed. "No one's bauble is Rora,
to be dandled and played with and warmed on a winter's
night. Pure enough to hunt the unicorn, our Rora, and too
good for comedy—No! No! No! Fitch, you mutton-headed,
wool-pated, poxy, dripping . . ." He ran forward, shouting,

to the stage, where Knave Fitch was standing with an elaborately innocent face while the rest of the cast collapsed in hysterics around him.

"It is no error of mine, Master Playwright, if my fellow actors cannot restrain their . . ." His voice, rippling with rolled r's, drifted to them from the stage, but the door behind them opened suddenly, and they both turned.

Framed in a wash of gray light from the door, Rora entered, and Liam thought his heart might have stopped. Even bundled in a warm cloak she was stunning, the fullness of her red lips and the perfect beauty of her white complexion etched in the gray light. It turned her hair to dusty gold, and Liam fleetingly compared her to Lady Necquer, dismissing the latter in an instant. She stopped when she saw them. Over her shoulder, Lons loomed curiously.

"Good day, Aedile Coeccias," she said in a rich, musical voice. Her eyes rested on Liam, however, smiling a little mysteriously and arching an eyebrow, clearly aware of her affect on him.

Maybe if I bring my jaw up from my knees, he thought ashamedly, and looked at Coeccias, who cleared his throat.

"Ah, y'are the actor Lons?"

The handsome man, not expecting to be addressed, did not reply at once.

"Aye."

"We'd have words with you, if you can spare a moment."

"But I've a practice—"

"Kansallus will not mind," Coeccias interrupted firmly, crossing his arms on his wide chest.

"Well, then, I suppose . . ." He edged his way in past Rora, who continued to stare at Liam. Liam, in turn, kept his eyes fixed on the other two men, horribly aware of the blush that was creeping up his long neck. He decided that it was a point in Lady Necquer's favor that she did not seem so keenly conscious of her beauty.

"What did you want, Aedile?" Lons seemed a little surer of himself, now that he was out from behind Rora and facing Coeccias. The Aedile gestured significantly at the woman.

"Would you not prefer to be alone?"

Lons stiffened, as did Rora. "Anything you can say to my brother you can say with me as witness," she said coldly.

"Well enough," he said agreeably, turning back to Lons. "Pray you, brother, do tell what business you had with Tarquin Tanaquil?"

Stammering, Lons clenched his hands. "Tanaquil? The wizard? He's called you? The bargain's not fulfilled, the terms not met, I—"

"Lons," Rora warned.

"Still!" Coeccias hissed at her out of the side of his mouth, but the moment was enough for Lons to regain his composure.

"Our business was that," he said formally. "*Ours*. And as it is not finished, there's no need for you t'interfere."

"I doubt but there is, goodman player. You'll have no more business with Master Tanaquil."

"What?" Lons exclaimed angrily. "You can't make me—"

Liam watched Coeccias draw the young man on, and scrutinized the handsome face carefully.

"None'll have business with Master Tanaquil. He's gone beyond business, Lons, sped on his way by a dagger."

Lons gaped, stunned.

"Tanaquil? Murdered?"

Liam had to remind himself that the man was an actor. His astonishment seemed unfeigned, real to a fault. Liam was disappointed, but not surprised. Much as he disliked the actor, he did not believe him capable of murder; Coeccias, however pressed on.

"So you see, sirrah, what was your particular business is now my business, and the question stands. Why did you have dealings with the wizard?"

Licking his lips, the young man looked from one face to another, Liam's and Coeccias's expectant, Rora's wary and warning.

"I needed his help in a . . . in a small matter of the heart."

Rora nodded approvingly, but the Aedile laughed heartily.

"A love potion? You sought a wizard for a love potion? My granddam could've made you a love potion!"

"The lady," Lons said with barely restrained anger, "required a great service of me. I lacked the power for it, and sought the wizard's help."

"She needs must have set you a great task," Coeccias said, angling for more.

"The Teeth. She wanted the Teeth removed, to protect her husband," the actor supplied, over his sister's hissed objection.

"You commissioned *that*?" The Aedile was clearly awed. "I hope the lady was worth it."

"She is," Lons replied, with a glance at Liam, who nodded agreement, allowing himself a sidelong look at Rora.

"And the lady's name? Her husband's station?"

"Is unimportant now," Liam said quietly, drawing a surprised stare from the Aedile and a sneer from Lons. "I'll explain later. For now, I've a question." He addressed himself to the actor.

"Tell me, how did you propose to pay Tanaquil? Wizards are costly, and I know the spell took a great deal of effort."

"I proposed no payment. He named a sum, and I agreed."

"What sum?"

"Ten thousand, in gold," the actor said, with a touch of pride.

Rora gasped and Coeccias gave a low whistle, but Liam only nodded thoughtfully.

"And he took you at your word that you could pay?"

"I presume he knew my state. He accepted my compact."

"But you don't have ten thousand in gold."

"No." Lons shifted under the questions, perplexed.

"And so you couldn't have paid him, but he undertook the spell anyway."

"Perhaps he knew he was doing a noble deed—helping true love find its course." Again, there was the touch of hard, wounded pride, the sense of disdain at having his affairs discussed. Liam barked a laugh.

"More likely you dressed yourself up in the richest costume the Golden Orb has and let him think you a rich merchant's son."

The young man blanched, but said nothing.

"And now that he's dead, you don't have to pay, do you?"

"I did not kill him," Lons said thickly, licking dry lips.

With the wolf's grin he had practiced, Liam agreed. "Certainly not, certainly not. No one's suggesting such a thing. It would not be worth murder to catch a beautiful woman, get rid of an unpayable debt, and avoid a powerful wizard's wrath. Certainly not."

The wolf's grin worked nicely, leaving the young man speechless and gaping.

"I think we're done here, don't you, Aedile Coeccias?" Liam raised an eyebrow to the officer, who looked intently at him for a moment, and then nodded once.

"Thank you, Lons, for your time. I don't think we'll be bothering you again." Smiling the wolf's grin again for effect, he ushered Coeccias to the door and let him pass out first.

Rora recovered before Lons did, and began stammering furiously.

"Who are you? How dare you question us—"

He dropped the grin and assumed a polite smile to match his words, which were offhand but firmly interrupted her.

"An interesting thing, Maid Rora. The knife that killed Tarquin was one that players often use. One of a pair, I'm told. It would be interesting to see if the theater were missing any, wouldn't it?"

With a friendly smile, he dipped his head to her, and then turned to Lons, putting his back to the girl.

"Stay away from Lady Necquer," he whispered quietly. "Do you hear? Stay away."

"I'll not," Lons said, trying and failing to sound firm. Liam's remarks had greatly upset him.

"Stay away from her," he repeated. "If Necquer hears—"

"Necquer," the actor interrupted eagerly, as if he had found an attack he could answer, "deserves her not! He's naught but a pandering, strutting—"

Rora hissed a warning and Lons stopped, glaring angrily and desperately at her.

"Just stay away from her," Liam said into the sudden silence, and received a sullen nod from the actor. Denying himself the last look at Rora that he wanted, he went out the door to join Coeccias.

CHAPTER 9

COECCIAS WAS WAITING further down the street, leaning against a wall and watching a group of boys scuffle around a leather ball. He looked up with a slight chuckle at Liam's approach.

"It should be branded on your front, Rhenford: 'Take no surprise; I may do anything.' Branded in bold letters, or sewn into your clothes in characters of red."

"What do you mean?"

They started off, leaving the boys behind and heading by tacit consent towards the Point. Coeccias ticked his reasons off on thick, blunt fingers.

"Firstly, you discount the player, and throw your weight behind the merchant. Y'ignore the player whiles we talk, to gawp and stare at his sweet sister. Then, of a sudden, you turn on the player again and fasten your teeth into his throat. You warrant him a motive and an opportunity, and show a familiarity with his affairs I'd have never guessed at. You fair prove him the murderer. And then—then you ask his pardon and go your way! You as much as say 'Y'are a killer, sirrah,' and then leave him at large!"

"You didn't argue," Liam pointed out, and the Aedile threw up his arms in exasperation.

"Oh, no, nor call you the wooden fool y'are, nor clap Lons in as I should! I've grown as wooden as you! And yet I give you my service. That of value I have in this I have from you, and all I see you do makes you out a bloodhound. Y'have an acute nose, Rhenford. Perhaps I'll just give you rein and follow you to the murderer."

Liam shrugged uncomfortably under the praise, and

glanced around the street before dropping his gaze to his boots, not looking at Coeccias.

"You could also follow me nowhere."

"I'd wager not. Y'are strange in thought and manner, but I'll be led by you in this, Rhenford, and I doubt not but it'll be to my profit."

They lapsed into silence, Coeccias satisfied and content, Liam wondering.

He *had* as much as said Lons was a murderer, and all the clues pointed that way. The knife, the debt, the timing—almost everything indicated Lons, but he was reluctant to accept that. For one thing, he was afraid his dislike had colored his judgement, that his connection with Lady Necquer made him anxious to find Lons guilty. For another, there was Lons himself—Liam simply could not find murder in the self-involved actor's character. Pride and arrogance, yes, but it seemed the sort he had often found in cowards, men who shrank from blood. And lastly, there was Lons's sister. Rora had taken a powerful hold on his mind, and he found it difficult to remove her. She was an amazing presence, he thought, and though he had felt something cold and disdainful in her, she drew him, her image fluttering around inside his head.

Now that he had warned Lons away from Lady Necquer, he was inclined to find his murderer elsewhere, and he favored the merchant prince. Marcius's motives were muddied, and the evidence did not single him out, but he had the sort of strength of will and capacity for violence that Liam expected to find in a killer. And his threats, even veiled and obscure ones, had the ring of truth.

Liam told none of this to the Aedile. Instead, he thought it out, eyes fixed on his feet as the two men made their way south through the city. Other considerations sprang to mind. He remembered Lady Necquer's comments on the Teeth, and heard now a note of morbid fascination he had not noticed at first. She had been so afraid of them and the danger they presented to her husband that she had agreed to sleep with the man who could remove them.

And Tarquin had been responsible for it; could she be

suspected? Or her husband? A series of questions formed themselves in his head, almost involuntarily, that he would ask her that afternoon. He felt instinctively that she was not involved, but her husband might be, if she had told him about Lons's courtship. That Necquer should strike at Tarquin and not Lons was strange, and argued against the suspicion, but the questions interested him in and of themselves, and he resolved to ask them.

"Your face's dark as the sky," Coeccias said finally, with a gesture that took in Liam's wrinkled brow and the cloudy sky. They were back in the neighborhood of the White Grape, and a pall of black hung over the sky.

"Thinking about murderers and rainy days make for a depressing combination."

"Truth, they do. Would a drink help?" The painted signboard of the White Grape hung further down the street, swaying slightly in the stiff, storm-bringing breeze from the sea.

"I think so."

A bottle of the tavern's watered-down white wine sped away the time, and Liam looked up from the dregs to hear the bells announce that it was time for his daily visit to Lady Necquer. He stood up from the table with mixed feelings. Coeccias reminded him of the next day's work, looking for the barmaid Donoé, and they agreed on an hour to meet.

It was strange, Liam reflected as he walked towards the rich quarter, how Coeccias's attitude had changed. Only a few hours earlier the Aedile had been highly suspicious of him because of his abrupt departure from the theater the evening before. Now Coeccias was practically giving up, throwing the weight of the whole investigation on Liam. Had his questioning of Lons been that impressive?

He was not entirely comfortable with the idea of himself as a sort of human bloodhound. He did not picture himself as particularly astute where people's darker motivations were concerned. If he were like that, he could not imagine why people accepted his presence; he knew that he would not want to be with someone who could smell out his deepest secrets.

Yet people did accept his presence. Tarquin had spoken freely around him, the Aedile shared meals with him. Lady Necquer actually seemed to look forward to his visits. Did that mean that, even though they felt he could see into their souls, they felt secure enough with themselves to ignore it?

Was that what Fanuilh had seen in him? The thing that made the dragon entrust him with finding Tarquin's murderer?

Liam Rhenford, human bloodhound. Liam Rhenford, before whom men's souls are laid bare. Liam Rhenford, the perfect investigator.

Suddenly he laughed harshly, repressing the grandiose thoughts.

I'm just asking questions, he thought, grinning, *and they just happen to be good ones. I'm carrying my Luck with me.* He laughed again, and felt better. The narrow street with its border of high walls where the Necquers lived was just ahead.

"Master Liam, at th'appointed hour, as usual!"

Lares's bow was small out of familiarity and friendliness, not disdain, and the old man ushered him in with a smile.

Well, at least the old man isn't uneasy around me, Liam thought with relief, and offered Lares a smile in return.

"It's becoming a ritual, Lares. They set the tolling of the bells by me."

Lady Necquer awaited him in the same upstairs parlor, and started up with a smile when Lares announced him. She came to him and, taking his hands, kissed him formally on the cheek. Thinking of the questions he wanted to ask and his unfavorable comparison of her with Rora, he coughed nervously and reclaimed his hands as soon as he could.

"Well, Sir Liam," she said, sitting gracefully, "what discourse have you prepared for me this day?" Bright color suffused her pale complexion, and a smile broke out uncontrollably on her face. She seemed intensely happy about something, and he smiled mildly, infected by her mood.

"I'm afraid I haven't prepared any talk for this afternoon. But you, I think, must have some news. If you grin any harder your face will split in two. What makes you so happy?"

Her grin widened until it took possession of her whole face, and she suddenly leapt up and danced around the room.

"Oh, Sir Liam, my husband comes home this day, and will not leave me again for winter entire! My heart is full to bursting!" She hugged herself, and Liam smiled at her childlike joy. He took a breath and spoke heartily.

"When does he arrive?"

"Soon, soon, soon! He'll dine with me this night!" She danced further, twirling around the whole room, and he thought of Rora's dancing in the theater, the exact opposite of Lady Necquer's pure, girlish giddiness. Favoring him with a radiant smile, she danced past his chair, laying a hand briefly on his shoulder.

"He is in the city even now, attending pressing business, but he'll be home soon, and mine for the winter!"

"That's excellent news, madam, and I think I have some other that will increase your happiness."

"Oh?" She came to a reluctant halt, her full skirts whirling around her, and beamed abashedly at him. "You must excuse me, Sir Liam. I'm hardly fit company. I can think of little else but Freihett. But come, your news." Eagerly, she came and sat beside him on the divan, placing a hand on his arm, offering her whole attention with a forced serious look that threatened to break into a wild grin at any moment.

"It so happens," he began slowly, "that I had occasion to speak with someone who I believe was causing you some discomfort."

She nodded, still seriously, but the smile threatened hugely. He went on.

"A young man, an actor, who was presenting unwanted attentions."

The threat of a smile vanished, and she took a deep breath.

"There are some things I know about him that could have caused him a great deal of trouble, and it so happened that I was able to . . . well, warn him off, if you see what I mean. I don't think he will be bothering you again. I did not mean to pry, madam, but the opportunity presented itself. I know it was not my place—"

Taking her hand from his arm, her voice was strained and her eyes downcast on her lap, where her hands were clasped fiercely. "No, it was not your place . . . how did you happen to speak with him?"

Liam stood and took a few steps to stand before an elegant hanging. He fingered its tassels absently, his back to her. "I was well acquainted with a wizard named Tarquin Tanaquil. He . . . died recently, and several things indicated that Lons was involved in the death. I spoke with him about his involvement, and took the opportunity to suggest he leave you alone."

"The wizard was murdered?" The strain in her voice was greater.

"Yes. And certain things indicate Lons was responsible." He turned to look at her, and almost flinched at the pain on her face. "Lons had commissioned Tarquin to make the Teeth vanish, but couldn't pay the price. The knife that was used was a stage blade. His guilt could be established with these."

"He would not do that," she whispered, almost choking on a sob. "He hasn't the strength."

Liam went and sat beside her. "I don't think so either. Tell me, why did you want him to get rid of the Teeth?"

Her words came slowly, with great difficulty. He writhed inside at making her talk about it, but was also grateful that she was speaking freely, and had not chosen to be angry with him. He had feared she would think he had tricked her, had wormed his way into her confidence just for information. But she seemed wrapped up in her sorrow and confusion.

"He . . . he wooed me, professed undying love. The summer entire, while Freihett was at sea. He spoke with such heat, so truly . . . he said he needs must, that he needs must . . . *know* me. I gave him no encouragement, no sign of returning his feelings, but he pressed and pressed. And all while Freihett was at sea, and those cursed Teeth waited to take him down, to crush him beneath the cold blue."

She gasped at the intensity of her vision, at the depth of her fear for her husband, and Liam waited silently for her to go on. Tears brimmed in her enormous blue eyes, but were not shed, and suddenly she smiled bleakly, looking defenselessly at him.

"I thought if I tasked him impossibly, he would give me peace. I claimed the destruction of the Teeth as my price, and sent him away, sure he could not achieve it. It was a fond and foolish thought, wasn't it?" Liam shook his head sadly, and she took a deep breath, steadying herself. "But he did it. The wizard succored him, and he saved my husband's life. What could I do? I could not surrender to him."

After a long pause, she looked earnestly at him and added: "I did not surrender to him, Sir Liam, though he continues to plague me. He was to come to me on the day the Teeth vanished, but I put him off, feigned sickness, and on the day after my husband was home . . . I broke my word, and did not pay him for my husband's life. I have transgressed doubly, in breaking an oath and entertaining a lover while my husband was away. You understand?"

It was important to her, and he nodded again, gravely. "Yes, I do understand. Does your husband know?"

"Yes. I gave him the whole story when he was well. The journey had taken much from him, you know."

"I can imagine. What did he say about it?"

"Naught, or very little. He credited me, and said he would not hold it against me. But he was terribly irked, I know. If Lons had been there, or he'd come across him, there'd have been more than harsh words."

It was time to stop, Liam decided. Lady Necquer's brave smile held, but her lip trembled, and he knew enough for now. She had not thought to wonder about his interest, nor to think that he might connect any of what she said with Tarquin's death. He hated himself for prying, but offered a directionless prayer of thanks that she had not realized what he was after.

"Come," he said, rising, "there's no reason to think on it any longer. Right or wrong, I think he'll stay away, and Master Necquer is back now to stay by your side."

At a sideboard he found wine, and filled two crystal goblets. He brought the goblets back to the divan and handed one to her. She took it gratefully and drank. Tears still brimmed in her eyes, dangling from her eyelashes. He wanted very much to brush them away, but was afraid it might seem forward. Instead, he walked back to the hanging and examined it, sipping his wine.

After gulping down her glass, Lady Necquer went to the sideboard and poured herself another, from which she took a smaller sip before speaking in a deliberately bright manner.

"Now, Sir Liam, enough of all that. Enough and too much. We must regain our wonted mirth, and find a way to pass the time more in keeping with my husband's home-coming."

"What shall we talk about? I'm afraid we've covered what I know of the rest of the world pretty thoroughly."

"Well then," she said with a smile halfway towards her earlier happiness, "we shall cover you. I know where you've been and what you've seen, but nothing of you. Come hold discourse on Sir Liam Rhenford."

Smiling apologetically, he followed her back to the divan. "That is a very boring topic, madam. The rest of the world is far more interesting."

"I'll judge that, Sir Liam. You may begin."

Folding her hands in her lap, she assumed a very grave demeanor, as if she really meant to judge him. He laughed, and she joined him tentatively.

"Come, go to, go to! Tell me about you!"

"Very well," he said, pleased to see her smiling. "What would you like to know?"

"What you do in Southwark," she answered promptly, and he had to pause and think.

"Nothing," he said after a while. "Nothing, really."

"Nothing? Naught? I'll not believe that. You certainly don't idle your time waiting to attend me in the afternoons!"

"Well, I suppose I am recovering. I have been a long time away from Taralon, and I thought it was time to get back."

"After your shipwrack?"

Had he mentioned that to her? He did not remember, but he was sure he had not told her the whole story. Now that he thought about it, he realized once again that he was not sure why he was in Southwark. The experience on the island had worn him out, and when he had finally reached Southwark, he was so grateful to be back in Taralon that he had settled there instinctively. To fill the time, he had half-invented the idea of writing, but that was not the real reason he stayed in Southwark. It was safe, a part of Taralon that held no memories for him at all, but that was a part of his home nonetheless.

"Yes. I'm also writing."

"Stories?" she asked eagerly. "Or a play? Or poetry? I'll wager your verse is passing fair."

"Neither, I'm afraid. History. Or rather, my history, with some of the history of the places I've been." He smiled at her obvious disappointment, and spoke with a hint of reproach. "You seemed to think my stories of where I'd been somewhat interesting."

"Well, and they were," she admitted grudgingly, "when you *told* them. But if you cage them with bars of ink and walls of leather, they'll be stuporous, sleep-inducing, for it was your tongue that gave them life. You'd do better to make of them a romance, or better, a string of poems. Yes! A string of poems addressed to the sweetling who awaits you on shore!"

"But I didn't have a sweetling on shore," he protested.

Brushing aside the objection, she went on. "No matter; invent one! Call her . . . call her Larissa, and pine longingly for her as you view the lusty beauties of the strange scenes you've visited! Mince your words and file your phrase, and harken back to her shining face whenever you mention some far-off wonder!"

They went on in the same vein for a while, as Lady Necquer mapped out the collection of poems she expected from him, and he objected to it every step of the way, laughingly complaining that he was no poet, and had had no girl waiting for him while he traveled.

The idea seemed to inspire her, and though she too giggled at her own high-flown fancies, there was a seriousness as well.

If I were a poet, Liam thought, *it* would *make good verse. But I'm not*, he reminded himself, and reminded her as well, an objection she countered with the suggestion that he perform vigils with the priests of Uris.

"Oh, and Uris-tide is nigh! If you begin tomorrow, you can complete the course of the devotions by midnight of the feast! The goddess'll surely inspire you!"

"I doubt that; Uris is not widely worshipped in the Midlands, and would hardly look favorably on me. Besides, don't men have to shave their heads to attend the vigils?"

"They do," she agreed, and looked at him for a long moment before bursting into giggles at the image of him without any hair at all, with even eyebrows shaved, as was required of supplicants to Uris.

"It sounds a high price to pay for poetic inspiration," he said, but she did not hear, trying to stifle her own mirth. She did, however, hear the heavy tread on the stairs and the voice that came from outside the door of the parlor.

"Poppae! Poppae! I'm home!"

The door swung open, and Necquer entered, still in his dusty traveling cloak and mud-spattered riding boots. Her giggles subsided in a gasp, and she leapt to her feet and ran to him, kissing him quickly and often without discretion. He staggered under her affection, and put his arms around her to steady himself, smiling indulgently. Then he noticed Liam, and greeted him with an ironic nod.

"I'd shake your hand, Rhenford, but mine are full at the moment."

Suddenly, Poppae cried out, and ran her hand delicately down Necquer's cheek. Just above the line of his beard, a bright purple bruise was blooming.

"You've taken a hurt!"

"It's nothing," he murmured brusquely, taking her hand

in his and drawing it away. "An unruly pair of highwaymen, without the sense to be afraid of my guards." She made to fuss about it, but he stopped her with a brief kiss. "It's nothing. You won't even notice it in a few days. Now, Rhenford, I must say I'm glad to see you here. I take it you've been entertaining?"

"Actually, I've just been trying not to be boring."

"Go to, go to," Lady Necquer scolded, shifting so that she could see both men, but leaving her arms around Necquer. "He has kindly borne my maunderings and incessant weeping over your absence, and entertained me most regally. He has even promised to pen me a string of poems!"

Necquer smiled at Liam's look of surprise. "Poems, eh? You're more talented than I realized, Rhenford."

"More talented than I realized, Master Necquer. I didn't know I was a poet."

"Well then, you'll stay to dinner and maybe Poppae can instruct you in the art."

"Oh, yes, do stay, Sir Liam!"

Liam was surprised to notice that Necquer honestly meant the invitation, though his wife's agreement had been hasty and not entirely heartfelt. And the merchant had not been at all disturbed to find his wife closeted with another man, even though he had recently found out someone was wooing her. Had he ruled Liam completely out as a threat?

Lady Necquer's obvious desire to be alone with her husband would make that a fair judgement, he thought wryly.

"I'm afraid I cannot. I promised I'd dine with a friend tonight."

Frowning, Necquer accepted the refusal, to his wife's ill-concealed delight. "Another time, then," he said, disengaging himself from his wife to offer Liam his hand.

"Certainly," Liam said, and took the merchant's slim hand, which was warm and moist with sweat. "You really should wear some armor, and a helmet." He pointed with his free hand at Necquer's cheek.

"I do," the merchant laughed, letting go his grip on Liam's hand. "They tried to sneak up on us in the night."

Liam smiled and headed for the door with a slight bow.

Lady Necquer, perhaps regretting her fickle change in interest, stopped him and kissed both his cheeks warmly.

"I'll expect you on the morrow, Sir Liam, though earlier. Say noon, if you've no objection. You'll not slip out of that string of poems so easily. We will discuss it then."

"Your servant," he said with a tremendous show of humility and a low bow, and backed out of the room.

At the bottom of the stairs Lares stood gazing reverently up.

"It's no small blessing t'have him back, eh, Sir Liam?"

"No," Liam said with a chuckle, thinking of Lady Necquer ecstatically greeting her husband. "No small blessing indeed. Goodnight, Lares."

A small wave of anger broke over him in the street. He had spent his afternoons entertaining her, turning his own life into an amusing tale to while away her waiting hours, and she had abandoned him the instant Necquer had come back. Necquer, who left her alone for months at a time!

The anger passed into reproach. It was foolish to think that way. Necquer was her husband, and obviously loved her dearly, despite what Lons had said, while he was only a recent acquaintance. And she had not simply abandoned him; she had asked him back the next day, as though nothing had changed.

Smiling a familiar, well-worn smile at himself, he wandered through the darkening streets. It was dusk, the clouds now beginning to shred into tatters beneath the onslaught of the sea breeze. Cold and stinging, the breeze scoured the sky and the rapidly emptying streets, molding his cloak to his back and legs as he walked north. Stars glittered, impossibly distant and small between the rents in the clouds.

Lady Necquer was, after all, almost a child. In her mid-twenties, he thought, and thus only five or six years younger than he, but different, in a way he sought to name.

Sheltered, he eventually thought. The only sorrows she knew were hers, while he had seen those of many others. In ports and lands Southwark had never heard of, on seas her merchants had never sailed, Liam had seen many other people's sorrows, and with an unconscious selflessness, he judged them greater than his. Greater than his burning home and his slain father, greater than being alone in a strange city and alone, for that matter, in the whole world.

It was for that reason, perhaps, that he had not objected to being linked with Fanuilh, or to finding Tarquin's murderer. One was a tie, a bond of sorts, and the other a duty that one might offer to family. He did not delude himself into thinking of Tarquin as a replacement for, or symbol of, his father; no thought could be more ridiculous. But it was a duty he wanted to fulfill, a purpose that went beyond food or shelter or survival, an unnecessary duty, and thus one gladly undertaken.

Liam thought of the house on the beach, and the quiet, dreamless night he had spent there, and decided that though it was not his yet, he would try to make it his.

But he did not want to go there yet. He wanted a drink, and something to eat, and the sound of other people enjoying themselves. And perhaps a glimpse of Rora, to take his mind off the weighty subjects he was now embarrassed to have thought about. He set his feet to the Golden Orb, the wind from the sea pushing steadily against his back, urging him on.

The theater was not yet open, he found when he arrived, his ears and the tip of his nose scarlet with the cold. It was too early for the evening's performance. Exasperated at his own foolishness, he searched the streets around for a tavern. There was no one to ask; the shops were closed and it was so early that the street in front of the theater had not yet filled up with the evening's audience.

He found a tavern on a side street only a few blocks from the Golden Orb, between a house like his landlady's, where the fourth and fifth stories leaned precariously out over the street, and a building with a crudely lettered sign that announced the school of a private teacher of rhetoric and grammar. Liam noticed with amusement that the sign had three misspellings. The tavern was called the Uncommon Player, and the wooden board that swung creakily over the door was painted with a figure in motley juggling three balls of flame. Noise trickled out, like the murmur of the sea from far away.

Inside, the common room was long and narrow, and the noise swelled to a din like battle. The tavern was packed to bursting with laughing, shouting, singing men and women, hectically enjoying themselves. Behind the bar, three men were busy trying to serve enough beer to keep the huge crowd happy. It was hot, and sweat streamed freely down many of the faces, but the smell was oddly pleasant, even with the thick banks of smoke that hovered overhead. Close, but not stifling, and fresh. The evening had only just begun, and the odors and the fun had not had time to sour. He wondered distastefully what it would be like in a few hours, and looked around for a place to sit.

There were only a few tables, inadequate for the large groups that were crammed around them, and all the standing room was taken by the raucous clientele. Even as he stood uncertainly in the doorway, however, four people stood up from the table nearest him, and Liam recognized them as actors from the rehearsal. One of them, a man, shouted loudly and waved towards the rear of the room, while the others settled with the harassed serving girl.

"Fitch! Fitch!" the man called, gesturing urgently. "Call!" Liam followed his pointing and saw Knave Fitch's flushed face nod comprehendingly towards the door and then resume talking with the group gathered around him. The man shook his head and led his three fellow actors out of the Uncommon Player.

Liam instantly installed himself at the vacant table, amazed that the four actors had managed to fit around it. He thought it barely adequate for one.

An earthenware tankard suddenly dropped to the table before him. He caught it instinctively and looked up at the hard-pressed serving girl, who nodded in approval at his quickness.

"I didn't—" he began, pitching his voice above the roar.

"All the drink we serve, master," the girl cut in, and turned abruptly to waltz away into the mass of thirsty customers.

Shrugging, Liam tested the drink and found beer, remarkably cold and far better than merely drinkable. He downed nearly half of it, looking idly around the room. The customers were not the same dour, quiet types as those in the White Grape, but they seemed better off for it, laughing and shouting and drinking hugely, unaffected by the cramped space or the din or the smoke from dozens of cheap tapers and even cheaper pipes. He liked it, assuming a blandly smiling expression while he wondered at the number of people and the pleasure they seemed to take in each other's company.

The serving girl appeared again, dancing gracefully through the unmoving crowd with a huge platter balanced above her head. She slammed the platter down on his table and breathed a huge sigh of relief before holding up her hand to stop his question.

"I know you did not order it, master, but you needs must take it, for that y'are at a table, and at the tables you needs must pay for food, even though y'eat not." She waited for a second and he smiled. She nodded and whirled away again to fight her way to the bar.

He had seen the public houses and taverns and restaurants and saloons of hundreds of cities, and had learned to be comfortable eating alone, so he turned his attention to the platter without a qualm.

Pleasantly surprised, he saw that the Uncommon Player offered nothing cooked, relying instead on quantity to make up for heat. There were three huge wheels of cheese, each spiced differently, and large loaves of flat bread. Cold meat, nuts, apple slices and butter were arrayed around the cheese and bread in workmanlike profusion. There was even a small pot of honey, and he remembered the knife at his belt with relief. The Uncommon Player apparently saw silverware as an unnecessary item.

As he ate, the crowd grew smaller, drifting out in a hail of noisy farewells, until it seemed there was only the small group gathered around Knave Fitch. He held court raucously, shouting witty obscenities and insults at his companions, who rewarded him with gusts of laughter and refillings of his tankard. Liam smiled at some of the clown's jokes, and noticed that there were three musicians at the far end of the room, playing furiously on lute, pipes and a small set of skin drums. They could only occasionally be heard over Fitch's constant stream of filth, mostly when he stopped to take monstrous gulps of beer.

Liam stared at the platter, which was still more than half full, and gave up. His stomach strained uncomfortably, and he felt short of breath; it was by far the most food he had eaten in a long while.

He pushed the platter carefully away, as though afraid some of the food might leap off it and try to run down his throat, and gave Fitch his full attention.

The clown managed two or three more rude jokes before the door of the Player burst in and Kansallus appeared like an angry god.

A *short*, angry god, Liam amended, and watched the proceedings with even more interest.

"Fitch, you bastard!" Kansallus screamed, his face purple with anger. "Call was an hour since! You've less than ten minutes to be on stage, you damned, double-damned, triply-damned ass!"

The little playwright stormed over to the clown, who was draining his tankard unperturbed, and clamped his fingers on Fitch's upper arm in a way that made Liam wince, remembering an old tutor who had done the same thing. With the thumb and forefinger pressing into the meat of the muscle, it could be exquisitely painful, but Fitch took it in stride, handing his empty tankard to a barkeeper and allowing himself to be dragged to the door. Kansallus propelled him through it with a vicious kick to his ample behind, and slammed it closed behind him.

Liam applauded softly, and Kansallus turned, his face suddenly calm and amiable, and bowed deeply. When he rose, he smiled agreeably.

"How now! It's the gentleman of the afternoon that appreciates true art! Might I?" He gestured at the empty chair across from Liam as he sat in it. "I know you not, sir, but you strike me as a man of some discretion, of some taste, if you'll allow me to say so."

"I will," Liam said, and signaled the serving girl.

Kansallus laughed loudly, and then again when the girl brought two fresh tankards to the table.

"Is it a problem when Fitch drinks before a performance?" Liam asked as the playwright downed most of his beer.

"Not in the least," Kansallus answered, smacking his lips and beaming happily. He had sharp eyes, Liam noted, but there were shadows in them, a sort of defensive mask. "He'll outshine the stars tonight, and send the groundlings to their knees weak as babes with mirth. He's best when pickled."

Noting the way Kansallus's eyes dropped to the half-full platter, Liam pushed it across the table and bade him eat, if he was hungry.

"As a rule, I don't sup on the leavings of men whose names I'm not privy," the playwright said with a smile, though the defensive shadows were thick, ready for rejection. "I'm Kansallus, scripter and part owner of the Golden Orb."

"Liam Rhenford." He held out his hand, which the playwright took briefly and with unshadowed eyes before digging into the platter like a starving man. "You seem hungry, Kansallus of the Golden Orb. Is it not so profitable?"

"Profitable enough," the little man muttered around a huge mouthful, "but not so luxurious that I'll refuse a freely offered meal. Pray you," he said after washing the mouthful down, "if I'm not too bold, what brings a man who walks the day with an Aedile to the Unco' Player at night?"

"I thought I might see your performance tonight. I enjoyed the other one I saw very much."

"Ah, then, y'are as much caught by Rora as any other."

Nettled by the man's amused tone, Liam feigned indifference. "Rora?" The other smirked, spilling a handful of nuts into his mouth, and Liam smiled guiltily. "You must admit, she's a beautiful woman."

"Oh, aye, passing fair, until you know her well. She can be hideous as a witch, if you take my meaning. I'll disappoint you further: she's not on tonight."

"No?"

"She's this night free and the next, for that Uris-tide

is nigh. She's a very zealot," he added, with a wink that suggested the opposite.

"No great temple-goer?"

"Not by half. Though no sinner, mind. Pure as the unsunned snow, our Rora." Strangely, he seemed to mean it.

"Then the way she dances is . . ."

"Intuitive," Kansallus supplied with malicious humor. "An imposture of a knowing wench. And all the more impressive for it, if you see."

"I suppose I do."

They fell silent, Liam pondering the idea of Rora's dancing while Kansallus wolfed down the rest of the platter. When he had finished it, he pushed away from the table and began picking his teeth with an immaculately clean fingernail. He was startlingly neat; though his artisan's smock was a little ragged and his thin, reddish hair unshorn, both were clean, and a slight smell of soap arose from him.

"If you do," he said, as though the conversation had not been interrupted, "I'll thank you for the meal with advice: stay clear of Rora. Any fancies you have on her she's sure not to fill, and more like to box your ears or scratch the jelly from your eyes."

"I'll keep it in mind," Liam said, laughing at the transparency of his interest. On the other hand, he imagined that Kansallus and Rora's fellow actors must be used to men showing that kind of interest.

"I'm no wagerer, friend Rhenford, but if I were, I'd have one for you." The playwright was looking at him with friendly appraisal.

"What?"

"I'd wager—though I'm neither snooper nor gossip— I'd wager that whatever else brought you to the Orb this afternoon revolved 'round a certain rich merchant's wife."

Kansallus was indeed the man he should have talked to when he first began investigating.

"And you might have won, had you phrased the bet properly. She was not the focus of the business, but a part of it."

The playwright nodded judiciously. "Lons is an arrogant, silly ass. He deserves to have panted after her, puppylike, for the whole summer. Strange, now, isn't it, that Lons, handsome piece of work that he is, should have such trouble getting what he wants, while his sister has so little getting what she doesn't?"

Liam agreed, and bent forward at the playwright's beckoning finger.

"Though there are some," he whispered furtively, "knaves and caitiffs all, mind, but some nonetheless, who say that Rora may get that trouble she wants, but only from a certain individual troubler." He nodded again and leaned back, finishing his tankard with an air of having imparted a great secret.

"And that troubler?"

Kansallus shook his head and sighed regretfully. "A cypher, a mystery, an unknown quantity of indistinct parts. None of the caitiffs and knaves and vicious gossips who say it can warrant it, and I'm of a mind t'ignore it, but there you are—it's been bruited about."

"I see." He rose to go, and dropped a handful of coins on the table. "It's been fascinating, friend Kansallus, if disappointing as regards a certain dancer. I think there's enough there for another few tankards, if you don't have to go back to the theater."

"I don't, bless you," the playwright said with a broad smile. "And for it, I'll tell you this—have ever seen Knave Fitch scratch at's ear while on the boards?"

"No," Liam admitted. He decided not to mention that he had only seen the clown three times, one of them within the last few minutes.

"Well, he does, from time to time, and the common run think it a pose of comic thought, but's not." Kansallus paused and smiled secretly. "It's a scar he's scratching—from the teeth of a maid."

"Rora," Liam supplied, and was rewarded with a firm nod.

"I know, to look at, Fitch's no rake—but he's a fair number of maids under's belt, and we all at th'Orb give

him first crack at any wench. So it chanced when Rora was
newly with us as a dancer out of some house on the Point
and on her brother's vouching, we stood back and let Fitch
go to work. The very next day he appears with a bandaged
head, and tells us all she's a hellcat for her virtue, and to
stay away. So, that's the dancer—and my warning. Go for
tamer flesh."

"I'll bear it in mind. Now I must go."

"Say, friend Liam," Kansallus stopped him again, "one
last. I note a writing case at your side. Y'are not, by chance,
a scripter as I am?"

"No," Liam answered, looking curiously down at the
playwright. "Only sometimes a scholar."

"Excellent news," Kansallus said, the smile deepening.
"There's enough of scribblers 'round the Orb, and I'd hate to
find this meal a sop for your taking away my livelihood."

Still laughing, Liam made his way through the darkened
streets, guided only by the stars and the occasional torch.
Kansallus made an excellent source of information, as well
as an interesting companion. Not that Coeccias was a bad
sort, but he lacked the playwright's good-natured but malicious tongue.

The night was cold, even colder after the warmth of the
inn, and he had to fight now against the freshening sea
breeze. The doors to the Golden Orb were still open, but
he passed them by, wondering what Rora was doing with
her evening off.

Sounds were few and far between, the streets empty, and
he started once at what he thought was the sound of feet
behind him. Then he heard the coo of a pigeon and the
flap of wings and smiled with relief. Coeccias might not be
very good at searching out murderers, but in four months of
frequent night walks he had never been accosted, and that
reflected well on the Aedile. The streets were clear of the
common run of villains, if private houses weren't safe from
the uncommon run.

Nonetheless, he found himself looking over his shoulder
more than usual, unable to shake the feeling that he was
being watched. Try as he might, he was on edge for the

length of his walk, and reached the stables with a genuine feeling of relief.

The boy let him stand inside, out of the cold, while his mount was saddled. Once on Diamond, he felt better, and trotted quickly out of the city towards Tarquin's house on the beach.

My *house on the beach*, he reminded himself, and smiled at the thought.

CHAPTER 10

ONCE AGAIN THE house was lit before he arrived, and the warm yellow light spilling from its windows helped him find his way down the narrow path in the moonless night. The surf was unseen but loud, crashing in the blackness like the shouting of giants. He tethered Diamond in the small shed, apologizing for the cramped quarters. He thought about bringing out a blanket to keep the chill off, but noticed that the air of the shed had already grown warmer.

Tarquin planned for everything, he thought, and patted the restive horse soothingly before going back to the house.

You are home early, Fanuilh thought at him as soon as he had closed the door. Liam bit off a retort and waited until he went into the workroom.

"Yes, I'm home early," he said pleasantly when he could see the tiny dragon's face. "I decided that even murderers must sleep, and that if they'd been avoiding me with as much energy as I've been searching for them, they must be tired."

That is not why.

"No, of course not. Why would I bother lying to you, when you can read my mind? I'm joking, though that seems to be as useless as lying, since you don't have a sense of humor."

I find different things funny.

"I'm sure you do." There was a long pause. Liam frowned, wondering what Fanuilh would find funny, and the dragon simply leveled its yellow cat's eyes at him. Dragon humor was beyond him, he finally decided, and thought back to his meal at the Uncommon Player. "Are you hungry?"

Yes.

"I'll get you something."

The dragon's head snaked in a sinuous nod, and Liam went to the kitchen and desired raw meat as hard as he could, discovering with a mixture of satisfaction and disgust that it was no longer so difficult.

Fanuilh tore into the meat with its usual gusto, and Liam watched for a few minutes before beginning to wander absently around the workroom. The empty crystal bottle still lay alone on the empty middle table. He picked it up.

'Virgin's blood.' It no longer held the same repulsion for him; it had become simply a relic, devoid of meaning, a jumble of letters that he should have been able to decipher.

He wondered why it was empty, and why the label was crossed out.

What is important about the beaker? It is empty. What can be important about—

"I don't know, but I might if you'd let me think," he said, and though he could not hear the words over the silent block of Fanuilh's thought, the dragon accepted it, and the block lifted. Liam crossed his arms and tipped the beaker at the dragon.

"The vanishing spell does not require virgin's blood, correct? It's not mentioned in the text of the spell. But he had it out on his table, and he never left things lying around; you said so yourself. This must be important."

The number of spells that require virgin's blood is enormous. Tarquin must have over a hundred of them in his catalogues. The uses to which they can be put are a hundred times a hundred.

"How can you read my mind and be so stupid? Maybe one of those was the one Marcius came about," Liam shouted, tired of the dragon's apparent obtuseness. "And Tarquin cast it—the bottle is empty—but not to Marcius's satisfaction!"

Why are you so certain the merchant is the killer?

"Because he *could* be a murderer!" He shouted louder, trying to justify what was really only a feeling.

Many men could be. You could be, the dragon pointed out. Though he knew the creature was incapable of real irony, Liam could not help feeling that its impassive face and toneless thoughts masked a greater sarcasm.

"But you know I'm not!"

Not of Tarquin, yes. But you have killed, and you could kill again. I know, as well as you do. You would regret it, to be sure, but you could kill.

"Enough! I'm in no mood for you to be my conscience. Did you do this to Tarquin? Small wonder he ordered you away so often. And that's not a question you're meant to answer!" he added hastily, and the dragon obliged by staying out of his head. He went to stand by the lectern.

The color and texture of the pages did not match, and they differed in size from spell to spell. Sometimes the inks varied, though most of the writing was in black, in Tarquin's clear, blocklike script. As he flipped idly through the tome, he noticed a page covered with red in a wildly different handwriting.

Another mage's spell, Fanuilh supplied, its back to Liam, still intent on the meat. *They can trade them back and forth, or steal them. It is the instructions that matter, not who wrote them. That book was only stitched together very recently. It contains all the important spells he had collected over his career.*

Liam tried to lift the heavy tome, and found he needed both hands. The chain clanked.

"These are all the spells he collected? What about the books on the shelves? And in the library?"

All the important spells, the dragon qualified. *The books behind you are instructions for mixing and preparing the elements of the spells, and one or two lengthy reports of experiments. The library contains thirty or forty texts on the enchanting of objects; the rest are histories, or poetry, or philosophy or collections of fables. Master Tanaquil liked to read a great deal.*

"I gathered as much from his conversation."

Fanuilh did not respond and Liam turned to the shelf, leaning back against the lectern to examine the books. There were few with marked spines, most of them unadorned leather or wood, many cracked and beginning to fall apart from long use.

He wondered which described the uses of virgin's blood. The empty bottle and its crossed-out label annoyed him.

"Tell me, Fanuilh, what spells do you know?"

The thought was a long time in forming.

I know very few. Only those appropriate to an apprentice, as they do not generally require speaking and use few precious ingredients. Master Tanaquil taught them to me from the spellbook he had when he was an apprentice.

"What can you do?"

Put a man to sleep, light a fire, stop blood flowing if the wound is fairly small, cause itching, or uncontrollable laughter. Maybe a dozen others. Useful things, and some that were merely for practice in the discipline.

"You can cause uncontrollable laughter?"

Yes.

Shaking his head with a smile, Liam left the lectern and walked to the door. He stood there and stretched luxuriously.

"How are you feeling?"

Better. The soreness fades. Soon I will be able to fly again.

Liam received the news with an approving nod.

"I'm going to go to sleep now, if you don't need anything else. Wake me two hours after sunrise, will you?"

The dragon's head bobbed gracefully and Liam left the workroom, suppressing a yawn.

He did not go right to the library, but wandered curiously through the house he had accepted as his own. The light was even throughout the house, but the empty, echoing sound was gone. The parlor, the kitchen, the trophy room all felt comfortable, almost welcoming. He did not disturb anything, just entered each room briefly and surveyed the furnishings, smiling the lightly bitter smile that even after ten years of use had not creased his face.

It's not Rhenford Keep, but it will do, I suppose.

Still smiling, as much at himself as at his house, he went into the library to sleep.

Fanuilh woke him precisely at the hour he requested, though there was no accompanying illusion of stone cities from his travels. The call in his mind felt normal, proper in a strange way.

I used to wake Master Tanaquil this way, came the dragon's thought as Liam sat on the edge of the divan, rubbing the sleep from his eyes. He did not comment, but went to the kitchen and imagined another platter of meat for it. He brought the food to the workroom and laid it on the table.

"Eat your fill," he said cheerily. "I want you well and whole soon, so you can begin holding up your end of the bargain."

You think you can fulfill your end soon.

Liam thought for a moment, his eyes on the intricate model by the window, and on the jagged Teeth that dominated it.

"Yes, I do. Today will answer a number of questions."

They were silent for a while, Liam lost in thought, his eyes unfocused on the model. Fanuilh did not eat, but stared at him. He grew aware of the dragon's gaze after a moment, and started with a guilty smile.

"What was I thinking?" he challenged.

Nothing. Your thoughts were diffused.

"What is that like? Looking at diffused thoughts, I mean? How does it appear to you?"

The dragon's stare impaled his, holding it till he grew uneasy, wondering. Finally, the block formed in his mind, and he realized the creature had been searching for a way to express the idea.

Like a flock of birds that explode suddenly from a city square, so scattered and intermingled that you cannot follow any single one. It is confusion.

With even more surprise, he saw that the idea was his, drawn from a memory he had of the birdsellers and their flocks in Torquay.

"I was daydreaming, not confused."

No, but you allowed your thoughts to fly apart. You do that often, letting many lines go their ways, not following any particular one. Master Tanaquil never did that. His thoughts were orderly, like the steps in a ritual. It was easy to follow them.

"Well, then, it's a good thing you won't have to look into my head much longer. We'll finish this business in the next few days, and you can teach me. Now, if there's nothing else, I'll be on my way." The dragon shook its head in wide, sweeping arcs. "Fine. I suggest you study up on what you have to teach me while I'm gone."

The dragon stopped moving its head, and tucked it down between its forelegs, like a dog preparing for rest.

"Good boy," Liam muttered, and went to get his horse.

The morning was colder than the night, and his breath plumed out in clouds that the sharp breeze tore to tatters. Diamond was not cold, but restive, unhappy with the cramped confines of the shed. He tossed his mane and snorted when Liam led him out onto the beach, kicking up spurts of sand that the wind caught and whirled, stinging, into Liam's eyes.

He calmed the horse with a soft word, and once they were up the cliff path, gave him rein. Thundering over the frozen ruts of the road, they passed fields dusted with frost, and Liam had to duck his face down into his cloak to escape the bite of the wind.

Cheeks tingling and scarlet with cold, he gave the snorting horse over to the boy at the stables, and set off briskly for the Aedile's house. The sun was bright and the sky a pale blue that reminded him of summer, but there was no warmth in the light, and a deep chill lingered in the shadows cast by the bleached gray stone and wood of the city.

Coeccias's servant let him into the house and directed him to the small kitchen at the rear. The Aedile was there, using a ladle to stir a large pot hung on a swivel hook over the fire.

"Rhenford, y'are here just in time. I'll have you test this brew, and escape it myself if it's foul." He filled the ladle with steaming liquid from the pot and shoved it in Liam's face. "Go to, go to! Drink!" he commanded.

Inclining his head, Liam sniffed suspiciously and then hazarded a small sip. It was mulled cider, and though it scalded his tongue, it slid down his throat smoothly, to form a warm, spiced ball in his stomach. He nodded appreciatively and took another sip.

"It's not just cider," he accused, to the Aedile's amusement.

"And should it be?" Coeccias pulled two pewter mugs from the mantel above the fire and filled them from the pot, which he then swung further away from the fire. He gestured Liam to a seat at the cluttered wooden table that filled most of the kitchen, and placed one of the steaming mugs in front of him.

"It's a hint of the very water of life, to add the inspirational tone. I've to make a greater batch for Uris-tide, and this is but a test." He took a sip of his own mug and smacked his lips with closed eyes. "It'll do."

A scent of cinnamon rose from the cider, mingled with the hint of liquor, and Liam sipped again approvingly. Coeccias called his servant, and when the man appeared, gave orders for his breakfast.

"You'll eat?" he asked Liam, and without waiting for an answer, told the servant to double the breakfast. Liam smiled into his mug as the heavy man took the seat across from him.

The servant busied himself cutting up bread and bacon and setting them to cook by the fire. The seated men sipped at their mugs for a moment. Liam let the spiked cider warm his hands and stomach, looking around the kitchen. It was messy, but well stocked, with bunches of herbs and vegetables hanging in no particular order from the rafters, pots and utensils scattered everywhere, mingled with half-eaten loaves and scraps of cheese and meat and dirty dishes. Reflecting on the Aedile, it did not surprise him, but it did not bother him either. The suggestion was not of filth, but of comfort and a relaxed attitude towards cleanliness. Liam liked it, in the way he liked Coeccias—

with tolerance for obvious faults.

"I thought we were going to look for the barmaid."

"Truth, so we are. But we needs must be fed, eh? And the cider calls for tasting. It'd be blaspheming to offer good Uris an untested brew. It likes you?"

"Yes, very much. But why do you have to make a bigger batch?" Liam gestured at the large pot, obscured by the servant's back as he knelt before the fire, prodding the crackling bacon. "You have enough there to last a while."

Laughing, Coeccias said, "Enough? I'll swear there's little enough there for the first libation! Why, there'd be none left for the worshippers, if that was all I put up. Know you nothing about the uses of Uris-tide?"

The servant began laying out dishes on the table.

"No, in the Midlands we never made much of Uris. She was a city god to us, of little use to farmers and husbandmen. There are not many mechanics or apothecaries there."

"What of your vintners, tanners, smiths, armorers, tinkers? Have you no brewers or candlers in the Midlands? Y'are yourself a scholar, and from the Midlands. Uris is patron of all these—how can Midlanders ignore her?"

"I suppose the trades just seemed less important. We paid more attention to the harvest gods."

Coeccias snorted and frowned his way through the rest of his mug. Liam decided not to mention that there were hundreds of places that had never heard of Uris, and that credited her gifts of craft and trade to other gods.

The bacon and toast were ready, and the servant placed them before them in silence, taking their mugs to refill them at the pot. Butter and salt were brought and Coeccias dug in, making huge sandwiches thick with butter. Liam, made hungry by the smell, copied him, and the kitchen was filled with the sound of their chewing.

The Aedile's frown deepened at each bite, and then broke out into a question.

"Truth, you know nothing of the rites of Uris-tide?"

"Very little," Liam admitted.

"And you a scholar," Coeccias marveled. "Well," he went on, carefully putting his third sandwich to one side, "the true rites are complex, and the sole sphere of the priests. Only the divines are allowed in the fane when they are performed, but there're numerous lesser rites for the common run of worshippers."

Solemnly, he described the lay rituals that led up to the actual day of Uris-tide. Daily processions through the streets began six days before, and every true worshipper was supposed to walk on at least one of the days. Some, the very devout, made more than one. Viyescu, the Aedile pointed out with no hint of sarcasm, walked every day, displaying an unparalleled devotion. Each day's procession was led by a progressively higher-ranked priest, and so more worshippers attended the later ones. The procession Liam had seen was one of the first, and consequently one of the smallest.

"Today's is the most important. I'll be marching, as the Duke's man, and the richest of Uris's images will go forth as well, gilt and jeweled. It was gifted the temple by the Duke himself, and cost a fortune. The Duke subscribes the old ways and worships right strongly."

Beginning at midafternoon in the square at the heart of the city, the procession would go from there around most of Southwark, offering Uris's blessing to all and particularly to artisans and craftsmen. It would be led by the second most important priest in the local temple and include the highest of the city's officials and the richest of her artisans, as well as a large number of commoners. The last procession, scheduled for the next day, would be comprised only of clergy, led by the hierarch of the temple, and carry a very simple image of Uris, ancient relic handed down from the earliest days of her worship. That night the secret ceremonies would begin in the temple, and the common worshippers would eat only the simplest of foods. Unleavened bread, sauceless meat, milk and water, to symbolize life before Uris gave her arts to the world.

"The cider is reserved for Uris-tide itself. It's a strange brew, liquor and cider and spices, but it goes well with the stuffs served. Look you, on that day, we eat fancifully, with sauces and pastries and dishes that are long in preparation and complex in design, like unto the arts Uris herself gave us, and we offer portions of all to her as grace. I'll bring the pot to my sister, and celebrate with her. She's a large get of children, and many others'll be there from her husband's family, so I needs must make a greater punch than this test here."

Coeccias stopped and picked up his sandwich again. He chewed absently, calculation in his eyes as he looked at Liam, who stared into the rich brown depths of his mug, wondering at his companion's obvious belief.

"Look you," the Aedile said at length, "would it like you t'attend the feast? At my sister's?"

Liam was surprised, but immediately interested. "I suppose, yes, that would be nice," he answered, trying to conceal the attractiveness of the idea.

"Come, come," Coeccias blurted impatiently, "Uris-tide is no time to rest alone. It'd be improper for you to spend it in that empty house. You'll come to my sister's."

There was no room for objection, so Liam simply nodded his agreement.

"Good, then," Coeccias said gruffly. "We'd best get to it, if we're to find this barmaid before I must prepare for the procession."

Gulping down the rest of his cider, Liam followed the Aedile out of the house.

There were seventeen inns, taverns and public houses in the Point, as well as a few private clubs and special establishments that Coeccias thought worth checking.

Though the streets of this quarter were as narrow as those in the rest of the city, the area was much better laid out, with something approaching a plan. They were able, therefore, to follow an orderly route, covering the relatively straight roads one by one. Further down in the city the roads twisted and angled in mazelike complexity, joined by uncountable alleys and hidden courts, all of which could harbor an eating house or wineshop, and Coeccias explained that his men had had to spend a great deal of time to cover a small area.

"I should have thought Tarquin unlikely to frequent the lower haunts, but it struck me not. Happily, there're not so many up here. We'll be through by an hour after noon, and if this Donoé exists, we'll search her out."

Polished paneling and expensive fittings, gilt and silver, foreign hangings and crystal goblets, intricately painted signboards—the inns and restaurants were expensively decorated, the rich accouterments proper for the neighborhood's merchant princes and giants of trade. Some even had their offerings painstakingly painted on large boards, for those customers who could read. The proprietors were quiet, polite men, singularly colorless, who could scarcely be bothered to remember the names of their wives, let alone their serving girls.

It was early in the day, and most of the places they stopped had not even opened yet, but Coeccias's title gained them entrance at every one. It was unfair, Liam knew, to compare these sophisticated restaurants and taverns with the Uncommon Player, but he could not help it. Two hours before noon, they could not be expected to have customers, but they still seemed unnaturally somber, depressing in the stilted formality of furnishings you were afraid to touch and proprietors who acted like courtiers in a tyrant's court. He silently praised the Player, and vowed to avoid the rich quarter if he wished to enjoy himself.

They were most of the way through Coeccias's mental list when they came to a stone building that fronted a stretch of street that was inordinately large for the quarter. It had a full portico with fluted columns a foot thick above which rested a triangular frieze, and broad steps made of carefully fitted blocks of white stone. There was no painted sign or nameplate to announce its purpose, and Liam laid a hand on the Aedile's arm as he started up the steps.

"What's this? It's someone's house."

"No house this," he muttered, and surprised Liam by flushing. "Come along."

Bas-relief panels adorned the double-leafed doors, but Liam did not have a chance to examine them, because the Aedile pulled one door open hastily and ushered him inside.

White and pink marble greeted them, totally at odds with the gray exterior, and Liam paused, unable to believe what he saw. A sweeping flight of marble stairs curved up and away from a huge foyer, lined with niches holding amorously entangled statues and potted plants. Banks of exotic flowers bloomed in vivid reds and oranges, filling the air with heady scents. Water danced and splashed in a fountain at the center of the room, two stone lovers entwining in the pool. Two young women appeared far away at the top of the steps and then fled, giggling.

"Gods, Coeccias," Liam exclaimed, "it's a whorehouse!"

The Aedile silenced him with a staggering punch to the arm and a frantic "Hsst! Not so loud!"

"Why 'Hsst,' milord Aedile?" The speaker appeared smoothly from behind a heavy arras concealing a doorway. She was tall and bore herself proudly, with an elaborately curled headdress of gleaming black hair and an artfully painted face. "Though we glaze it over with 'house of pleasure' and 'night palace,' we are indeed a whorehouse. The man has the right of it."

She stepped in front of Liam and gazed with imperious amusement at him. "He needs must have seen one before to recognize it so quickly." She held out a ringed hand coolly, and Liam bent over it, suddenly embarrassed.

"Liam Rhenford, lady," he stammered. "Your servant."

Her laughter was loud but not harsh. "Your pardon, sir, but men rarely say that here. In this house, it is more often a woman who gives that office." She turned to Coeccias, leaving Liam crushed and flustering in her wake. "Coeccias," she said warmly, giving him a lingeringly formal kiss on both cheeks. "What brings you to my house?"

"Business, Herione. A few questions for you, if you've the time."

"Ever business, Coeccias," she murmured, and slid her arm through his to draw him towards the arras. "Come along, servant," she called over her shoulder to Liam, who followed along hanging his head.

Behind the arras a corridor led towards the rear of the palatial whorehouse, and Herione went directly into the first

room they came to. Walking side by side, arms linked, she
and Coeccias seemed matched in size and height, appropriate to each other. Herione was broad, but not fat, statuesque,
even in a girl's gown that had no hint of girlishness.

The room was her office, a fact attested by the ledgers
in racks on the walls and the tidy columns of coins on a
small writing table. A slate board bore a painted diagram of
the house, with a woman's name and a blank line chalked
into each room; Liam read the women's names and smiled;
each was a princess or queen from history or legend. After
the lavish entrance hall, the office seemed spartan. Herione
gracefully motioned them to a pair of straight-backed cane
chairs, and settled herself in a more comfortable padded
seat behind the writing table. She traced Liam's gaze to
the slate board, and gave a smile that did not reach her
eyes.

"Y'are impressed, sir? Blue blood and true, one and all.
Only royalty here."

Noting the coldness of her smile, Liam spoke nonchalantly, peering with studied consternation at the slate lists.
"I was just wondering if you knew that Princess Cresside
was a hunchback in life."

Her smile began touching her eyes. "Well, sir, with no
queen worth a whit in Torquay, we needs must take our
royalty where we can."

"Well, how can there be a queen in Torquay?" Liam
responded, grandly flinging a hand at the slate board. "You
have them all here!"

The smile reached her eyes finally, and Liam thought he
might have made up for his gaffe in the hall.

"Tell me, Coeccias," she said, turning to the officer, who
had fidgeted through the exchange, "is this your business?
T'upbraid me for the naming of my stable?"

"A scholar, Herione. It's his business to know such things.
He meant no offense."

"Coeccias, y'are wooden," she sighed. "I know't, he
knows't; why make you amends? Now come, your business." She steepled her hands before her on the table among
the coins, and became serious.

"Have you a girl named Donoé here? A barmaid, or serving wench?"

"None such," she replied instantly.

"Not perhaps one of your empresses?" Coeccias asked, raising an eyebrow at the slate board. Herione shook her head definitely.

"None such. Why do you ask?"

The Aedile glanced at Liam, who shrugged absently, still looking at the slate board. "We're looking for a girl of that name, who may've known the wizard Tanaquil."

"The murdered wizard." She did not seem fazed by the news, but she did look curiously at Liam. "Do you always string along a scholar when you con a murderer, Coeccias?"

"No," the Aedile rasped at the playful tone in her voice. "He knew the wizard best of any, and's proved helpful. So, no Donoé, and we're to't again. Come, Rhenford."

He stood, but Liam waved for him to stop.

"Wait a moment, if you would. I've a question or two the lady may be able to answer, if I may ask."

Coeccias muttered, " 'Take no surprise' " to himself, but remained standing behind his chair. Herione shifted polite interest to Liam, who moved his gaze from the slate board to her.

"Your questions, sir?"

"Has Ancus Marcius ever come here?"

"Ever? More than ever, sir. Quite often. Twice, thrice a moon. And's good for a solid gold each visit," she added meaningfully to Coeccias. "I'd hope this won't reflect on him."

"If he's a murderer, bawdry won't soil him any more."

Herione offered a slight nod in agreement.

"Truth," she exclaimed softly.

"One other question, if I may. Has Freihett Necquer ever come here?"

"Necquer?" She frowned into her memory.

"A Freeporter merchant."

"Oh, yes, yes. Necquer. Once, perhaps, a long while since, over two years. He took a wife not long after, and has not returned since."

Liam nodded, gratified. "Thank you, lady."

Coeccias muttered his thanks and the two left, going unescorted through the empty foyer with its gurgling fountain and out into the cold street.

Liam paused for a moment on the steps to look closely at the bas-relief panels set into the doors. They depicted strange scenes, large groups of people engaged in uncertain acts. The carvings were not explicit and, in fact, were strangely tasteful, almost artistic. He tried to trace the intricacies of one scene with the point of a long finger, and then gave up and went down the steps to join Coeccias.

"An acquaintance?" He phrased the question as casually as he could, though he was more than a little curious. There had been undercurrents running rampant in Herione's office that went beyond Coeccias's responsibility for keeping tabs on the local houses of pleasure. Yet he could not imagine the stolid, bulky Aedile having anything to do with the quick-witted madame.

"What's Necquer in this?" Coeccias shot back, ignoring the issue. "Is his wife Lons's taskmaster?"

"She is, but I don't think Necquer's involved. I asked for . . . personal reasons."

Liam took it as a measure of how little the Aedile wanted to talk about Herione that he did not press about Necquer. That was all right; it was Coeccias's business, after all, and the visit had dispelled his suspicions of Necquer. If the merchant had been unfaithful to his wife, as Lons had suggested, he would have done it in Herione's house, clearly the most expensive in the city and, from its unassuming front, the most discreet.

So discreet, Liam thought, *that in four months I never heard of it. What else is there in this city that I've missed? The Golden Orb, the worship of Uris, Herione's house— so much I've missed, and so little I can say I've seen.*

Preoccupied with his own morose thoughts, he did not hear Coeccias the first time, and had to ask him to repeat his statement, which he did after clearing his throat.

"I said she was somewhat of an acquaintance. The Duke requires a man to register the houses. The office is mine."

Liam accepted the tight-lipped explanation with a non-committal sound and remained prudently silent. Coeccias strode along the street with a heavy thunder in his thick brows.

The owner of the second-to-last inn on their list somewhat nervously said that yes, he did have a serving girl named Donoé. When Coeccias had allayed his fears that the girl was a criminal, and convinced him that they only wanted to ask her a few questions, he bustled off, shouting her name.

"Fortune bears us only a small grudge," Coeccias growled at the innkeeper's retreating back. "She saved us from one last house; quite generous of Her." Liam nodded absently.

The inn seemed appropriate to Tarquin. It was comfortable, without the ostentation of the others in the rich quarter. The woods were blond, and light flooded in from a large window, and it reminded Liam slightly of the wizard's home on the beach. For a man who had chosen to live outside a city, it would be a good place for a quiet drink when he had to be there.

Donoé, when she was dragged from the kitchen by the anxious proprietor, was the girl he remembered. Hiding her fidgeting hands in a wet cloth, flushed and eyeing Coeccias subserviently, she was a far cry from the laughing young woman Tarquin had so gallantly sent on her way in the summer, but he could not mistake her looks. She was very young, perhaps only sixteen, and had the sort of prettiness that is mostly youth and innocence, and only really noticeable when informed with happiness. At the inn, confronted with the Aedile's bearlike scowl, her prettiness faded into fear, and she was not worth a second look.

Liam regretted it, recalling her happy smile in the summer, on Tarquin's veranda. Coeccias made it worse by snorting as soon as she appeared, which frightened her even more than her employer's peremptory summons.

"Herself?" Coeccias asked him, and when he nodded, went on gruffly: "Well then, to't. You wanted her."

Wincing at the words' effect on the wilting girl, Liam cleared his throat and spoke to her as pleasantly as he could, indicating one of the tables.

"Perhaps you'd care to sit? Coeccias, could you get us something to drink?"

The Aedile trudged grudgingly off to the proprietor, and the girl reluctantly took a seat at the empty table, staring wide-eyed at Liam, who smiled reassuringly.

"Do you remember me?"

She shook her head vehemently.

"You're sure? On the beach, maybe? You were there a few times."

Though her eyes could not get any wider, they changed expression from fear to recognition, her hands clapping to the tabletop to emphasize it. "From the beach! You were at the wizard's!" Recognition changed back to fear, and she practically wailed. "Oh my lord, is that the matter? I swear I'd nothing to do with his taking off, I swear!"

"I know, I know," he assured her hastily, aware he was handling it badly. "I only want to ask you a few questions, Donoé. I know you haven't done anything."

"I was sore sad to hear he'd died, sore sad, my lord!"

"Yes, yes, I know, but I have to ask you a few questions."

He patted her hand gently, which seemed to calm her a little, and Coeccias brought two cups of wine with ill grace, which gave her some time to collect herself. The Aedile retired to the bar, leaving them alone.

"Now, Donoé, I have to ask you a few questions," he repeated, when she was more sure of herself. "About Tarquin. I need to know if you knew anything about his affairs."

"Oh, no, my lord, I never pried nor gossiped, my lord, I swear!"

"Let me ask that a different way. Do you know if he saw any other women?"

"Other women?" She was clearly puzzled.

"Did he bring any other women home that you know of? Any, maybe, that he met here, or elsewhere?"

She thought for a moment, and suddenly looked full into his eyes in shock.

"My lord!"

"What?"

"You think I . . . I . . . you think he *knew* me!" She whispered it fiercely, in disbelief and accusation, and Liam colored instantly. He was handling this very badly, he knew, but took comfort from the fact that Coeccias probably would have bungled it worse.

"Well, I suppose, I—" he stammered.

"He did no such," she stated indignantly. "I'm only a poor serving girl, I know, but I'm chaste, and Master Tanaquil was a true gentle! He'd an oath of purity himself, he said!"

Momentarily stunned by her vehement defense of her virtue, Liam sought for words, and finally asked tentatively, "Then what were you doing at his house?"

It was her turn to color, and though he had thought the question natural, it seemed to deflate her rage at his insinuation.

"He wanted blood," she whispered, lowering her head in shame.

"Blood?"

"The blood of a virgin."

He had to strain to hear the words she spoke into her lap, but they disappointed him deeply. The empty decanter had held *her* blood, and Tarquin had probably crossed out the label because he had used it all. A hundred uses for virgin's blood, Fanuilh had said. Tarquin might well have gone through gallons of it, and the clue he had thought so much of was nothing.

Donoé lifted her head and glared defiance at him again. "But it hurt not a bit, and Master Tanaquil was a true gentle, and paid me well, and there's naught wrong with what I did! I'm chaste, you, and Master Tanaquil was a true gentle! He'd an oath! I tell you, you've no right to slander me nor him, serpent!"

She was standing by the end of her tirade, though he thanked all the gods he could remember that she did not raise her voice. She did, however, turn on her heel after labeling him a snake, and stalked back to the kitchen with all the terrible dignity of an affronted and wrathful teenage girl. She even shouldered her employer aside.

Though he had not heard all of their exchange, Donoé's abrupt exit and Liam's chastened expression told him enough, and Coeccias laughed loudly, coming to the table.

"Come along, 'serpent.' Y'have insulted enough of Southwark's maids." He propelled Liam out of the inn to the street, leaving the cups of wine untasted.

"That," Liam sighed, "was very bad."

"Y'have no talent for searching into the innocent," Coeccias commented cheerfully, drawing him along the street, "and if that's a murderer, I'll scale the Teeth. Now, if she'd been a killer with blood on her blade and it at your throat, you'd have battered her to her knees with questions. No shame not to hone your wit on girls, Rhenford. Now, what'd she relate?"

Still unhappy with the way he had conducted the interview, Liam told what he had found out: the origin of the virgin's blood, the purpose of Donoé's visit to the beach, and most importantly, the oath Tarquin claimed he had taken.

"A vow to remain chaste, eh? I've heard wizards do stranger," the Aedile said. "It fair puts Viyescu's mystery maid out of thought."

"And leaves us with Marcius, and Lons."

"It leaves us with Lons," the Aedile said. "There's naught that's proved against the merchant."

"Hmm."

Coeccias rolled his eyes in exasperation, but Liam did not notice. A piece of Donoé's story had lodged itself irritatingly in his head.

"If you were a wizard," he suddenly asked, "wouldn't you have to test to know if your virgin's blood was good?"

"What?"

"Do you think Tarquin had a test? A way to know if she were still a virgin?"

"Truth," Coeccias answered with a smile, "I scarcely know her, but I'd wager that trull'll be a virgin on her deathbed."

Liam ignored the Aedile's joke; he had not been thinking about Donoé at all. He pushed the idea to the back of his head, and took up considering more immediate questions. They walked towards the outskirts of the rich quarter, the Aedile smiling at the warmthless sun bright in the sky, Liam staring at the cobbles, tracing his thoughts there.

Why had he mishandled Donoé so badly? Was the other man right, he could only be sharp with people he truly suspected? In a certain way, it was comforting to think that he was not completely suspicious, that only those who deserved it called out the bloodhound in him. And in the end, he had gotten the important information.

On the other hand, they were left with Lons, a conclusion he could not believe.

They left the confines of the rich quarter without saying a word, passing into an area of smaller buildings of poorer construction and pushed closer together. Suddenly remembering his appointment with Lady Necquer, Liam stopped.

"I just remembered; I am supposed to meet someone soon, back there."

Without a trace of anything more than casual curiosity, Coeccias said, "Poppae Necquer?"

"Yes," Liam answered shortly, refusing to be surprised by what the rough-looking man picked up.

"Then we'll part here. I'm to prepare for the procession. We ought to meet later, to see if there's any current news."

"The White Grape for dinner?"

"No, the Grape grows stale for me, and I've all that cider to finish. Come to my house after the procession. You'll know it's done by the bells. The priests'll toll all when the procession gains the temple."

"Your house, then," Liam agreed.

Coeccias smiled and suddenly stuck out his heavy hand, and Liam took it firmly.

"Though y'are only a scholar, y'are a good hound, Rhenford, and a better man. Don't fret so over a silly girl, nor over the player. We've got to see justice done— I for my office, and you for the wizard. Whatever we do, whatever we've done, is to a higher end."

Liam fidgeted, but Coeccias would not let go of his hand until he relented.

"I suppose so. I suppose you're right."

His hand was released, and the two men bid each other goodbye diffidently, as if embarrassed by their words and thoughts. Coeccias went down the street to the city's heart and his procession. Liam turned around and traced his way back towards the Point and the Necquers' house.

CHAPTER 11

LIAM WAS NOT far from the Necquers' when he left Coeccias, and the bells had only just begun to announce noon when he knocked on their street door. Lares received him as usual, but did not usher him up to the parlor. Instead, he motioned for Liam to wait and, avoiding his eyes, hurried up the stairs himself.

A few minutes later, Lady Necquer came down in a whirl of skirts, her face drawn and pale. She stopped on the bottom step and shot a fearful look back up before coming quickly to him.

"You must away, Sir Liam," she whispered anxiously. "I cannot receive you this day." Her eyes kept returning to the stairs, as though she were afraid something horrible would come down them.

"May I ask why? Are you ill?"

She laid a hand on his arm, and quickly withdrew it. "My apologies, Sir Liam, but I beg you not to press. I simply cannot receive you. You may come tomorrow, at this hour, if y'are careful."

"But—" He did not move, not understanding, and her face screwed up suddenly before she burst out:

"My lord would not have you so much about! Now please, Sir Liam, do not ask the wherefore; only go!"

Bewildered, Liam hesitated in the face of her distress, shifting from foot to foot.

"Please," she begged. "Come tomorrow, and let none see you."

His thoughts scattered, and he retreated, sketching a hasty bow. She shut the door firmly behind him. Standing in the

169

street, he stared at the closed door and blew out a heavy
breath.

"Necquer won't have me around so much," he wondered
aloud, then turned away down the street, shaking his head
and muttering. "And just the other day he asked me to
dinner. Freeporters. Hah."

The afternoon stretched emptily before him, with nothing
to do. He had hoped to fill a large part of it with Lady
Necquer, listening to her outline the series of poems he
could not write. The odd hour he could fill with wandering,
or maybe a visit to the Uncommon Player. Now there was
nothing, and it was far too early to go to a wineshop.

A long lunch was a poor second, he decided, but it was
all he had. Over the course of the morning, he and Coeccias
had been into every tavern in the Point but one, and he
chose this last one to eat in, solely because it was the far-
thest from the Necquers' and would take the longest time
to reach.

It did not take as long as he wished to get there, but the
service made up for it by being extraordinarily slow. He
could almost feel the minutes creeping away.

In a way, his impatience for the afternoon to be over
amused him. It had been quite a while since he had anything
to wait for, and he had watched so much time slip profit-
lessly away that it was strange to begrudge the hours.

He was anxious, he saw, for the whole business to be
over. For Tarquin's murderer to hang, for Fanuilh to be
shut out of his mind, to resume his quiet life. The activity
that had brought him bouncing out of bed only a few days
before was now tiresome. It had brought him the contact
with other people that he belatedly realized he needed, but
the investigation had begun to color the contact.

Lady Necquer had sent him packing, after all, and he had
grown used to their daily conversations.

*So much so that now my afternoon seems empty as a
keg after a feast*, he reflected ruefully. Heartily sick of
the search for Tarquin's killer, and even sicker of his own
maudlin thoughts, he gratefully turned his attention to the
lunch he had ordered.

The meal was huge, and the cost equally large. Just past the soup, a thick broth delicately spiced, and into the fish, sole with a fiery-hot sauce, he managed to put his concerns away and keep them at bay for the rest of the meal. The afternoon light crawled slowly across the front of the nearly empty tavern, and when he was done, over an hour had passed.

"Not late enough," he cursed. Hours still lay in wait before him, and like stubborn crows, his thoughts swung back to pick at what he had learned from Donoé. By her report, Tarquin had sworn an oath of chastity which, if true, effectively destroyed any theories about the wizard having gotten the hooded woman pregnant.

Or did it?

He had a happy inspiration concerning the rest of his afternoon, settled his score quickly, and set out for Northfield. His stomach groaned for time to deal with the heavy meal he had put down, but he gave it as little thought as possible.

Viyescu was in his shop, and clearly wished he hadn't been. He twitched when the door opened and Liam walked in, and set down the mortar and pestle he had been using with a heavy thud.

"Hierarch Cance," he grated unhappily.

"Master Viyescu. I'm sorry to bother you again."

The druggist shrugged to indicate that it did not matter, but there was no fluidity in the gesture: his shoulders were a single block of tension.

"I wanted to ask you some more questions about the wizard, and the pregnant woman who mentioned him."

"I'm afraid I can't spare the time, Hierarch," the druggist said, in a strange tone that bordered on pleading. "I must prepare for the procession."

"Ah, the procession," Liam answered airily. "Of course. You'll be marching?"

"I always do, Hierarch." Viyescu sounded almost miserable, and Liam fixed his gaze squarely on the man's eyes.

"Of course. I only wish more followed your example. But I must detain you for only a few moments, and as you know, the business with the wizard is quite important to the temple in Torquay."

"As you wish," Viyescu acceded nervously. Liam noted with mild astonishment that the druggist had actually begun to sweat.

"It has to do with the woman who mentioned Tarquin to you. I think I misunderstood you when last we spoke. I thought you implied that the wizard had gotten her pregnant, but I have it on the best of information that he had sworn an oath of celibacy."

The words seemed to strike Viyescu with physical force. He stammered for a moment, and then controlled himself with visible effort. "I apologize, Hierarch, I did not mean to imply that. *He* did not get the girl pregnant; *he* did not sleep with her."

"I see. So some other man was the father, then? Not Tarquin?"

"No, Hierarch. Not Tarquin."

"You see, I've been trying to figure out what has happened to him, because he was important to us, if you take my meaning. Tell me, did this woman ask you for any virgin's blood?"

The question drew a complete blank from Viyescu, who shook his head as if he might have misheard. "Virgin's blood, Hierarch?"

"Never mind. She only asked for santhract?"

Viyescu nodded eagerly. He was being more cooperative than he had been before, and Liam wondered why.

"How does one take santhract?"

"Powdered, Hierarch," the druggist said instantly, "in wine or cider to cut the taste. But I never sold her any," he added quickly. Indecision suddenly flickered behind his eyes, and he began to add something before cutting himself short. Liam waited for a moment and then went on, disappointed.

"And she wanted it to terminate her pregnancy?" Viyescu nodded again. "She must be very deep in sin, Master Apothecary. Very deep." He intoned the words deeply, with as much of the piousness of a Torquay priest as he could

remember. It sounded silly to him, like a poor imitation
from his student days, but the sound clearly hit Viyescu
another way.

He began to speak, faltered, and gazed deeply into Liam's
face, searching for something. Liam willed himself to remain
impassive, hoping that whatever was sought would be found,
but apparently he disappointed the apothecary because he
only said, "Yes, Hierarch, very deep," before snapping his
mouth shut.

"Did you know the woman when she came to you?"

"No, Hierarch," Viyescu said, firm once again, but Liam
knew he was lying. "I had never seen her before."

The sound of a horn echoed out over the city, and Viyescu
looked up in alarm.

"The procession! I must go now, Hierarch, if I'm to be
on time. You'll excuse me?"

Liam gestured graciously, though inwardly he was angry
and frustrated. The druggist had been on the verge of telling
him something of importance, something about the woman.
Watching him pull off his stained apron, Liam cursed himself mentally. It had been very close. What was Viyescu
hiding?

"I must go upstairs to change," the druggist said when
he had hung his apron on a peg, pointing vaguely towards
the rear of his shop. "Don't you have to prepare for the
procession, Hierarch?"

"I have a dispensation for this Uris-tide," Liam said
smoothly, and allowed himself brief mental congratulations
for having thought it out earlier. "I will be watching, of
course, but the business Torquay has sent me on is terribly
important."

"No doubt. I, on the other hand, must prepare myself."

Liam understood the dismissal. "Certainly, certainly. Perhaps we can talk again?"

"I do not know what else I can tell you, Hierarch."

"Of course. Well, then, I'll be on my way." He turned
and started for the door, and then stopped, his hand on the
latch. "Master Viyescu," he said, smiling pleasantly, though
he wanted to shake the man until he spoke. "My prayers

will go with you in the procession today."

If it was not what the druggist had been looking for in his face a few moments before, it was certainly very good. Viyescu's expression softened, and he nodded once.

"Thank you, Hierarch" he said, his voice suddenly thick.

"Perhaps you would do me two small favors, Master Viyescu," Liam risked. "Perhaps if you see this woman again, you would not mention my interest in her? And perhaps you would pray for me as you go in the procession?"

"I am not worthy," Viyescu said, his eyes dropping to the floor.

What does that *mean?* Liam wondered.

"Who is? Nonetheless, I would appreciate both."

"As you wish," Viyescu mumbled, and then quickly left the room.

Liam paused for a moment in the empty shop, wondering about the man's strange behavior. The sound of the horn being winded again called him back to himself, and he went out into the street.

The horn sounded twice more, and he noticed a few people hurrying towards the center of the city. Towards the forming procession, he guessed, and set his steps to follow. He had, after all, told Viyescu that he would watch.

Ordinarily the square at the heart of Southwark bustled with people, selling goods or buying, gawking at jugglers or clowns or musicians. Rival birdsellers sent their disciplined flocks charging into each other from either side of the square, the object to confuse the other birds into joining the strongest flock. It was a game Liam had never tired of watching, and he had never passed through without stopping for a moment.

There were no flocks that day, however, and no men with elbow-length gauntlets urging on their feathered soldiers with whistles and high-pitched cries.

The squat stone bulk of the jail and the imposing, columned facade of the Duke's court on the western side of the square did not usually deter the chattering crowds, and on most days the wineshops, cafés and stores scattered around the other sides did a brisk business.

The square seemed less active today though it was thronged with people who spilled into the sidestreets and approaching lanes. Hundreds obscured the pavement, most dressed in their brightly colored holiday finest, but they were hushed, expectant.

By discreet pushing and taking advantage of his thinness, Liam managed to edge his way into the square proper, but the crowd was so thick that he found it uncomfortable, and shoved his way along the fringes of the square until he came to a two-storied wineshop. It was empty, and his footsteps echoed loudly as he entered.

All of the staff of the wineshop were at the galleries on the second floor, gazing in reverence out over the square. Liam coughed politely, and the barkeep whirled in fury at the interruption, then stopped himself when he saw Liam's expensive clothes.

"Ah, my lord," he fawned, "you'd grace us to share the process with us. If it please you, sit here." He shooed a crowd of serving girls and tapboys from the table in front of the central gallery and installed Liam there, cheerfully ignoring his employees' sullen looks.

"Something to go with, my lord?"

"Just wine," Liam said.

The barkeep brought it quickly, smiled obsequiously, and dashed to another gallery, forcing a spot for himself between two angry serving girls.

Liam sipped at his wine, turning his attention to the square below.

A platform had been erected at shoulder height against the grim stone steps of the jail, and Liam noted with a wry smile that there were fixtures that would allow it to be changed to a gallows. Around the platform, a small space had been cleared by members of the Guard, resplendent in black surcoats emblazoned with the Duke's three foxes and polished, ornately useless ceremonial armor. Inside the circle of armored men several people had gathered. A small knot of shaven-headed acolytes of Uris talked quietly amongst themselves; Ancus Marcius held silent court over three other prominent merchants; and Ton Viyescu stood alone in a blindingly white full-length robe, his face screwed up in a sour expression beneath its encroaching beard. Coeccias, his shaggy hair painstakingly combed, his own surcoat and armor crumb-free, scowled at a man dressed in the everyday uniform of the Guard. The man was speaking at length about something, and in the middle of his speech, Coeccias began scanning the crowd impatiently. As Liam watched from the gallery, the man finished his report and the Aedile dismissed him offhandedly, his eyes still searching the crowd. Then he looked directly at the second floor of the wineshop, started, and grabbed the departing man, pointing in Liam's direction.

The man nodded and pushed his way into the crowd, crossing the packed square towards the shop. The gathered worshippers parted silently for him, their attention still held by the empty platform. Liam, however, watched him with interest until he disappeared below. Then he turned his gaze to the stairs, expecting the messenger to appear at any moment.

When he finally heard footsteps on the stairs, he rose himself and walked towards them, meeting the man at the top.

"Are you looking for me?"

The messenger stared at him, obviously not having expected to be met at the head of the stairs.

"Y'are Liam Rhenford?" he asked suspiciously.

"Yes. Coeccias sent you?"

"Aye, to carry you these news. The rent's paid on the lodgings, sir, and so not by the wizard. Someone else keeps the hooded woman."

"That's all?" Liam said after a moment. It did not surprise him—Viyescu had just told him that Tarquin had not kept the woman.

"Well, sir, just that the owner said the coins used were the most fantastic he'd seen, though neither clipped nor light. Good gold, but strange."

Liam raised an eyebrow in politeness, but was not interested. He was more concerned with figuring out Viyescu's strange behavior. What had the druggist been about to tell him? More importantly, was it connected with Tarquin's death?

The sound of the horn called him to his surroundings, and he turned back to the gallery, the messenger following behind wordlessly.

The horn was winded only once this time, and Liam saw that one of the shaven-headed acolytes was standing on the platform, raising a silver-chased ram's horn to the sky. He sounded it twice more, and a clash of cymbals answered the third, at which he hurriedly left the platform to join his fellows below. All eyes in the crowd turned to the north, where the main point of the procession was approaching.

Two young boys led the way, crowned with wreaths of laurel and dressed in short white tunics despite the cold. They spread rushes in the path the crowd cleared for them, walking solemnly. Behind them followed a single man in complicated flowing vestments of white sewn with pearls and gold and silver threads. He wore a tall scarlet mitre and carried a golden lantern and an oversized book bound in tooled, painted leather. His massive belly bobbled beneath the vestments, and his beard straggled over three extra chins, giving rise to Liam's blasphemous thought that Uris's second-highest priest would not enjoy the next day's fast.

The priest did manage to look grand, however, pacing measuredly on the carpet of rushes strewn by the pageboys, aloof and proud under the silent scrutiny of the crowd.

Behind him, borne in a litter carried on the muscular shoulders of eight bald acolytes, came Uris's image, shrouded in a snowy tarp. Last in line was a group of musicians, piper and drummer and the man with the cymbals, marching unobserved in grave lockstep. The attention of the crowd was divided equally between the fat priest in his magnificent clothes and the covered statue.

Only the rustle of sandals on rushes and the sigh of the wind could be heard as the procession moved into the circle of Guardsmen. The pageboys went up the narrow steps to the platform, leaving rushes behind, and the priest followed them, moving to the edge to face the crowd. The litter bearers brought their load to rest in front of the platform, neatly turning around so that Uris, when uncovered, would face her worshippers like the priest. Coeccias, Viyescu and the merchants stood in ranks to the left of the litter, looking up at the priest; the other acolytes knelt to the right. Finally the musicians took up their position at the bottom of the steps leading to the platform.

When they were ready, the piper nodded to the priest, who handed the lantern to one boy and the book to the other. Liam was struck by the awe with which they received their burdens, and the way they held them firmly in their hands but away from their bodies, as if afraid to soil them.

Just a book and a lantern, Liam thought. He had never had much use for organized religions, though he knew the gods were there. Meet the Storm King face to face, he thought somewhat scornfully, and see how much you care for a book and a lantern.

The ceremony was interesting, he had to admit, if only for its aesthetic and historical value. Once rid of his book and lantern, the priest raised his hands and began a chant in a high-pitched voice that swept over the silent square. Rising and falling in a stately, cadenced rhythm, the chant described the wondrous gifts Uris had bestowed on the world in an obscure, highly refined dialect of High Church Taralonian. Liam vaguely recognized it from his student days in Torquay, and was able to follow haltingly along, despite the complex syntax and the strange, inverted poetry. He wondered if anyone there besides the priest, the acolytes and himself understood a single word of it.

After several verses lauding Uris in general and her two major gifts—medicine and writing—the chant broke into song. The shaven acolytes raised their voices with the priest's, ranging around his high tenor in a complex and surprisingly merry harmony. At first the drummer was the only musician playing, giving the singers a simple beat, but then the piper began, and the man with the cymbals joined in as well with carefully muted crashes. They were, however, only the framework of the music, a steady undercurrent for the voices of the celebrants.

The singing went through two repeated verses, and then subsided into just the priest's chant, though the drummer continued to beat out a more subdued rhythm for the chanter to follow.

It went on for almost an hour, breaking from chant to song back to chant, going into detail about Uris's contributions to almost every civilized craft, illustrating the gifts with old myths and legends. First the piper wove into the chant and then the cymbalist as well, until the only way to tell chant from song was by the participation or silence of the shaven chorus. The crowd of worshippers remained silent, and Liam gave a moment's admiration to their stoicism, packed closely into a cold square listening to a long service in a language they could not understand. For his own part, he was too absorbed in translating it to himself to notice the length, and he grudgingly admitted to himself that it was beautiful in a strange way.

Finally, with the sun little more than an hour above the western horizon, the singers and musicians brought their last burst of song to a halt, and an imposing silence descended on the square. Flushed with his exertions, the priest on the platform retrieved his book and his lantern from the pageboys and raised them high for the adoration of the common worshippers. He let a suitably dramatic pause go by, and then pronounced a blessing they could understand.

"Uris, Light of Our Dark and Teacher of the World, bless this city and this gathering!"

A muttering of "So be it" rose from the assembled crowd, and every person in the square and the wineshop galleries where Liam stood bowed their head. On cue, two of the acolytes caught hold of the immaculate tarp that covered the image on the litter and pulled it back, so that it slid up the front of the statue and then fell back from its shoulders.

Liam almost whistled, but checked himself. The statue was incredible, an eight-foot-tall woman bearing a book and a lantern and a benign expression. Uris had been rendered in exquisite detail, but what struck Liam was the obvious cost of the image. Carved of wood, barely an inch was free of some expensive decoration, from the cloth-of-gold robes to the chips of jade that were inset in her fingers to stand for nails. Her eyes were multifaceted diamonds, her hair uncountable wires of beaten silver; the book and lantern were gold, and in the heart of the lantern, representing the flame, was an enormous winking ruby. Countless smaller gems glittered from her robes, sewn into the cloth-of-gold.

Absurdly, Liam thought of a thief he had once known who would then and there have resolved to steal the statue, and then made good on the resolution. Thievery, however, was far from the minds of the worshippers in the square, who could not decide whether to gaze devotedly on their goddess or hang their heads in humility.

Once he judged the people had had their fill of the statue, the priest walked down off the platform and allowed the procession to form behind him. Without any discernible scurrying, everyone found their places; the pageboys once again in front, joined by the acolyte with the horn, followed by the priest, the litter, the rest of the acolytes, then Coeccias and his Guardsmen dressed in their ceremonial armor. As the only layman who had made all the processions of the week, Viyescu walked alone next, with the musicians behind him. Last in the official procession came Marcius and his gaggle of prominent merchants.

The horn sounded again, the musicians struck up a tune, and the procession began to move fairly quickly out of the square to the south. As soon as Marcius and his group were past, the general crowd fell in behind them, beginning to raise up songs and shouts. Instruments appeared among the hitherto silent worshippers, and the noise swelled into a happy celebration, loudly heralding the unveiled Uris through the city.

The procession was headed down towards the harbor and moving rapidly, the hundreds of worshippers pressing hard after, bearing their noisy celebration with them.

Liam watched until the last had straggled out of the square, leaving a loud silence in their wake. A long pent-up sigh escaped from the messenger, calling attention to him.

"Where will they go?"

"To the harbor, sure," the man said, as though it should be obvious. "And then they'll up through Auric's Park and Northfield, and so back to Temple's Court."

"I've never seen the celebrations for Uris-tide before," Liam said, thinking with pity of the litter bearers and their heavy cargo.

"They're every year," the man said, looking at him like he was an idiot. "How could you not?"

He began to explain, but then decided not to bother. If the man couldn't figure out from his accent and his name that he was a Midlander, why bother enlightening him? Instead, he simply shrugged and sat down at the table, pulling his unfinished wine to him.

The messenger stayed for a moment to bestow a pitying look on him, and then left.

Liam stayed at the wineshop for another half an hour, reflecting on the ceremony through two more cups. Few other Taralonian gods required processions, even in Torquay, which was noted for its zealous maintenance of ancient rituals.

At length, however, he could not keep his thoughts from the investigation, and he felt compelled to do something, even if it was just to walk—which he did, at length.

The procession's taking a long time, he thought as he strolled the nearly empty streets, with even more pity for the litter bearers.

He walked west from the square, past the outdoor theater he now realized was the summer home of the Golden Orb's company, and into the Warren, the sprawl of narrow, twisted streets and tortured lanes that housed most of the city in ramshackle houses that stretched impossibly high. They seemed to rely on each other for support, leaning forward across the streets, almost touching as they reached four and five stories.

Ordinarily he would not have gone there, but the spirit of the celebration must have taken hold, and there were few people in the streets, some of whom looked like they might actually have been cleaned to honor the goddess. Even the ranks of the beggars were thinner, many undoubtedly gone to try their luck with the processors.

And besides, Coeccias had told him that the apartment rented by the hooded woman was in the Warren. He pondered Viyescu's strange behavior once again. For some reason, his questions about the woman had upset the gruff druggist, but Liam found it difficult to understand why. It might have something to do with Tarquin, but it might have been that the druggist was simply unwilling to discuss the intricacies of sin with a priest. He might well have tripped himself up again with his religious imposture, closing off an avenue of investigation with an ill-chosen ploy. Or maybe Uris herself was frustrating him, as a punishment for pretending to be one of her Hierarchs.

Still—Viyescu had wanted to tell him something, and had not. Until he knew what it was, he could not dismiss the inkling at the back of his mind.

His thoughts as aimless as his footsteps, he was well into the Warren before he heard the bells tolling from far to the east in Temple's Court. On hearing them, he pulled up short and immediately turned around. There was little for him and Coeccias to talk about—the news about the rent being paid made little or no difference, and his impressions of his conversation with Viyescu were better kept to himself—but at least his afternoon of waiting was over.

Liam began to hurry through the city to the Aedile's house, and had to concentrate to slow down, to give Coeccias time to get home from the Temple of Uris. He even managed to make himself stop to buy a jug of wine, thinking it appropriate to bring something with him.

He need not have bothered. Coeccias opened the door himself when he knocked, and there was a steaming mug of mulled cider in his hand.

"Ah, y'have brought a small something, have you?" Relieving Liam of the jug, he ushered him in and then led the way back to the kitchen, which was considerably neater than it had been in the morning. Noticing Liam's appreciative glance, Coeccias laughed. "Burus was busy all the day, setting straight for the morrow. Cleaning's forbid on the eve of Uris-tide."

The servant looked up from stirring the steaming pot of cider and smiled sourly, handing Liam a cup without preamble.

"If it please you, Rhenford, we'll save the wine for another time, and finish this batch of cider. I'll not drink it tomorrow, and by the next it'll be fairly undrinkable." He sat at the table, motioning Liam to sit opposite him, and raised his mug. Liam touched his mug to the Aedile's, and they drank in silence for a moment.

"Truth, it's a blessing to be out of that infernal armor," Coeccias said after a moment. He had changed into his usual stained black tunic, though his hair had stayed perfectly in place. As though reminded of it, he ruffled it with his free hand. "I'd just as soon make a trifling donation than march that process again. It's a passing trouble."

"I imagine it must be worse for the men who have to carry the statue."

"Oh, aye," the Aedile agreed. "I'd sooner wear the armor than carry the goddess, but I'd even sooner just worship from afar. Not for me are pomps and displays, I'll tell you, though I'm as deep in for Uris as any other."

Burus apparently decided the cider was sufficiently stirred, because he stood and left the room.

"Now say, Rhenford, what think you of the moneys handed out?"

"The rent? It's paid, so we know for sure that the woman was not Tarquin's—though I never really thought she was. We're still left with Lons."

"Ah, I note y'omit Marcius from your accounting, at last. Y'are convinced, then?"

"I can't imagine or prove anything else, though I still think Lons doesn't have it in him."

He did not mention Viyescu. What he had discovered— what he *thought* he had discovered—he could not put into words. He thought the druggist wanted to reveal something, wanted to come forward, but it was only a fleeting feeling, a hunch. Not worth bothering Coeccias with.

Coeccias shrugged. "I'd agree, for argument, but thinking's no place here—the *knowing* is all. We know the player had a right good reason, and the knife was that of a player. All points to him, though why he's not fled is beyond me." For a moment, the Aedile stared into the depths of his mug, then looked up and spoke in a different tone.

"There's another thing, though, that'll interest you. The druggist recommended himself to you."

"Viyescu? He mentioned me?"

"Aye," Coeccias nodded. "At the fane, after the procession. He must have seen me post the messenger to you, for he came to me when all was done, and asked if I knew the hierarch. It took a moment, but then I recalled your imposture, and said I did. He said there was something he'd thought of to tell you since your last talk, something that might interest you."

"Well?"

"Truth, he mumbled and muttered and jigged around it, saying he'd only come to tell it through pure meditation on Uris and a lot of other pious rambling, but the pure and straight of it is that 'the woman' had come to him again, just the other day, and begged once more a dram of the poison from him. Now this is our woman, is it not?"

"Yes, but we already know Tarquin wasn't keeping her," Liam said, shaking his head.

"Remind me: what was the herb?"

Santhract, but it doesn't matter. Tarquin was dead, not pregnant."

"That's true," Coeccias admitted. "Though here's more on it: this hooded and cloaked beldame must've put a mighty fright to our druggist, for that he was shaking leaflike, and pale, and looked around him oft."

"So?" Liam could barely restrain his frustration. Viyescu's information was scarcely to the point, gone the way of his interviews with Marcius and his decanter of virgin's blood. Wasted breath and effort poorly spent. He was annoyed with the business, and with Viyescu. The puritanical druggist's problems had nothing to do with Tarquin's death, of that he was suddenly sure. Lons was the killer, though he did not want to believe it. "So some temple-soft fanatic is frightened by a woman? It's not proof, it's not *knowing*, and the *knowing* is all, isn't it?"

Was that what Viyescu had wanted to tell him? That he was frightened of the woman? It did not matter.

He regretted his tone, but fortunately the Aedile did not take it amiss.

"Truth, you've the right of it. More like Viyescu was afraid to talk with me, or to utter ungodly thoughts in Uris's fane. The knowing is all, and we know it's our player. Perhaps we'll clap him tomorrow." He fell to pondering his cup of cider, and when he saw it was almost empty, lumbered over to the fire to refill it, taking Liam's cup as well. Bending over the pot, he muttered heavily. "I'll say, though, that I'm wondering wherefore he hasn't fled. If I were him, I'd to the heath before we were a street away."

Liam accepted his refill. "He has probably guessed you have someone watching him, and that the proof is circumstantial. It is circumstantial, though damning."

"Enough to hang him, if need be, though I'm loath to do't," Coeccias said ruefully, resuming his seat. "A confession'd do my heart good."

"He probably guesses that as well, and is hoping we'll give up. Or maybe he thinks my warning was all the punishment he'd get."

"Ah," Coeccias said, his eyes lighting with malicious humor, "then that was the matter you had when you let him off! To keep him off the Lady Necquer!"

Nodding miserably, Liam cursed himself. He had bungled it, bargaining with their best suspect for an unimportant tangent.

"Y'have a soft spot for the gentler sex, Rhenford, that much is clear. Perhaps he thinks we'll not take him for the murder because you're overfond of his sister, eh?"

The jibe stung, though a smile lit Coeccias's eyes, and Liam hung his head.

"Well, on the morrow we'll clap the player, and the matter'll be done."

Liam drank unhappily to the resolution. Strangely, he thought of Fanuilh. With Lons's arrest, he would have fulfilled his part of the bargain, regardless of his numerous missteps; he wondered if the dragon would carry out his part as ineptly.

They sat for a while, drinking the cider. Coeccias refilled the mugs twice, and Liam's face flushed with the spiked drink.

Suddenly the Aedile boomed out a laugh and slammed his mug to the table.

"Why sit we here like maudlin old crows?" he shouted, his teeth beaming hugely in his black beard. "We've conned and caught our killer! It's done! We're done with it! On the morrow he'll take up residence in the jail, and I'll to clearing drunken tars out of taverns, and you'll to your books! We're clear! Come! Bring the pot!"

The Aedile jumped to his feet and careered out of the kitchen. Liam stood more slowly, and felt the blood rush dizzily in his head. He had drunk more than was good for him, but he had the sense to use a rag to hold the hot ring of the pot he took from the fire. Coeccias's sudden good cheer both surprised and amused him, and he gratefully allowed it to distract him from his melancholy mood.

Calling for Burus to light a fire in the parlor and to bring food, Coeccias then saw to the fire himself, and cursed the servant good-naturedly when he appeared.

"Damn your slowness, Burus! I've the fire in hand! You to the food, and mind you bring your pipes as well, and a third mug! Now, Rhenford," he called when Liam came in, carefully carrying the pot, "hang it on the fire, and see yourself to another mug!"

Burus came back with a huge tray covered with cold meat, cheese and bread, and a flute under his arm. Liam perceived through the rapidly descending haze of the cider that the servant's smile was sour by a trick of his face, and that he was well acquainted with his master's sudden moods.

He left the food on a chest that stood by the fire, and stood back to check his flute.

Though his lunch had been large, Liam attacked the platter, both because the spiked cider had given him a new appetite and because he was afraid of the haze it had imposed.

"Now, Burus," Coeccias said while Liam stuffed sausage, cheese and bread indiscriminately down his throat, "it's not yet Uris's appointed fasting time, and Rhenford and I've finished up a business the like of which I've never seen in my office, and there's most of a pot of cider to down. So, you'll have a mug, and we'll have a tune." Gesturing imperiously, he filled the extra mug and thrust it at the servant, who took a deep draught before setting it down and commencing a high, lively air on his flute.

Coeccias burst out laughing and applauding at once, and stamped his feet in a ragged approximation of time.

"Go to, go to, Burus! He knows," the Aedile bellowed confidingly to Liam, "that that's my favorite." Liam was busy with the food he had heaped in his lap, but he managed to look up and nod appreciatively, though he had never heard the tune before.

By the end of the song, Liam had finished a large portion of the food on the platter, refilled his mug and begun beating out the rhythm on his knees. Burus was more than a fair musician, and Liam recognized his next song with a bright grin and an emphatic nod of approval. The servant had started in on "The Lipless Flutist" over the strenuous objections of Coeccias, who wanted to hear the first song again. As soon as he saw that Liam was engrossed in the song, however, he stopped shouting for the old one, and came and sat by him, slurring his question slightly.

"It likes you?"

"Very much," Liam replied, running over the obscene words to the song in his head and noticing the mischievous glint in Burus's eye as he cocked his head over the plain wooden flute. It seemed as though the servant was daring him to sing.

"Then sing it," Coeccias roared in his ear, swaying perilously.

"I can't sing."

"Play?" When Liam, wanting only to hear the song and recall its lyrics, ignored him, the Aedile grabbed him and shouted his question again. "Can you play?"

"Yes, yes."

"The lute?"

"Yes, the lute, a little," Liam said, willing his friend to be quiet. To his great disappointment, however, it was Burus who was quiet, laying aside his flute and looking at his master with an unvoiced question. Coeccias lurched to his feet and went to the chest. Dropping the platter on the floor, he flung the lid open and rummaged for a moment, coming up with a much-battered lute case. He opened it tenderly, and revealed a rosewood lute of tremendous craftsmanship, with ivory pegs and silvered edges. He presented it to Liam and then took a seat on a caned chair off to one side of the room.

"Will you, sir?" They were the first words Liam had heard Burus say, and he was surprised to hear a courtly voice issue from the sour face. He noticed suddenly that Burus was older than Coeccias, the thin hairs that straggled across his bald head a dirty gray.

"I suppose, yes, just let me tune it."

"It'll need no tuning, sir."

Shrugging, Liam picked out the first few notes of "The Lipless Flutist," and heard that Burus was right. Encouraged, he went on more confidently, and the servant joined in soon. After a few minutes, the rust in Liam's fingers wore away, and the two matched each other. Coeccias started singing the most common verse once they had run through the main theme twice. His range was poor, and he shouted more than sang, but the words came out clear and loud, and the words were the most important part of "The Lipless Flutist." Liam entered the singing almost right away, and though the mix of the two men's voices was hardly pleasant, it was not outright offensive, and seemed to fit the ruder lines quite well.

The variations on the song's basic theme—the adventures of a flute-player with no lips—were almost endless, and

Coeccias and Liam diverged radically after three verses. The Aedile tried to return to the beginning, but Liam went on, into a verse he had once heard in Harcourt. Coeccias joined him on the refrain, though, and they brought the song to a rousing finish, shouting and laughing, with the heavy official jigging across the parlor.

Laughing, Liam flexed his fingers, pleased that he had remembered how to play. Another thing he had not done in a long time.

"Y'have a fair hand for the lute," Burus commented, cheeks red from playing the furiously paced song.

"And y'have a saucy, impertinent tongue, rascal!" Coeccias shook with laughter and clapped his servant on the shoulder, rocking the slighter man.

"I only learned because of that song," Liam said. He had indeed learned to play because of "The Lipless Flutist," taking up the lute to fill long hours on deck and as a way to remember the countless verses that had amused him in taverns and wineshops and camps in a hundred lands. He smiled at the pervasiveness of one song, and recalled a particular version.

"There's a variation to it, if you'd like to hear it."

Coeccias loudly left no doubt that he was in favor of it, and Burus smiled indulgently.

He led them through the variation, called "The Lipless Flutist and the One-Armed Lutist," laying out each new line for Coeccias to roar along. He included a few of the special rills that went along with mention of the Lutist, and found Burus accompanying him easily, while Coeccias clapped with drunken joy. They sang the new verse twice, and then paused, drinking much more cider and laughing with the Aedile as he tried and failed to remember the lines Liam had just taught him.

"You'll write them out for me, Rhenford," he said angrily, and then called for another song.

Liam began one of the few others he knew, a sailor's song, high-spirited but relatively clean for the normally filthy genre. Burus picked it up effortlessly, and added a number of flourishes that enhanced the simple melody. As he bent his head to check his fingering, Liam marveled at the gnarled old servant's skill. He was a true musician, not a dabbler like Liam, who had only learned individual songs and not the theories or ideas behind them. He could play the songs he knew, but Burus could learn a new one easily, and make it better.

They played two more songs that Liam knew, and Coeccias remained silent, staring fixedly at a space between them. When they were done, Liam bowed over his lute at Burus.

"You're a fine player, Burus. A really fine musician."

The servant flushed and scowled, and the Aedile roused himself from his stupor to take another gulp of cider and fix his attention on the lute Liam held.

"And so he should be, Rhenford! My father had the teaching of him, and my father was the rarest that ever served the office of Duke's Minstrel!"

Burus's scowl deepened, but he did not speak angrily. "That lute was his," he said, pointing with his flute, "and though you do it no disgrace, he was as far your master as a king is a swineherd's."

"Aye, a rarer there never was, a rare man for a song," Coeccias muttered morosely, and then suddenly burst out laughing. "And the rankest time-server and flatterer the Duke's court ever saw! How think you I came to my own office? Son of the Duke's favorite, and good for naught but chucking tosspots into the street—so off with him to Southwark, and create him Aedile!"

"Y'have done credit to it, Coeccias," the old servant said mildly, and the Aedile nodded firmly.

"Truth, I've done my all, and few could do better. But go to, another song!"

Burus began a slow, mournful song, a dirge to Laomedon, the God of the Worlds Beyond. He peered questioningly over his flute, but Liam shook his head and smiled, carefully putting the beautiful lute back into its case before refilling his mug.

The pot was finished by the time Burus had gone through four more songs, three of which Liam did not recognize.

Finally, the servant put aside his flute and drained the last of the only cup he had taken.

"If there's nothing else, I think I'll to my cot."

"No, naught else, good Burus, beside my thanks." Coeccias seemed to be over his earlier wild drunkenness, and nodded gravely at his servant's bow.

Liam whistled after the old man had gone, now far worse off than his friend. The haze was fully extended now, and he was glad the pot was empty, because the thought of even another sip made his stomach ache.

"He's a fine musician," he whispered in awe.

"Truth, a fine man as well."

Unsteadily, Liam made his way to his feet. "It's time for me to go."

Coeccias did not argue, but he did stand and open the door for him with a wide smile.

"Y'are no poor player yourself, for all Burus's round-about way of saying it. Y'ought to come again, and let him teach you some other tunes."

"That would be good," Liam said thickly, trying force-fully to regain control of his reluctant legs. Their talk of Coeccias's father had brought to mind his own, and he felt inexpressibly sad beneath the numbness of the cider.

"On the morrow, then," the Aedile said, as Liam went out the door.

"Yes, tomorrow," he muttered, waving a hand over his shoulder.

There was a cold breeze in the street, and it thinned the haze enough for him to realize that trying to ride out to Tarquin's would be pointless, if not dangerous. With that muddled thought, he forced himself to start for his garret.

The stairs seemed to stretch interminably ahead of him, but eventually he reached the top, bumping from wall to wall. Sad, fuzzy thoughts of his father and muddled curses for Coeccias's wickedly spiked cider echoed in his head. Fully clothed, he collapsed onto his pallet and into sleep.

CHAPTER 12

AS USUAL WHEN he was even slightly drunk, Liam slept poorly, plagued by nightmares.

In Tarquin's house, which the dream meant for his father's keep, a wild revel was going on, and he, as a crippled jester, was being baited like a bear. Hounds snapped savagely at him, biting his legs and hands. Blood streamed down his legs, but he could not move to defend himself. This greatly displeased the revelers who circled him. The wizard himself, Donoé at his side, his face a demon-mask with the flickering orange candlelight, laughed disdainfully at Liam's pitiful gestures. Coeccias tossed a seemingly endless supply of lutes at his head and growled encouragement to the dogs. Lons and Lady Necquer, lying together on the same couch, shrieked with delight as a particularly large bite was torn from his leg. Others he had met—Viyescu and Marcius, Kansallus and his actors, even Mother Japh the ghost witch—gorged themselves on wine and roasted meat, screaming for the dogs to dispatch him.

Weaker and weaker, Liam tried to avoid the pack, but the laughter and the hatred of the revelers discouraged him, and he allowed himself to fall.

The dogs pounced on him from all sides, rolling him over with the pressure of their attack, and he gazed up into Fanuilh's eyes. The dragon was hovering high above him, gazing imperturbably down on the dog's feast. Suddenly, it flapped its wings gently, and at each downstroke a sound like thunder echoed through the suddenly silent chamber. The revelers stopped indulging themselves, and looked in awe at the dragon as more peals of thunder rang out. Liam looked helplessly into the creature's eyes, searching for something he could understand.

Knocking at his door, subtly like thunder, woke him up, and he left the dream with a muffled gasp. He jumped to his feet, disentangling himself from his blanket with difficulty. He could not have slept very long; it was still dark out, his candle was still burning, and he was still slightly drunk. There was another knock and he jumped, then took a deep breath to steady himself and hurried to the door.

Rora stood there, a concerned look on her flawless face. Liam recoiled in surprise and her concerned look grew troubled.

Must be a dream, Liam thought; *where are the dogs?*

"Master?" she said, taking his sweating palm in her own cool one. "Is all well? Your face's a fright." Her voice was a wellspring of good intentions and honest worry, and her hand felt wonderfully cool and smooth, but he pulled away roughly and turned into the room, soddenly aware that it was wrong for her to be there.

"Nothing. Just a dream." He scrubbed at his hot face and swiped his hair back, knowing enough to know his wits were not with him. He did not hear her come up behind him, and jumped again when she laid her hand on his shoulder.

"Master, is all well?"

He saw his chair by the window and, convinced it was a refuge, threw himself into it.

Rora followed, dropping her heavy cloak on the bed, and knelt by him. Her skirts ballooned out from above her waist in a black mushroom, and he focused on them, sternly forcing himself to ignore the low cut of her bodice. She laid a light hand on his knee.

"Master Rhenford, y'are not well, I fear." Her hair was held away from her face by a simple clasp, and rippled down her back. A sweet perfume crept like a thief behind what was left of the cider's haze, and he stirred and shoved at her hand.

"I'm fine, fine. What do you want?"

She took his bluntness in stride.

"Faith, Master," she said, rising smoothly and pacing a few steps away, "I must beg a boon." She turned on him, her eyes sparkling with tears, pressing her hands tightly palm to palm.

I'm not up to this, Liam thought, feeling very stupid.

"You'll clap my sweet brother in for a crime he had no hand in, Master, and I must plead his innocence! On my body I swear his soul's free of taint!"

Oh, gods, why did she swear on her body? I'm going to regret this.

"Plead to the Aedile," he snapped, shaking his head in wide arcs he almost could not control. "I can't do anything for you."

"The Aedile! Even I can see y'are his genius! I pray you, Master, speak with him! Plead my brother's half, bespeak his innocence, I pray you!"

She knelt again squarely in front of him, claiming his wandering attention. He could not look at her for longer than a few seconds; the only thoughts that came to mind were dangerous.

If only she'd go away, he thought vainly, *I could stop worrying about looking at her breasts.*

Two tears welled up, and then traced perfect courses down her fair cheeks, and he knew he was going to make a mistake.

"I'm only a common player, I know, Master, but I've as much honesty as a gentle! Lons is guiltless in this, I swear! By Uris I swear, Master!"

"Don't call me that; I'm not your Master," he protested feebly, waving his hand at the entrancing vision, hoping it would go away.

"Y'are, Master," she cried, and her hands flashed spontaneously to his knees.

Much higher than before, he thought with alarm, and though he tried to move them, could not. She tried to bury her head in his lap, beginning to weep in earnest, but he managed to fend her off.

I can't let this happen.

"I pray you, Master, bespeak the Aedile as you can! You know you can turn him off that track! I'd do anything to prove Lons honest!"

Anything? No.

She managed to get her head onto his lap, and continued to plead, though her sobs were muffled.

This is so wrong, he thought, and tried to stand up, which was a mistake.

Rora came up with him, and somewhere in the confusion of rising, her lips met his. The cider and conversation had left him flushed and hot, his lips dry, and hers felt cool and moist, tasting slightly of salt from her tears.

Damn cider, damn Coeccias, damn Lons and Poppae Necquer. I'm making a mistake.

"I'd do aught," she whispered, her voice suddenly low and throaty in his ear.

Damn me.

Sometime later, she stirred beside him on the pallet, and then, even later, Liam rolled over and found her gone. The cider, too, was gone, and his head was clear enough to allow him to curse himself soundly.

"Damn, damn, damn, damn," he chanted into the darkness, with his hands knotted behind his head. He had made a mistake, he knew, and tried to console himself by cursing Coeccias's cider and thinking about how long it had been since he was with a woman. It did not work. Would she expect him now to leave her brother alone? That was ridiculous, of course; Lons had had every reason to kill Tarquin, and despite his alibi, everything pointed to him. There was no way he could convince Coeccias otherwise without some new piece of evidence, and it was entirely unlikely that one would come his way. If only Marcius had done something, or if Donoé had told him a different story, then he might have supported his belief that Lons was not the killer. As things stood, though, there was no other conclusion.

But Rora would not see it that way, naturally. With his foolish, stupid, damnable drunken acquiescence, he had as

much as told the tearful, pleading innocent that he would
help her brother.

Innocent? Her perfume lingered, and he imagined his
blanket and mattress still held a hint of her warmth. Naive,
perhaps, but not innocent. She had been . . . *amazing*, he
thought guiltily, so that even a half-drunk man might look
back on the experience and shake his head in wonder, and
regret that it was over. And doubly regret that it had happened at all. Kansallus had only partly guessed about Rora.
No virgin, certainly.

Liam groaned out loud, trying to express the mix of sen-
sual reminiscence and self-condemnation, or at least drive
it away.

Poised over him at one point, she had looked down on
him, flushed and deeply involved in what she was doing to
him with her body, her hair in wild disarray.

"You're going to get fat," he had murmured, running his
hands over her silky, sweat-damp skin.

"Too much wine," she had laughed. "You know players. . . ." The rest was lost, spoken into his throat as she
arced downward to begin again.

The memory was so vivid that Liam had to sit up in bed
and rub his eyes to keep from actually seeing it.

It had been so long that he only wanted to revel in it,
but he could not allow that. He had to do something, anything, to avoid remembering, or it would only strengthen
his guilt.

He had effectively pledged to help her brother, and racked
his brain for a way to do it. He went over the investigation point by point, rethinking every clue, reexamining
each possibility. Was there something he and Coeccias had
missed? Some old idea they had put aside that might be
dusted off?

The sky outside his window had taken on the deep royal
blue of predawn before he thought of even one thing he
might check. Viyescu's hooded woman, and her desire for
new poison. It was almost surely pointless, but the druggist
had for some reason thought it worth telling. And there
was Coeccias's report of Viyescu's nervousness and, more

important, his own strange meeting with the druggist. What if the mystery woman had threatened him? What if they had gotten closer to the truth with Viyescu, and then passed it up for the easier explanation that Lons afforded? What if, what if. Since Marcius had not seen fit to confess, it was the only thing he could imagine as a possibility, however slim. He decided to visit the apothecary again, to ask the questions he should have asked before, and just then noticed the color of the sky.

It was far too early to go to Viyescu's, he knew, but he was afraid to sleep, afraid that Coeccias would arrest Lons before he could unearth a new clue to protect the player, and his sister. He shifted uncomfortably on the pallet, wondering how to occupy the time before he could go to Northfield and, worn out by the hard cider and his exertions, fell instantly asleep.

Panicking, Liam woke all at once, jumped up from his pallet, and ran to the window. The sun was still low; he had only been asleep for a few hours. Still, he felt a tremendous pressure to be out and on his way to Viyescu's. He stripped and splashed the entire contents of his washbasin over his body, then dried himself patchily with his blanket.

Lying directly in front of his door was a folded piece of paper, pure white and of good quality, one of the sheets he had bought on his arrival in Southwark. Sunlight from the window slanted onto it, and he frowned as he knelt to pick it up. It was too far into the room to have been shoved beneath the door; Rora must have left it. There was no name on the outside of the paper, and he opened it as if it might contain a dangerous animal.

Wincing, he read the short note through twice. The writing was crude, the letters poorly formed, the spelling atrocious, and the message painful.

> *I know you won't fail me, Master, not now. Pray you, bespeak the Aedile on my sweet brother's part. I swear his innocence!*

There was no signature, but the note did not need one.

Growling, he almost crumpled the page, but instead threw it towards the table. He did not wait to see it flutter to the ground like a wounded dove, several feet short of the table.

He hurried passed the shrinking drudge and out into the street, buckling his belt as he went and haphazardly tucking his breeches into his boots. Outside, the sky stopped him for a moment. It was a fine morning, just cold enough to chill the wet spots left by his uneven toweling, and the vault of the sky was unbroken blue, pale and bright. A line of black clouds, however, like waves in the sky, were building up far out over the sea, and he knew that by afternoon the day would be shattered by storms.

It made little difference to him. He was concerned with his own stupidity, and the obligation he had foolishly assumed. He found he was grinding his teeth, and he strode through the streets like an ill wind, cursing himself. Beggars, seeing his clenched fists, did not try to stop him, but he did not notice.

Gods, let the druggist have something.

Liam was grasping at straws, and knew it, but when he allowed himself to consider the fact his mind dropped back to the night before, and to what he had tacitly agreed. So he tried to reorder what he knew, and cast about for new constructions that would, if not find another murderer, at least clear Lons.

Viyescu turned white beneath his untamed beard and began shaking when Liam entered. Dismissing it as the product of his own undoubtedly grim appearance, Liam crossed to the counter.

"Hierarch," the druggist whispered anxiously, "what brings you here again?"

"I spoke with the Aedile yesterday, and he gave me some news from you."

"Yes, certainly, but surely there's no need to—"

Liam cut the strangely distressed apothecary off. "The woman who mentioned Tarquin came back?"

"Yes, Hierarch." Viyescu was subdued, accepting questions much more easily than before.

"And asked for more santhract?" Viyescu nodded. "You didn't sell her any?"

"I've said, I don't sell it; it likes me not."

"But she frightened you?"

Startled, Viyescu goggled at him.

"She frightened you. The Aedile said you looked frightened."

"Oh," he hemmed, "it was naught; I just—"

"Did she threaten you?"

"Perhaps she spoke some in anger, but it was naught, if it please you, she—"

The apothecary was lying, Liam felt sure; the woman had threatened him, but he did not want to admit it. Liam let it go.

"I see, I see. I've just one more question for you, then." Viyescu was visibly relieved, and Liam wondered at his change of attitude. His stern, puritanical righteousness was gone, as well as the subtle hinting of their meeting the day before. Viyescu clearly regretted having said—or having begun to say—anything. "Santhract is used only to . . . terminate pregnancies, correct?"

"Yes, Hierarch."

"And then only in small doses?"

"Yes, Hierarch."

"What if someone was given a larger dose? Could it kill a man, say?"

Sweat broke on the druggist's brow, and Liam had to try hard to keep calm. What was making him so nervous?

"Could it?"

"I have so heard," Viyescu stammered softly. A hot stab of hope and relief went through Liam. He had latched onto something.

"How much did the woman want?"

The druggist leaned forward with wide eyes, as though he had not understood the question.

"I'm wondering if she wanted enough to kill a man," Liam explained.

"But—but Master Tanaquil was stabbed, was he not?"

Liam shrugged, as though the question meant nothing. "It doesn't matter, of course—you don't sell santhract; it likes you not, eh?" Here was something much more than he had hoped for, and he could not avoid lacing the question with acid irony. Viyescu shook his head instantly.

"And of course, you still don't know who this woman is?" Viyescu shook his head again, obviously unwilling now to speak, not trusting his tongue.

Liam did not care. New ideas crowded out the druggist's worried face, a hundred possibilities spun half out of the few small revelations he had gotten and half out of his guilty need to exonerate Lons.

"Of course," he murmured. "Thank you, Master Viyescu. Your help will not go unnoted." He turned and left the druggist behind his counter.

The black line of clouds was noticeably closer but Liam paid them no attention, his thoughts fully occupied with the web of suppositions he was weaving. He ambled out of Northfield back towards his garret, staring with unseeing eyes at the cobbles. Beggars let him go again, frowning at the tall, distracted figure.

What could the poison mean? And what had Viyescu so upset? It must have to do with Tarquin, or the druggist would not have sent the news to him through Coeccias. So the woman and her poison must be connected with the wizard's death. That was a thorny problem, because if Donoé's story was to mean anything, Tarquin could not have gotten the woman pregnant, and besides, he had been stabbed, not poisoned.

A thousand new questions rose from that. If Tarquin had not gotten her pregnant, who had? And why was the wizard involved? Could the murderer be a person he and Coeccias had never considered, namely the hooded man who came to the unknown woman's sometime lodgings?

Too many new questions. The neat fabric of their solution seemed likely to unravel beneath the weight of his new thoughts. And to further complicate matters, he suddenly wondered if Rora might perhaps have been far less innocent than he thought. The encounter could easily have been planned as a sort of blackmail, to try to turn him away from Lons.

She could not have known he would be drunk and thus vulnerable, but his admiration for her had been obvious. If Coeccias had commented on it, she must have noticed it, and Kansallus had said that she was used to being sought after. What if Lons had sent her there? If he had, it put the guilt firmly on his shoulders.

"Gods," he groaned, "I've been so stupid."

There was nothing for it, though, but to go on trying to clear the actor. Rora might have come to him on her own, unsure of her brother's innocence but determined to protect him in her own way. Again, the possibilities were enormous, and a hundred lines of thought stretched away into uselessness. He and Coeccias had settled, however reluctantly, on an explanation that now seemed simple-minded.

Looking up, he saw that his feet and his musing had carried him to the street where his lodgings were. He stopped uncertainly at the corner and gazed with mild distaste at the high, dark house and the tiny window that fronted his garret. He thought how much better it would have been if he had gone to Tarquin's the night before. Remembering the house, he remembered Fanuilh. He had given no thought to feeding the little creature and, feeling guilty, headed for the stables.

The mass of new and complicated questions weighed heavily on him as he rode, and he attempted to sort it out by going over the information he had, and poking holes in it.

The mystery woman was still looking for poison, and Viyescu somehow connected it with Tarquin's death, and was frightened about something. Lons had not tried to escape, but his sister had tried to turn suspicion from him. The decanter, his treasured decanter with the crossed-out label, suddenly seemed a clue again, unreadable but nonetheless a clue. And the illusion spell Tarquin had marked in his book might hold significance. Marcius had done nothing, but Liam would not dismiss him. Despite his inactivity, he might still fit into the puzzle's unexpectedly wider dimensions.

All he needed was a way to fit everything together. His mind revolted at the new complexity, somehow feeling that simpler explanations were better. Still, he juggled the pieces around, hoping for a way to clear his conscience.

He saw the mounting clouds from the beach, and put Diamond in the shed. The wind had picked up, scouring the beach with cold, stinging sand. He let himself into the house.

I did not think you would come.

Liam waited until he was in the workroom before answering.

"I almost forgot. I've been busy."

I know. Fanuilh's flat cat's eyes and toneless thought stung more than the wind-flung sand. *Sleeping with the dancer was not wise.*

"It was the cider," Liam muttered abashedly, unable to meet the dragon's gaze. "Are you hungry?"

Yes.

He hurried out to the kitchen and fixed his thoughts on the oven. When the raw meat was ready, he brought it back and laid it silently on the worktable.

Coeccias thinks the player killed Master Tanaquil, Fanuilh thought after several large mouthfuls. It moved more easily, and Liam wondered how long it would take to recover completely. *But you do not think so. Your thoughts are scattered on the subject.*

"That's because I'm not sure now why I think he didn't do it," Liam admitted. He went to the second worktable and picked up the empty beaker with its obliterated label. "I don't think Lons is the sort who would kill, but now I have to wonder if I think that because of Lady Necquer, and because of Rora. That's why my thoughts are scattered. If you'd let me tell you things," he said more strongly, "instead of picking them out of my head at random, this might be easier."

Even as he spoke, he knew it was foolish. The dragon would know—because he knew—that his thoughts would be scattered whether or not it invaded them. Fanuilh let it pass, putting all its attention to the meat.

Staring at the beaker, Liam suddenly struck his forehead with his free hand and cursed. It was such a simple question, but he had never thought to ask it.

"Fanuilh, when did you first see this decanter?"

Master Tanaquil had it for many years.

"No, I mean, when did you first notice it here, on the table? Empty?"

The morning after Master Tanaquil removed the Teeth.

"The morning after the woman visited him."

Yes.

Liam set the decanter down on the worktable and went to the book of spells on the lectern. It was still open to the spell that had caused the Teeth to vanish, and he ran his finger along, looking for a list of ingredients.

Symbol components, appeared the thought in his head, and he looked over at the dragon, which had its back to him and was busy gnawing bones.

"What?"

They are not called ingredients; they are called symbol components, and there is no list. Where they appear in the text, they are underscored.

Shrugging at the unresponsive scaled back, Liam rechecked the spell, and saw that the dragon was right. After the initial abstract paragraphs came the actual instructions, and several words were underlined: pitch, purified water, a white-hot brazier of coals, and others, some of which he could not identify. But there was no listing for virgin's blood. Disappointed, he scanned the spell again and found nothing, then flipped through the book to the illusion spell.

There, to his relief, the words "an ounce of virgin's blood" were underlined. He barked a triumphant laugh that brought Fanuilh's head around.

What have you found?

"Well," he said, repressing his grin and going over the words of the spell, "virgin's blood is not called for in the vanishing spell, but it is in the one for invisibility. And since the decanter wasn't on the table until after the woman came, we can reasonably suppose that she requested the spell."

That does not necessarily follow.

"Not necessarily, no, but for the sake of argument—"

It might have been for Marcius.

"Yes, it might," Liam said impatiently, "but we're not going to work that idea just yet. We're going to focus on this woman."

It would help if you knew who she was.

Liam closed his eyes and massaged his brows. "Fanuilh, how is it that you can read my thoughts and remain so impenetrably stupid?" His eyes snapped open and he held his hand out, palm up, to stop the dragon. "Don't answer. Just be quiet."

In blessed silence, he checked the ingredients—symbol components, he reminded himself—for the spell of invisibility, and then compared them with those for the other spell. Both called for pitch, water and coals, and two of the unidentifiable items from the latter were required by the former. The only difference was that virgin's blood was listed under invisibility, while there were three items underlined in the vanishing spell whose names he did not recognize.

The theory behind each spell seemed the same; the difference in effect was accounted for by the three unknown components in the more powerful one. Intrigued, he checked the texts with more care. The vanishing spell often referred to a "representation" or "model" as the focus of the spell, while the casting of invisibility centered around a "homunculus" or "mannikin."

"Fanuilh," he began, but the dragon's thought cut him off.

Invisibility is usually cast on a person, hence the homunculus; a doll, really. Vanishing is for objects, hence the model.

It was looking at him, the long neck twisted sinuously over its shoulder.

"So Tarquin would have had to have a little doll of a person to cast the spell—or could he use this?" He pointed at the model, and Fanuilh's wedgy head shifted to look on the miniature Southwark. No thoughts came for a while, and Liam began to fidget. Finally, a tentative thought snaked into his head.

He might have. I believe the spell can be cast on an object. Before Liam could say anything, another thought came in. *But I am not sure.*

"Of course not," Liam said, "nor am I. But I've one more question. Did Tarquin have a test for Donoé?"

For her blood? No. He trusted Donoé. He trusted people often.

"As he trusted Lons," Liam mused. "To take a man's word for that much money. . . ."

The player did look like a rich merchant.

"Yes, yes, but what man—no matter how rich a merchant—will pay that much gold for a woman? Why just take his word?"

Master Tanaquil was a powerful wizard. He had no need for money—he called the fees he charged "gauges of need." How much someone would pay, or what they would be willing to do, for his spells indicated how much they needed them.

"So when Lons agreed to 10,000, he showed his need. Now the question is, what did the woman agree to? How great was her need?"

I do not know. I cannot follow your thoughts on this. They are very scattered.

"Of course they are," Liam agreed, smiling broadly, already on his way out. "It's a tenuous connection at best, very tenuous." He stopped to stroke the dragon's clothlike scales, and feel the creature arch happily under his hand. "I'll be back tomorrow morning."

Do not forget.

"I won't," he called from the hall.

Do you really think this is important?

He stopped in the doorway and shouted back. "I hope so. I'd hate to think I came all the way out here just to feed you."

Diamond safely stabled, Liam went back to his garret to get his writing case and the letter from Rora. He did not really need his writing case. The letter was more important. He did not want it lying around for his landlady to see and,

thinking of the way Coeccias had gotten hold of his list of
suspects, he did not want the Aedile to find it. They had
become friends, to a certain extent, and he was ashamed to
think of the things he had to hide.

His landlady was holding court in the kitchen, ordering
the drudge around when he walked in. She smiled broadly
and began speaking at once, almost as though she had been
expecting him.

"Master Liam! Uris bless us, you've just missed some
gentlemen who came calling for you."

"Really? Who?"

"None I'd ever seen," she said, pitching her voice in a
whisper that seemed to invite the exchange of confidences.
"And they'd not leave their names, or business," she added
significantly.

Liam grunted noncommittally and went up the stairs, glad
to frustrate her and thinking of the letter and the rest of
the day. There was still an hour before noon, when Lady
Necquer had told him to come back. He was not sure if he
would bother. First he had to see Coeccias, and find out
what he thought, and then he would decide if he could
spare the time to go up to the Point.

With the letter secure in his writing case on his belt, he
started back down the stairs.

"Master Liam," his landlady called peevishly from the
kitchen. "The men who're asking after you are here."

He thought more of her irritated tone than of the visitors she had announced. *I really shouldn't go out of my
way to annoy her*, he thought. *She's just a harmless old
gossip.*

The man who stood just inside the kitchen door was a
stranger, though Liam knew the type from his short-cut
hair and the way he smacked his fist into his palm. The
Rat stood behind him, and as Liam came off the last step
into the kitchen, Scar stepped through the door, his ghastly
smile wide and unpleasant.

Damn, Liam thought. *At least they're not armed.*

The three toughs began moving in, the Rat around one
end of the table and the unknown tough around the other.

Liam waited until all three were away from the door, and then moved.

"Run and fetch the Aedile," he shouted at his landlady and her drudge, and ran at the Rat. The drudge, young and smart, dodged past Scar, but the older woman found her way blocked by Scar's widespread arms. She backed away, gaping and goggling like a landed fish.

The Rat was not prepared to be attacked, and Liam hit him twice in the stomach, doubling him over. Liam was surprised how easy it was; the Rat was obviously no brawler. The man he did not know, however, was, and came up behind him before he could turn and caught his arms.

Scar grabbed the terrified landlady and thrust her angrily at the gasping, teary-eyed Rat. "Hold fast, jack; the woman'll not harm you," he sneered, and shoved past the other man to confront Liam.

With his arms tightly held behind him, Liam could only kick at Scar, but the bigger man swatted his leg away easily. The man who held him wrenched at his arms and hooked one foot around his, drawing him off balance. Scar snorted with laughter and waded in, slamming his fists into Liam's stomach with a sound like the thump of heavy sacks.

Liam's face mottled with pain and sickness, his sight grew blurry, and he became aware that the man behind him had eaten onions. The strong smell washed over his neck and face.

Onions, gods, he thought, and closed his eyes against two more punishing blows. Then he felt himself slipping to his knees, let go, and a rough hand grabbed his hair and jerked his head back. He opened his eyes weakly. Scar's face was only a few inches away, and he focused with difficulty on the puckered edges of the man's disfigurement. It was a livid purple, a shallow trench across the face.

"There's a man we both know of that's not pleased you've been to another man we both know of," Scar said, "and this man fears y'ought to part Southwark soon. Y'understand?"

He shook Liam's head by the hair he held, which did not help Liam's concentration.

"I haven't been to anyone else," he managed over the roaring ache that was his stomach and chest.

Scar stood up and let go of his head, sending him straight to the ground. The stone floor of the kitchen was wonderfully cold.

"You lie, Rhenford."

"Aye, and at full length," the man who had held him laughed, and aimed a perfect kick directly between his legs. Liam tried to curl up, but his stomach screamed in protest and he simply lay prostrate. Somewhere in the room, the Rat giggled.

"Remember," Scar's voice came to him, close to his ear, "part Southwark soon. This day." A rough hand cuffed his ear, but the stinging was nothing compared to his other pains.

He heard a number of footsteps hurrying out of the kitchen, and then the slamming of the door, but he did not open his eyes. The floor felt good against his burning face, and his muscles would not allow him to move much.

"Oh, Master Rhenford, what've they done!" His landlady was kneeling over him, tentatively touching the back of his head, but he was aware of it only as an annoyance.

Well, he thought dimly, *at least Marcius has done something.*

CHAPTER 13

BY THE TIME Coeccias came bustling in with the drudge, Liam was sitting up on the stairs, hugging his stomach. Mistress Dorcas hovered, pestering him with unwanted attention.

"You're awfully quick," he said sourly to the Aedile, moving an arm to wave away the piece of steak his landlady was shoving at him, and wincing at the movement.

"You don't seem to've taken much hurt," the Aedile said. "The girl had you drawn and quartered three times over." He gestured with a wry smile at the drudge, who was staring unashamedly at Liam's pallor. "Who was it?"

"Some of Marcius's playfellows." He finally pushed the landlady gently aside as she tried to probe a particularly delicate area. "Please, madam, I'm fine. And steak is only good for black eyes." He wondered where she had gotten the steak; she never served anything so good to her boarders.

"Y'are all right, then?" Coeccias moved to his side, and Liam quickly nodded, not wanting the Aedile's blunt fingers added to his landlady's.

"I'll be fine. Just winded."

He was much more than winded. Bright yellow and dull blue bruises blossomed in his imagination, counterparts to the ones he knew would soon appear all over his torso. Still, Scar had done his job remarkably well, for all the apparent indiscriminateness of his blows. No broken ribs, nothing damaged internally. He had checked himself over as thoroughly as possible, and saw none of the telltale signs he remembered from seeing more badly beaten men.

"And soon to bruise," he added. "But then, I bruise easily."

"I've heard scholars do," Coeccias said in a strange tone, as if something else was occurring to him. "So, Marcius has thrown's hand in?"

"It seems so. Why don't we discuss it upstairs?" He nodded significantly at his landlady, who was wringing her hands and clucking with sympathetic concern as well as watching them greedily and pricking up ears for every word. Amused, the Aedile bent forward to help him up, but Liam forestalled him with a grunt.

He made it to his feet and then began to sway, seized with dizziness. The Aedile casually steadied him, and gave him his arm to lean on as they went slowly up the stairs.

"Our thanks, madam," he said over his shoulder, "if you'd send up some wine?"

Liam lowered himself gingerly into the chair by the window and slumped slowly over the table, unspeakably happy he had not eaten that morning. The nausea was receding, but bright points of light still squirmed at the edges of his vision. They merged with the motes dancing in the mild beam of light lancing through the window, and he closed his eyes and leaned into it, trying to warm away the dull pain.

Coeccias paced silently around the room, waiting, apparently, for the knock at the door that revealed Mistress Dorcas herself with a jug and two mugs. He took them and pressed a coin into her hand with a stern look.

"For the girl," he warned. "A good lass, and quick-legged. Our thanks again."

The landlady let him shut the door in her face without so much as a word.

With his own cup filled, he put one down by Liam's open hand, and began pacing again.

"Truth, I'd have never thought Marcius to be so open in his businesses."

Liam gave a questioning grunt and tilted the mug to his mouth without raising his head. The wine slid coolly down his ragged throat, and quieted what was left of his dizziness.

"It surprises me that he'd only beat you, and leave harsher measures by. If I were Marcius, and I thought you could finger me a murderer, I'd've had my roughs beat you more than senseless."

What started as a laugh turned to a drawn-out "oh" of pain, and Liam gave it up. "Marcius didn't have his roughs beat me senseless because Marcius isn't worried about being connected with Tarquin's death. One of them said that Marcius was terribly unhappy with me for having seen a man we both knew."

"And what of it? The man's me, and Marcius wanted to fright you from helping me."

"No," Liam smiled limply, his head still on the table. It would have been ridiculous, if his stomach and chest did not hurt so much. "Marcius wanted to fright me from helping Freihett Necquer. Remember the maps I used as such a clever pretext for seeing him?"

Coeccias's face went blank, and then broke out in a sheepish wince. "It liked him not that you might sell the same over again, to another merchant. We misjudged how slight a thing would draw his ire. For mere mappery he'd beat a man; but think what he'd've done to a man who failed him in an important spell. It argues against him with the wizard."

Speaking was less of an effort now; even as Liam listened to the Aedile his body was reconciling itself to the beating. "It does, a little, but I don't think it's in any way we've imagined, if at all."

Coeccias glowered and crossed his arms.

"Pray you, Milord May-Do-Aught, how not? What news have you to change your mind and redraw the whole argument? No, don't tell, I'll guess—now you think the player's the man, accompliced by the high priest of Uris. Well? Do I hit the mark?"

"Not even close," Liam laughed, and regretted it instantly. He quickly told what he had learned that morning from Viyescu, and what he had figured out from Tarquin's spellbook. The Aedile pursed his lips at the new information, as if he had just sucked a lemon.

"And so we're not done. You'll want to search out this woman, and hope to substitute her for the player. You never gave him up as guilty, did you?"

"No," Liam admitted, annoyed that Coeccias had struck so close to home. There was no need to mention Rora, he figured. It would only lessen Coeccias's confidence in him.

"Then what would you? How do we gather her in? Do we set a crier out, begging all cloaked and hooded women gather in the square this day week?"

"I don't know," Liam said, ignoring the sarcasm. "I think we could talk with Viyescu again, and maybe have him followed. I think he knows her better than he lets on; perhaps he'll lead us to her."

"And what with the player? Do we take him, or leave him loose?"

"That's up to you." He forced himself to say it, though his conscience firmly admonished him. "Take him if you like. He's still the best suspect."

Throwing his hands up in a familiar gesture of exasperation, Coeccias began his heavy-footed pacing again. "If you'd your way, I'd have to leave him forever, while you con the town for some unfaced woman who, by reason of some broken clues, only *may* have a hand in this. You see what you put me to?"

"Are you satisfied that Lons killed Tarquin?"

"Truth, satisfied enough!" He was clearly not satisfied however, and let his anger fall away, deflated. "If you'd a plan, it'd be easier to let this play on. Have you any plan?"

"I still think Viyescu knows more than he says. He's frightened of her, though."

Coeccias snorted. "Of a maid! Ha!"

"Not of violence, obviously, not from a pregnant woman. But she may know something about him, some secret sin, that keeps him from telling."

"The threat of revelation?"

Liam shrugged. "Maybe. He was all bluster the first time I went to see him, and changed his tune when I said I was a

Hierarch in disguise. He accepted it right off, as if he was expecting me to pronounce divine judgement on him."

"And he so devout," Coeccias breathed. "It would mock his pious marches and professions. An interesting turn."

"If there were a way we could find out more about him, something about drink, perhaps, or women . . ."

"Herione'd know it, if it's to be known, or she'd know who might know. I'll to her now. Is there anything else I should ask?"

"Oh, anything that comes to mind," Liam said airily, drawing a grin from the Aedile.

"Perhaps I should ask if she knows who killed the wizard."

"It couldn't hurt."

"Truth, it couldn't! I'll do it." Chuckling, he paused in the doorway, and looked back thoughtfully. "Perhaps I'll send some men to look for Marcius's roughs to boot. We can't have our poor, milky scholars beaten in their own homes. What were they like?"

Liam described Scar and Ratface vividly, and gave what he could remember of the third man.

"A scar so big should shout itself about the city. We'll have them in soon enough."

"Tell your men not to be too gentle with them," Liam called as the Aedile closed the door behind him.

Less than twenty minutes later, Liam was closing the door himself. Much to his landlady's dismay and the drudge's obvious admiration, he managed to clear the kitchen without falling over.

The clouds, and with them a bleak chill, had reached the city from the sea; the blue sky was only a thin memory to the north. Still, the cold air cleared his head and took the edge off his aching. He kept to the side of the street, trailing his hand along the walls of stone and wood, unsure of his wobbly legs.

On reaching the Point without collapsing, he counted it a minor victory. It was undoubtedly stupid to go out, but he felt less sick. Leaning against a wall a hundred yards from

Necquer's house, he caught his breath. The stone of the
wall spread numbing fingers through his cloak and around
his back, reaching to dull his throbbing muscles. The cold
would feel even better if he turned around and let it touch
his chest directly, but that would not do. People were already
giving him strange looks as they passed.

Can't have people making love to walls in the Point, he
thought, and kept the laugh in his head to save the pain.
Maybe in the Warren, or even Auric's Park, but certainly
not the Point.

The wall he was leaning against was a real wall, not just
the side of a house, high and smooth, the stones closely fitted. From Tarquin's model he knew that inside the
wall lay a small garden, lovingly tended. The miniature
in the workroom was perpetually in bloom, with two tiny
rosebushes and three flowerbeds like intricate needlepoint.
Now, the real thing would be on its last legs, drawing in
on itself for the approaching winter.

Idly, he wondered who owned the garden. It might be the
woman he was looking for, a pregnant woman who casually
asked for poison and frightened fanatic apothecaries and
might think nothing of murdering a powerful wizard. He
imagined her like some warrior-queen, tall and broad and
spectacularly pregnant, her belly swollen to the size of a
cauldron, with a dagger in her hand shaped, for some reason
known only to his imagination, like an icicle. The picture
was surprisingly vivid, and he closed his eyes and sculpted
more, a face stern and without beauty, shrewd eyes blazing
thunder. A chin ships could be wrecked on. He smiled. She
might own the garden he rested outside.

Or she might not.

He shook his head and forced himself slowly away from
the wall. Though twelve bells had rung half an hour ago, he
did not hurry, shuffling the last yards to Necquer's door at
a comfortable pace.

Lares was long in answering the door, and he allowed
himself to slump against the door frame while he waited.

The old servant's face screwed up when he saw Liam,
and he ushered him in reluctantly.

"Good day, Lares."

"And to you, Sir Liam."

They stood facing each other in the foyer, Liam bracing himself with his legs spread wide so he would not fall, Lares shifting his weight uneasily and studiously examining a small section of the floor.

What's wrong with you? Can't you see I've been beaten by a merchant prince's toughs and can barely stand up? Isn't it obvious? Liam's face twitched at the questions he left unasked, stifling a laugh.

As Liam cleared his throat, Lares finally spoke, and he sounded miserable.

"If it please you, you should not've come, Sir Liam. I know I'm a mere pantler, and y'are a very gentleman, a good and noble, and you mean no harm. And Uris knows you've kept the lady's spirits high and diverted. But you should not've come. The Master's said he'd be gone the most of the day, but if he were to spy you here . . ." He left off, shaking his head woefully, and Liam spoke soberly, his lightheadedness effectively crushed.

"I won't stay long, Lares, I promise."

The servant looked him full in the face for a moment, as if judging how much his promise was worth, and then nodded.

For once, Liam did not mind the slowness with which the old man ascended the staircase. It covered his own weakness, and gave him time to think. He probably should not have come; but had not Lady Necquer told him to? And he wanted to know why her husband did not want him around. If she would just tell him that, he would leave.

Lady Necquer did not rise to meet him, but heard Lares's introduction in silence and waited on her couch. She sat in a simple, unaffected beige frock, her hands folded in her lap, and Liam was surprised by the depth of unhappiness on her face.

Maybe Marcius had her beaten as well, he thought, and instantly felt distaste for the joke wash through his mouth. Her eyes were puffed with tears barely restrained, she was unnaturally pale, and her voice caught when she spoke.

"Sir Liam."

She was not being cold, he knew, but keeping her reserve in order not to lose control completely. Necquer must have impressed his wishes quite forcefully.

"I won't stay long, madam," he replied, and remained standing.

"Pray you, Poppae," she blurted, and then regained her composure. "I think you might call me Poppae."

"Very well, Poppae." He wanted to sketch a bow to accept the intimacy, but had to settle for a nod. "I won't stay long, and I certainly don't want to cause any trouble between you and your husband. I just wondered . . . well, I wondered why Master Necquer would so suddenly want me kept away."

Her eyes fixed on the patterned carpet at her feet, she took a deep breath. "He says I've been too free with my confidences."

Liam pretended to take his time digesting this, though he knew exactly what she was talking about. "You mean about Lons," he said at length.

"About the player, yes."

His long silence this time was genuine. "But I helped! He won't bother you anymore."

"You misconstrue, Sir Liam," she sighed heavily. "My husband feels th'affair more than you can fathom, and so attaches more import to its every aspect than he should. He . . . he introduced Lons to our home."

The sentence came from her mouth like lead, a bare recital of facts. Liam found nothing to say, and she went on in the same way.

"Before he left for the ports on your charts, he went to the Golden Orb, and there saw a spectacle that he said had amused him no end. He commissioned a number of the players to give a private performance here. Lons was among them, as well as the clown, Fitch, and the beautiful dancer, and the other chief actors. Some two days after, Freihett parted, and Lons commenced his calls. I thought it no harm at first. . . ." She stopped suddenly, and then resumed quickly: "But you know the rest."

"Yes," he murmured.

"And so my husband feels it partly his shame that all this has come about. He was most grieved that I took you into our secret. He guards his privacy jealously, Sir Liam, you must understand."

"I do, I do." Liam stood, torn. She looked extremely young, and unhappy, and he compared her unwillingly with Rora. The two were probably the same age, somewhere in their early twenties, but while the dancer was a mere actress, the lowest of the low, she faced her problems with fire and determination. She had sought him out, and gained his assistance, while Lady Necquer, her superior in wealth, breeding and position, allowed him to be sent away. Strangely, he felt only a grudging admiration for Rora's spirit, but he pitied the woman he was with, and wanted somehow to console her.

He would have gone to her on the couch and tried, not out of any desire to be near her, but because he sensed that was the way it was done, with quiet words and innocent caresses. However, he was not sure how she would interpret it, and moreover he did not know if he could carry it off. A lifetime in the company of men, a widowed father and scholars locked in musty books, and then rough mercenaries and sailors, had given him little chance to practice. The few women he had known would never have submitted to Lady Necquer's lot, and had never needed that kind of comfort.

So, he cleared his throat and managed a small bow, despite the twinge it sent through his bruised body.

"I will leave you then, madam."

She did not move, so he turned and moved slowly to the door.

"Sir Liam!"

He stopped and turned around, to discover her on her feet right behind him. Before he could say anything she brushed his cheek with her lips and then backed away.

"You are very kind," she said wistfully. "I would I could hear more of your stories. Perhaps when you've written them?"

"When I have finished them, I'll send you a copy," he said, bowed again in haste, and left.

• • •

A last, thin strip of blue sky limned the northern horizon and, as Liam walked back to his garret, the clouds were rushing down to blot it out. They were coal black, roiling and angry, but the cold wind that bore them felt good. The clean salt smell supplanted the odor of Mistress Necquer's perfume.

He walked a little faster, but not much, and still kept close to the walls. The streets were emptying rapidly in anticipation of the approaching storm, and even the beggars were throwing foreboding glances at the sky. Imagining the purple bruises soon to appear over most of his upper body, he allowed himself a groan, and when he reached his house, sank into one of the kitchen chairs.

Mistress Dorcas was nowhere to be seen, but the drudge edged up to him and shyly inquired if there was anything he needed. Touched, he got a coin from his pouch and asked her if she could get him something to eat. She snatched the coin and disappeared out the door before he could specify what he wanted.

The drudge was back quickly, with a covered pot and a few loaves.

"Broth," she explained, laying the pot and the bread before him. "All that can be got on Uris's Eve, but best if y'are ill about the stomach," she added, biting her lip, afraid she might have gone too far.

He nodded. "You're wise, girl. I've known warriors who showed less sense."

She blushed and brightened at once. "Y'have?"

Dipping a spoon into the broth, he laughed. "I once knew a prince—the envy of armies, the hope of his country—who won a great battle, though he took a wound to his stomach. Afterwards, he stuffed himself full of wine and roast meat, though I advised him not to, and was so sick that he missed his own victory celebration."

"Then he died," the drudge whispered, fascinated.

"No, he just lay in his bed for a day, moaning and groaning, sure someone had poisoned his food. They had to postpone his triumph, and his reputation was greatly diminished.

The defeated army sent a present to the cook."

She giggled, and stopped, remembering his money. From the pocket of her smock she produced a sweaty handful of coins.

"Your money, Master," she said, and laid the change down beside his pot. He eyed it for a moment, and tasted his soup. It was only lightly spiced, not too hot, and the warmth soothed his throat. He waved his hand at the money.

"Keep it; you've done me a great service. The broth is just what I needed."

"Oh no, Master, I daren't." She shook her head and backed away from the table as though he had suggested something indecent.

"Go ahead, take it. Consider it my thanks, please."

She only shook her head and gazed fearfully at the street door, through which suddenly stalked his landlady. The thin, angular woman shot the drudge a commanding glance that sent the young girl scurrying away.

"Y'are better, then, Master Liam?"

"Much, madam, thank you. Your girl has been good enough to get me some soup, and I took a short walk that has cleared my head a great deal."

"Huh," she sniffed, and Liam sensed that she was unhappy about something. "I only hope the Aedile has nabbed the monstrous roughs who did this shameful thing."

It was not a question, but he answered it anyway. "He is looking for them right now."

"Then he'll have them, that's sure." She frowned again, but he was busy with the soup, which was doing wonders for his stomach. She puttered aimlessly around the kitchen while he ate. "Perhaps it's none of my affair, Master Liam," she said at length, "but, might I ask, why did they assault you?"

"A small disagreement, of no importance," he said, waving his spoon airily.

"If it please you, Master Liam, I think it could be of some note, for my part at least."

There was a tone in her voice he had never heard before, and it surprised him; it was firmness. She had always been such a sycophant, flattering and sucking up to him because he had money and had allowed her to believe him a scholar. He set his spoon down and steepled his fingers, looking at her curiously over the tips.

"It was a disagreement over the terms of a sale. I sold their master some information, and he thought I had sold the same to another man. I had not."

"Well," she said doubtfully. "Well, you needs must see my position, only a widow, and with my name to protect and this house to manage. I can ill afford any smirch to be attached to this house by the general opinion, you see."

"It won't happen again."

"Faith, how can I be sure, Master Liam?"

If he hadn't been conscious of his tender sides, Liam would have laughed. She was trying to find a way to throw him out—him, her star boarder, the eminently respectable scholar. Then he thought about the last few days, and realized how it must look to her. Tarquin's murder, the Aedile suddenly calling, fights in her kitchen.

And midnight visits from beautiful young dancers, he thought with dawning comprehension. She must think he had grown depraved.

He decided to make it easy for her.

"You can't be sure, madam, and I see your point. Your house's reputation must be protected, and even though I haven't done anything in the least improper, I can see my presence is disturbing. I'll pack my things, and leave in two days, after Uris-tide."

She was taken aback, clearly not expecting this sudden capitulation. He allowed himself a small smile, and returned to his soup.

"You may keep the deposit for the room."

"Faith," she stammered, "I meant not that—"

"No matter," he interrupted with his spoon, "I wouldn't dream of damaging your reputation. Consider me gone."

For a few moments she lingered while he studiously ignored her in favor of his broth, and then she skulked off unhappily.

Liam could not tell why she should be unhappy. He had agreed to leave in order to protect her "reputation," or what little she had. Near the bottom of his broth he thought of an answer. She would probably have been willing to sacrifice her good name for an increase in rent. Shaking his head at her malleable virtue, he pushed aside the empty pot and tried to make himself comfortable in the rigid wooden chair.

The money the drudge had left caught his eye. The rungs of the chair's ladderback pressed into a sore spot, and he leaned away from it to pick up one of the coins.

A small silver piece, stamped with the face and name of Auric IV, dead a hundred years but still well-defined on his currency. The noble profile and the laurel wreath were easily made out, despite a century's use, and most of the inscription of his name and title could still be read. The other coins, mostly copper and of more recent minting, showed age, worn smooth, simple discs of cheaper metal. They made better coins in the days when being King in Torquay meant something.

Someone had mentioned coins to him recently. Who? He moved the coin over the back of his hand, from finger to finger, wondering, a trick he had learned in his youth. It helped to have thin fingers. The silver piece made the trip from index to little finger and back three times.

He had it: the messenger Coeccias had sent him in the wineshop above the square, who had told him about the mystery woman's rent being paid. He had said something about the coins being strange, the strangest he had ever seen. Why would he say that?

Southwark sent ships as far as any other city in Taralon, trading in lands as far apart as Alyecir and the Freeports. A certain amount of foreign currency could be expected to come in from those places; besides, since the decline of the monarchy, any local lord could mint his own, thus adding to the mix. Provided the coins were really of the metal they claimed, no one would be interested in the origins. The coins would have to be strange indeed to arouse comment. So why had the landlord mentioned it to the messenger?

If the gold was good, it would mean the engraving was strange, which must mean that it was not impressed with the profile or head of the minter. One head on a coin was much the same as another, Liam knew, and he had seen a greater variety than most. So the coins must have been carved with a different image.

Some of the lands he had been to engraved their coins with local animals or buildings or landscapes that would seem strange to the people of Southwark.

To most of the people of Southwark, he thought, except for Freihett Necquer, whom Liam had sent to some of those lands in search of trade.

Perplexed, he missed his fingering and the coin slipped to the floor, where it rolled away under a heavy cupboard. He ignored it, cautioning himself against his own thoughts.

Just because Necquer had been to lands no one from Southwark other than Liam had ever heard of did not mean that the coins were his. They might have come from a member of his crew, or from some tradesman to whom he had paid them. They might not even be from one of the cities on Liam's maps, but from the mint of a Taralonian noble with strange tastes. It might mean nothing, and Necquer might not be involved at all.

But it might mean that Necquer kept the hooded woman. Lons's comment came back to him. He had said that the merchant did not deserve fidelity.

It could not hurt to check. If he was right, he could tell Coeccias who the hooded woman was, and that would settle a great number of things. With trembling fingers, he gathered up the coins, shoved them in his pouch, and left.

The bells were tolling three as Liam passed the city square. The sky was alive with writhing black clouds, but he did not think about the imminent storm. Coeccias had told him where the woman's apartment was, deep in the Warren. He would look there, and try to find out what made the coins strange.

He walked faster, and though he still kept close to walls, the dizziness was almost gone. The soup had settled his stomach, and all that was left was a steady, uniform aching. It was relatively easy to ignore.

The Warren was less uninviting than usual, the poor being smart enough to clear the streets well in advance of the storm. The lodgings he was looking for were located off a court that was approached from two separate streets by long, narrow alleys. His footsteps sounded like the slithering of wet snakes on the slick, gritty stones, slipping on mounds of sodden refuse. In the summer, he knew, he would not dare enter the hidden court for fear of the stench, but with the rains the smell was held down, and all that reached his nostrils was mildew. He hurried into the court, gazing wistfully up at the thin ribbon of gray sky far above him.

Even on a sunny day, little light would have filtered down to the tiny courtyard, ringed in by topheavy buildings. With the clouds, he had to squint to make anything out. Fragile porches climbed the walls like ivy, hung with washing. There were few windows in the walls, and those were small and showed no lights. A heap of broken furniture and staved-in casks took up nearly half the floor of the courtyard. Two thin children, a boy and girl as far as he could tell, clambered over the jumbled pile with the agility of mountain goats.

Liam called to them, and they approached silently, arm in fearful arm, with wide, respectful eyes. The girl, no more than ten, took in his clothes and attempted a clumsy curtsy. At a pinch from her, the boy knuckled his forehead. Liam asked them if they knew the owner of the building at the east end of the courtyard, the one whose entrance was almost blocked by the wooden junk they had been playing on.

The girl shoved the boy, who turned and ran, nimbly climbing over the pile and disappearing into the building.

"My brother'll fetch'm m'lord," the girl said, curtsying awkwardly again. Liam nodded and looked around the courtyard. There was nothing to see, so he turned his eyes back to the girl, who still stood before him, staring with unabashed greed at his rich clothes. He blushed under her scrutiny. She was no more than ten, with dirty, colorless hair and a child's smock, but her eyes seemed to take him in and dissect him, weighing every piece of him for value. Apparently she rated him high, because she shared a confidence with him.

"He's a fat rascally knave, m'lord, is th'owner. For that he's so long in coming."

"Mmm." Liam did not know what to say. He had never penetrated this far into the Warren, never left the larger streets, and he had never felt at ease talking with children. He was relieved to see the boy clambering back over the pile and to hear behind him the cursing of a full-grown man trying to make his way around.

The girl had told the truth: the owner was fat, and sweating heavily despite the chill. He had the poor man's haircut, shaven until just below his ears, and he cursed like a sailor until he caught sight of Liam. Then he stopped and wiggled his way past the last projecting piece of garbage and bowed as deeply as his belly would allow. He knuckled his forehead as well, with the ease of much practice. The boy and the girl drifted back to their playing.

"How now, my lord? If it please you, what office can I perform?" He was obsequious in exactly the manner Liam disliked, rubbing his hands together with an oily smile.

"The Aedile Coeccias sent a man to you recently, about one of your lodgers."

The fat man nodded eagerly, dropping his grin for an expression of considered interest.

"You told him the rent had been paid this month in foreign coins."

"Faith, m'lord, the strangest coins I ever saw, most strange."

"Can I see them?"

The man stiffened, and his face alternated between suspicion and contrition. "No, if it please you, my lord, for that I've spent them. On wood, my lord, and warm clothes, with winter almost on us, my lord."

"Well, never mind; can you tell me why they were strange?"

He scratched his bare neck and shuffled. "Strange indeed, strange indeed. They showed beasts the like I've never seen, even in the menageries as travel down from Torquay and can be seen for a copper. Great beasts, my lord, like—well, like naught so much as a bull, but with a whip in place of a muzzle, and so large that a city stood on its back."

"Were there others?"

"No my lord," the man said regretfully, "only those."

"Well, thank you."

It did not matter; he knew the coins to which the man was referring. They came from Epidamnum, one of the ports on the maps he had drawn for Necquer, and represented what were called elephants. The Epidamnites used them for war, and put towers on their backs. He had only seen elephants on coins from that land, which meant that it was likely that only people from Necquer's crew could have them.

The man still shifted from foot to foot, as though expecting something. Liam cleared his throat and dug into his pouch.

"Thank you again," he said, pressing a coin into the owner's hand. The fat man smiled and knuckled his forehead, then retreated behind the mound of junk where the children played, bowing his way.

Liam called to the girl, and she reluctantly climbed down from her playground to stand before him. The boy stayed perched atop the pile, poised and watchful.

"Thank you," Liam said and held out two coins for her. She snatched them, dropped a quick curtsy, and ran back up the pile to the boy, holding the coins high like a prize. The boy smiled shyly.

It had grown darker in the courtyard, and Liam hurried out one of the alleys. The street it opened on was broad, marking the edge of the Warren and the beginning of the waterfront district. A row of brick warehouses stood across the way. Necquer's offices were only a few streets away.

The clouds had grown angrier, agitated by the harsh wind from the sea; it would rain soon, but there was time to visit the merchant before it broke. Necquer would not be happy to see him, certainly, but what did that matter? He would simply ask a few harmless questions, and make sure Epidamnum had been one of the ports the merchant traded in. And since Necquer was already displeased with him, he could afford to annoy him a little more.

Necquer's warehouse was more attractive than Marcius's, red brick and long-fronted with a wide strip of clean windows near the roof. There was a large sign as well, painted in elaborate letters, announcing "Freihett Necquer, Factor and Merchant." Liam had been there before on three occasions, while selling his maps. There were no guards, only an old doorkeeper who seemed to recognize him. He let Liam in, and bid him wait while he went to announce him.

There were more goods in the warehouse than in Marcius's, kegs and boxes and bales reaching to the raftered ceiling in tidy stacks, and they filled most of the floorspace. Between the stacks at the center of the warehouse, an aisle had been left that led back to the offices. The doorkeeper appeared again after a moment, and waved Liam on.

"He'll see you," the old man called.

Liam went down the aisle and passed the doorkeeper into the merchant's offices. There was a large area with tall secretaries and the high stools that went with them. The other times he had been there, clerks had perched precariously on the stools, busily scratching away at ledger entries and bills of lading, making jokes and speaking among themselves. Now there was no one, all gone for Uris's Eve, Liam supposed, and the silence was eerie. Necquer's private office was beyond the clerks' area, behind a stout wooden door. He knocked at the door and then went in.

Necquer sat at a simple table, papers piled neatly before him, pen and inkpot and blotter arrayed with military precision. Sea charts and maps of Taralon hung on the walls, but Liam did not see his own charts. Too valuable to be displayed, even for Necquer's own clerks.

"Rhenford. What may I do for you?" He spoke formally, sitting rigid in his chair, his affability replaced by a brisk, businesslike demeanor.

"Well, Master Necquer," he said, smiling brightly, "I had the afternoon free, and it struck me that we never really discussed the outcome of your journey."

"Yes?"

"Naturally, I'm interested to know more about it. The maps, after all, were mine, and I'm glad to have heard you did well by them. But I'm really more interested to know how you found the lands themselves. Some of them I have not visited in a long time."

"Really?"

"Yes. For instance, I was wondering how things were in Domy—I spent six months there, and found it a very pleasant place. Did you find it so?"

"The trade was good."

The merchant's apathetic answers were exasperating. He decided to simply ask.

"Ah. And Sardis? And Epidamnum?"

"We did not make Sardis. Epidamnum was fairly profitable." He mentioned the second port without hesitation.

"I would like to discuss your journey in more detail, Master Necquer. Compare notes, you understand. Perhaps if you could spare an hour or so?"

"I am occupied at present, Rhenford. I have work to fill the afternoon."

Liam could sense that Necquer was getting impatient, but he wanted to know how far he could push him. It couldn't hurt, as the merchant's attitude towards him was already obviously negative.

"I see. Maybe this evening, then? Only an hour or so, I promise."

"Tonight is Uris's Eve, Rhenford. I will be working until eight, and then I must attend the vigil at her fane. I cannot spare you any time."

He spoke the last in such a way that the word "ever" was clearly attached, and Liam decided to take the hint.

"That's too bad. I would have liked to hear what you thought. Well, perhaps some other time."

"Perhaps," Necquer said coldly, and pointedly picked up his pen and began writing.

Liam nodded and left, still smiling brightly to show that he had not taken offense. The merchant paid him no attention. The doorkeeper was waiting outside the clerks' room, and escorted him out.

A fat drop of rain stained Liam's cloak. The storm was only a few minutes away, and he walked as quickly as he could towards the city square and the jail.

Lay worshippers were not allowed into the Uris's Eve vigils, Coeccias had told him. Necquer knew he was a Midlander only recently arrived in Southwark, and would not expect him to know that. But why then say he was going to attend the vigils? A convenient lie to avoid meeting with him, or did Necquer have somewhere to go at eight? More likely the first, but it was just possible that the merchant had a rendezvous scheduled. And if it were in the Warren, with a certain hooded woman . . .

Liam hurried faster, happy Scar had left his legs alone. The drops of rain began to fall sporadically, spotting his cloak, and by the time her reached the jail, it was a solid drizzle.

Coeccias was not there, but the Guardsman on duty let him sit on a hard bench in the small, cold antechamber.

"Th'Aedile's to be back soon," the Guardsman said, and left him alone. As he waited, he thought through what he had found, and how he would present it to Coeccias.

If the hooded woman was Necquer's mistress, then he had gotten her pregnant. It would make sense, in a way, for her to want to get rid of his child—it would not do for a prominent merchant to have an illegitimate child in the Warren. Therefore the santhract, which Viyescu had presumably sold her, though he denied it. There was nothing, however, that tied the affair to Tarquin's death, except the fact that the woman had mentioned his name and had, perhaps, visited him.

What did the virgin's blood mean, and the second spell for invisibility instead of total disappearance? It seemed as though he had stumbled on a separate mystery altogether, in which Tarquin's death was only a secondary event. There were too many extras for them all to revolve around one set of circumstances. The hooded woman, he feared, would turn out to be nothing more than a pregnant mistress, and worse, a dead end.

For a moment, he thought about ignoring Necquer's appointment and letting Lons stand guilty. The player's knife and the motive were enough to damn the young man, and Liam could explain to Rora, if he had to, that there was nothing he could do.

He rejected the idea at last, though not because of any debt he felt he owed to the dancer. He admitted he owed her the effort, but the real reason he was interested was because he wanted to know who Necquer's mistress was. He wanted to compare the hooded woman with Lady Necquer, and even more with his own image of her.

When the Aedile tramped grumpily into the antechamber, soaking wet, Liam had figured out what he would tell him.

"The very sky's cracked, and the gods weep themselves dry in wetting the earth," Coeccias complained, spraying sheets of water from cloak, hair and beard, and taking Liam's presence for granted. "You were not at home when I called. Should you be walking, after your heavy exercise of the afternoon?"

"It didn't turn out to be as bad as it felt," Liam replied, standing up. "I found something interesting."

"Truth, I've news as well, if you'd hear it."

Liam nodded over-graciously for Coeccias to precede him.

"Come in first," the Aedile said. "I've need of something, for it's cold and wet."

Liam followed him into the headquarters of the Guard. It was essentially a barracks, with a couple of rough cots and a number of pegs on the wall, some holding cloaks and hats. Halberds huddled in every corner, and there was a huge keg in the center of the rush-strewn floor. A door in the far wall, bound in iron and barred by a thick wooden beam, hid the jail proper. Two cavernous hearths flanked the room, and the Guardsman who had kindly allowed him to shiver in the anteroom was busy building a roaring fire. He barely nodded at Coeccias, who nodded back and went straight to the keg, catching up two tin cups from one of the cots. He filled them at the keg, and handed one to Liam.

Expecting beer, Liam drank deeply. It was some kind of hard liquor, and he almost coughed it up before it burned out his throat. Coeccias sipped appreciatively, and his eyes twinkled at Liam's distress.

"You'd be wise to drink small, Rhenford."

Liam coughed and spluttered his agreement.

"Now, for what's been discovered to me. Herione relates that Viyescu had indeed been to her house, perhaps twice, but it was long since, perhaps two years. She did not remember what he wanted, or what he did—she sees the whole book and catalogue of vice there, so the sins of a wretched apothecary would not impress themselves strongly on her mind."

"Still, even a single visit would impress itself strongly on a fanatic prude like Viyescu. Particularly if he enjoyed it, or maybe went somewhere else afterwards. Herione's women are expensive, aren't they?"

"To bed a princess or a queen should be," Coeccias laughed, but he was following Liam's thoughts avidly. "Y'are thinking he found out a form of entertainment less dear, and the memory plagues'm?"

"Anyone who knew would be able to hold it over his head. It would destroy his little part as Uris's prime lay worshipper, wouldn't it? At least in his own head, and that's where his devotion carries the most weight."

Coeccias laughed again, this time in half-mocking wonder at Liam's conclusion. "Y'are a seer, Rhenford, better than a bloodhound. Y'are an eagle, peering down into the puny souls of men, and reading their hearts like open books. So, we've some proof that Viyescu may be led by the hooded woman—what of it?"

"Nothing, yet. We have to know what she wanted of him, other than santhract, and why. And we'll know that when we find out who she is." He paused, he admitted to himself, for effect. "And I think I know how we can do that."

With the cocking of a bushy eyebrow, Coeccias invited him to explain how.

"I may be wrong, but I think the woman will be meeting her benefactor tonight. I'd like to be there." He did not say how he had guessed at the rendezvous. If there was no connection between the hooded woman and Tarquin's death, there was no reason for anyone to know of Necquer's infidelity.

"To peer deep into her soul and pry her inmost secrets to light? You'll want company, then, I'd guess."

"No," Liam said slowly. "As I said, I may be wrong, and I'd rather be wrong alone, with no one to see."

Coeccias laughed hard and walked over to the Guardsman, who was still tending the fire. "Truth, well said, Rhenford, well said! 'I'd rather be wrong alone,' that's well said. Withal, the Warren at night in a storm's no place for even a bloodhound. You'll take Boult here with you," he said, indicating the kneeling Guardsman with a thick forefinger. Liam began to object, but the Aedile ignored him and began talking to his underling, who had looked up sourly. "And Boult, my lad, if you see anything that Master Rhenford tells you to forget, say, if you see a man going somewhere he oughtn't, you'll clean it from your mind, like a forgiven score on a tavern board, wiped away. Won't you, my good Boult?"

The Guardsman nodded with ill-disguised displeasure, and the Aedile grinned up at Liam. "What time should my good Boult join you?"

"A little before eight." Once again, Coeccias had anticipated him and had understood Liam's sensibilities better than he had himself. Why the Aedile did not solve the mystery on his own was beyond him. The blunt, rough-looking man could be as perceptive as anyone Liam knew.

"Well then, Boult, can you make the schedule?"

Boult acquiesced with ill grace to his commander's light-hearted question.

"Then you'd best to your garret, Rhenford, before the storm waxes too great to walk the streets, and await the ever-cheerful Boult there."

Liam agreed, and left the rest of his liquor untasted on the keg.

CHAPTER 14

THE STORM HAD moved beyond mere drizzle when Liam left the jail, but it did not achieve its full strength until after he had reached his garret. As he shook out his cloak, thunder exploded and the patter of rain on the roof swelled into a constant drumming, then one continuous rumble, like the passage of a herd of horses. He cursed Necquer soundly for choosing a night like this for a meeting.

It was warm in the garret, and he looked at his bed, thinking how little he had slept the night before. Ignoring the reasons why, he decided to make up for it. He carefully spread out his cloak to dry and threw the rest of his clothes onto his chair, pleased that the new cloak had kept out most of the wet. When he blew out his candle, a flash of lightning lit the room, and he stopped for a moment before settling down on his pallet. The rain was coming down so hard that it was difficult to tell it was rain at all in the darkness, falling like a curtain across his window. It was quite a storm.

Even with the constant rumble on the roof, or maybe because of it, and his own missed sleep, he dropped off almost as soon as he crept beneath his blanket. The last thing he managed to do was turn onto his back, to spare his abused front.

A slackening in the rumble overhead woke him. The worst of the storm's fury had spent itself. Having been unable to wash Southwark away, it gave up, and wasted itself in a rain that seemed almost gentle in comparison with its previous power. The change woke him, and he thought for a moment as he sat in the dark that the storm had stopped altogether.

He felt more clearheaded for the nap, but his body was a solid ache from neck to waist. He debated dressing in the dark, to avoid seeing the damage Scar and his friends had done, but fumbling for his clothes without a light would undoubtedly lead to bumps that would aggravate his bruises. With a wince at every movement, he fumbled around in the dark for his tinderbox, and got a light the first time.

Bruises had bloomed all over his chest and stomach, a dark purple that was intriguing and revolting in the flickering yellow light of the candle. His body looked like an abstract tattoo, and he shuddered at the thought while he climbed gingerly into dry clothes.

Boult had not arrived yet, so he presumed it was before eight, and he was glad he had not had to be woken by Coeccias's surly Guardsman. He wondered what time it was, and a knock at his door satisfied him. It would be Boult, and it was time to go to the Warren. He went to the door.

Not expecting Rora, he stood for a moment in shock while she slipped into the room. Her cloak left a trail of water behind her, and beads of rain gleamed in her thick golden hair.

"Master," she said breathlessly, nestling close to him.

Speechless, he backed away, holding her shoulders to keep her at a distance.

"Forgive me, I could not stay away," she pleaded, ignoring his shock. "Have you bespoke the Aedile?"

What was she doing there? He forced his frozen jaw to open, and to speak. "No—yes, in a sense. I've spoken to him, but—"

"You've not!" The fury in her eyes at his betrayal, and the accusation in her tone, frightened him.

"Yes, yes I have, but in a different way." He hurried to pacify her. "I couldn't just tell him not to arrest Lons; he'd have been suspicious. I have to find out who really did it, or at least come up with enough evidence to suggest that it might have been someone else." He wanted to shout at her, to push her out, but the anger in her eyes stopped him;

and yet she was pouting in a way that was irresistible. And
the memory of her, panting over him in the dark, rose like
an ugly ghost in his mind. What time was it? When would
Boult get there?

"But what if you can't find the killer? What then?" She
spoke with an effort, though he could not tell if it was
because of her anger or the fact that the possibility frightened her.

"Then I'll make Coeccias leave Lons alone," he lied,
unable to say anything else. "But not till I've tried to find
the real killer."

"Who did it, think you?" The question, and the intense
way she asked it, startled him.

"I don't know," he stammered. "I have an idea, but I need
time to prove it." That was a lie as well: he had no ideas,
only clues that did not lead to conclusions. What would
Boult say if he saw Rora there? Would he tell Coeccias?

To his immense relief, she relaxed. "It was wrong to
come, I know," she said sorrowfully, then looked at him
with forlorn hope. "But you'll help, will you not?"

"Of course I will," he assured her, and began herding her
to the door. "Now you must go; I'm expecting someone
who must not see you."

"I'll go. I must to th'Orb in any case." Without warning,
she flung herself at him and kissed him soundly, feverishly,
letting him go reluctantly. "Grace you, Master," she said,
and slipped out the door, her large, promising eyes turned
over her shoulder at him until she was out of sight down
the stairs.

Liam let go an explosive breath, and walked shakily over
to his chair to collapse. While she was there, he had been
aware of her closeness only because of the stupid desires
it had raised. Now his chest throbbed painfully where she
had hugged him. He could not slump, because it bent tortured muscles, so he had to sit upright. Instead, he heaved
several sighs.

Gods, I'm a fool, he thought, *a lucky fool, but a fool
nonetheless*. He offered several undirected prayers of gratitude that Boult had not walked in on the middle of the

conversation. He had no idea what he would tell her if he could not prove Lons innocent, and could only hope it would not be necessary.

To avoid wondering about it, he forced himself to think about the night's business. If he could find out who Necquer's mistress was, it might give him a start. He doubted it, but would not allow himself to consider the doubt.

The hooded woman was pregnant, most likely by Necquer. She had told Viyescu she would go to Tarquin, and then done it, speaking to the wizard in a seductive voice. She had presumably commissioned a spell, an invisibility spell that would have been cast on the Teeth, because there was no other model in Tarquin's workroom.

That, he thought with consternation, made little sense. Whether Lons had intended it or not, it was the spell cast for him that had saved Necquer's life. If the hooded woman wanted Necquer dead, why not just entice the wizard to cancel the spell entirely? Why choose another spell that would make it look like Lons's had worked? And where had the virgin's blood come from? A pregnant woman would obviously not have any virgin's blood around her. He imagined the woman as he pictured her, nine months gone, handing Tarquin the decanter over her swollen belly and calmly proclaiming it virgin's blood, and her own.

Liam listened to his own laughter, and was scared to detect a note of hysteria in it.

Two hard knocks on his door steadied him, and he took a deep breath before granting entry.

Boult came in, dressed in a heavy riding cloak and high boots, as unconcerned with showing his unhappiness as before. "There's still a heavy storm, and the gutters run like a river in spate. Y'are sure you wish to attempt the Warren this night, Questor Rhenford?"

"Questor?" He was used to the indiscriminate way the people of Southwark flung titles about, but he had never heard this one attached to himself before. Questor was an old name used for special agents of the king in Torquay; it had lain unused for decades. As long unused, Liam realized, as the title Aedile.

"Aedile Coeccias said I was to call you that, for that it signified you were an officer of his, and gave you the right to command me." Boult could not possibly have cared less, and Liam found he liked him for it. He was almost perfectly average for Southwark—black hair shorn to just below his ears, neither short nor tall, skinny nor fat, with a blank face and heavy-lidded, black eyes. He looked bored, in a way that suggested he could be put to better use.

"Well, I'm afraid there's nothing for it, Boult. There's something I need to see in the Warren, and the good Aedile doesn't think I should go there without an escort."

Boult shrugged, with more than a hint that Coeccias might be right.

"I appreciate your confidence, Boult," Liam said sarcastically. "Let's go." Secretly, he was delighted with the taciturn, insolent Guardsman. He would not be the sort to talk about what he saw.

Boult had exaggerated his report of the weather: the gutters were full, but not overflowing, and the storm had resolved itself into a steady, icy downpour. The drumming gave rhythm to the gurgling melody of the rushing gutters. Snug in his cloak, with the Guardsman at his side holding a shielded lantern, Liam was strangely elated. The prospect of discovering just who the hooded woman was filled him with excitement. He began to feel confident that it would solve the mystery to his satisfaction, and he would be able to fulfill his obligations to Coeccias, to Rora, and to Fanuilh. He envisioned the explanation in vague terms, and saw himself giving it to each in a suitably modest way. He smiled behind the hood of his cloak.

The rain, though still thick, allowed the light of the lantern and the glow from the occasional window to play over the street. There was no one to be seen, and the hissing and drumming of the water closed in on his ears, shutting off all other noise, but twice he faltered, an itch between his shoulder blades. He felt watched, but put it off to the rain and the dark, and submerged the anxiety in thinking of what was to come.

Once they reached the Warren, Boult let him take the lead and the lantern, winding through the streets heading for the courtyard. It seemed to take longer than he remembered, and he was afraid he had gotten them lost in the maze of streets, when suddenly the swinging beam of the lantern showed the mouth of the alley he remembered from the afternoon. Breathing his relief, he turned down the alley, Boult at his back.

Lights showed in many of the windows surrounding the courtyard, but none on the ground floor. The yard was left in darkness, which suited him well. He had not given much thought as to how they would wait for Necquer and the woman, and he began to plan.

Beckoning for Boult to follow, he squeezed around the left side of the pile of wreckage, jabbing his sore body several times, and once walking hard into a piece of wood at chest height. He had to stop for a moment, tears springing to his eyes, before he could go on. It had looked much easier in the dry daylight, and the lantern did not help much, illuminating only a tiny section of the heap. Finally, however, he was around, and standing before the door of the tenement, which sagged on leather hinges. He handed the lantern to Boult and pushed at the door, which moved a few inches and then ground to a stop. He could see from the gap between door and jamb that it was neither locked nor barred, so he grabbed at it and shoved up and back. It moved easily, lifted over a pile of unseen rubbish. A single candle flickered high on a wall in the room beyond, casting suggestive shadows over a railless staircase and more rubbish, heaped against the walls like talus at the foot of a cliff.

Not the most likely place to house a mistress, Liam supposed, but convenient to Necquer's warehouse, and well out of the sight of his social peers on the Point. He only took a few steps into the room, to look up the stairwell. It rose in flights far up the building, to the top floor as far as he could tell. There seemed to be no other entrance to the stairs. Boult prodded at a large, unidentifiable mound with his toe, and muttered, "The Warren," with disgust.

"All right," Liam said in a low tone, "here's what we'll

do. We wait outside. When the person we're looking for arrives, you follow them inside, at a decent distance, and go up the stairs with them. Find out which door they go to, and pass them. As soon as they're in whatever room they're headed for, come back and tell me. Clear?"

"Most obvious, Questor, " the Guardsman said with only the slightest trace of irony, "except, if it please you, how'm I to know who we're looking for?"

Liam grinned, and Boult granted him a small one in return. "I'll let you know when he arrives. Now come on."

Boult shrugged and followed Liam back into the courtyard and beyond the pile. They settled themselves between the wall of the court and the right side of the high tangle of used furniture and rubbish. Liam could see the doorway of the building, and hoped that with the garbage and the rain, they would remain unseen. As a precaution, he took back the lantern and hooded it completely, leaving them in the dark.

They waited interminably, but Boult said nothing, and Liam tried not to allow his high spirits to ebb. It was difficult, with the rain seeping slowly through his cloak, the wet chill setting his bruises to aching, and the mental itch returning to his back. He thought hard on the clue he was about to get, and succeeded at least in pushing the last worry away. There was no reason for anyone to have followed him, or to be spying on him. There was no way for anyone to know how close he hoped he was to catching Tarquin's murderer. He thought of Marcius, but dismissed the idea. Having delivered his warning, the merchant would surely wait at least a day to see if it was carried out.

So he convinced himself that the suspicion was merely his nerves, and began to turn over his clues again.

Why the second spell? If Tarquin had cast it, it would have meant Necquer's death; surely his mistress would not want that. But what if she had? Ignoring the why, which he hoped he would understand when he knew who she was, he focused on the how. She had gone to Tarquin for the spell, but the wizard had not cast it, and Necquer had made it to port safely. Was that reason enough to kill him? Again, he would know better when he knew who she was.

The waiting dragged on, and several times Liam was sure he heard the bells tolling eight, though he knew hearing them through the rain was impossible. They both shifted their positions several times, trying to minimize the discomfort of rain and projecting garbage. Liam was in the middle of an extensive rearrangement when Boult laid a hand upon his arm and he froze, one leg raised, searching for a secure spot in the unseen mess underfoot. Boult steadied him without a word.

A figure glided out of one of the alleys, shrouded in a voluminous cloak and hood. The woman, Liam knew at once, and squinted at her through the rain, willing her hood to fall away. It did not, and she came on, slipping around the pile like a ghost, mere yards from them. She was shorter than he had imagined her, but the cloak billowed so much that it could easily have hid the prodigious belly he had given her. Only when she had gone through the door did Liam realize she had not carried a lantern, and had negotiated the streets easily in the dark. The idea disturbed him.

Beside him, Boult let out his breath, and Liam did the same, allowing his weight to settle back on both feet with relief.

"That our man?" the Guardsman whispered, touching Liam's arm again for his attention.

"No. Wait."

It did not take as long the second time, and Necquer announced his presence well in advance with the light of a lantern. He came hurrying down the same alley the woman had used, but with none of her weightless grace. They heard a distinct ripping sound as he negotiated the rubbish heap, followed by a curse, startlingly loud. Liam placed a restraining hand on Boult's shoulder, and waited while the merchant opened the door. He stood in the doorway, threw back his hood, and examined a large tear in his cloak, shaking his head and spitting in anger. Liam recognized his face for certain, and gently shoved Boult.

Necquer entered, and the Guardsman disappeared around

the pile, to reappear seconds later at the door. He paused a second, listening, and then went in. Liam waited as long as he could stand it, and began creeping around the pile himself. By the time he managed to cross the garbage, Boult was back, leaning with crossed arms against the doorsill.

"In th'attic," he said, gesturing up with his thumb. "I near followed him up, but stopped in time."

"Did someone greet him?"

"He knocked thrice, in a peculiar way, and a woman's voice bid him enter. You can hear through the walls as through the thinnest kerchief."

"Better and better." He would not be able to see the woman, but he could hear her at least, and their conversation might give something away. "Shall we?" He started for the stairs. Boult obediently followed with an apathetic shrug that seemed his only method of expression. At least it was dry indoors.

The stairs creaked ominously as they walked, and Liam winced even on the first flight. Going slowly and planting his feet carefully only seemed to make it worse, and the cries of old, creaking boards flew straight up, he was sure, to the attic where Necquer waited. He was struck by what he was doing—spying, basically, invading the most private moment of another man and woman. The parallel with Fanuilh did not escape him.

There was a candle on the second-story landing, but none beyond. Light showed from underneath some of the doors on the floors they passed, but this only emphasized the pitchy blackness of the stairwell. Liam's heart began to beat faster, and his skin was damp beneath the cloak. Sounds came from some of the apartments they passed, bodiless in the dark: a young girl singing to a crying child, a hissed argument between two men, the sounds of a meal in progress. The two men crept on, and the sounds died away as they reached the fourth floor, accompanied only by the creaking of the treads. Above him, Liam sensed space, a black void where the stairs to the attic would be.

Boult stopped him, and leaned close to whisper. His breath was warm in Liam's ear.

"It's the next flight. Your boots, Questor. The boards fairly shout here. The quarry made Hell's own clatter going up."

Did the Guardsman think Necquer was his quarry? He did not bother to correct him. He was after the hooded woman, and what she knew about Tarquin.

She tried to get Tarquin to substitute Lons's spell, he thought, bracing himself against the unseen wall to pull off first one boot, then the other.

"Wait here," he whispered to Boult, and wondered if he nodded in the darkness.

Switching spells would have meant Necquer's death. Why would she want that? And why would she kill Tarquin when he didn't perform the spell?

The darkness was absolute, palpable in a sense, like warm water pressing around him. He put his stockinged foot on the first step, and hesitated. His heart beat loud, his mouth was dry. It was just spying; he had done it before in a dozen places. In wars. This was not a war; this was the merchant Necquer betraying his wife in adultery, which was entirely his business, and none of Liam's.

And why didn't Tarquin perform the spell? He had the virgin's blood, and if he had been stupid enough to believe Lons would pay him, he would certainly have believed the seductive voice.

He forced his other foot to move, and gained two steps. There was a thin line of orange above his head, the bottom of the door to the attic. It was a goal. He made two more steps with only a single stifled squeal from the decrepit wood. Suddenly he imagined the door above swinging open, and Necquer glaring angrily down at him.

I'd piss my breeches, he thought, and had to clap his hand to his mouth to stifle a giggle.

The door stayed closed, and he forced himself up three more steps. Sweat trickled down his face. He heard a voice from above and stopped, his heart hammering.

It was Necquer's, from the sound of it, though he could not discern the words.

Had she killed him because he did not cast the spell? Was

that reason enough? Or had he figured out why she wanted the spell cast, and threatened to reveal it? If he knew why she wanted Necquer dead, he could understand.

If she wanted Necquer dead. If that was what the spell was for. If—

He cursed himself viciously and silently. He would never know if he did not go further. Three more steps, stooping, his hands groping for the treads in front of him, the wood brittle and ridged beneath his fingers. Traces of wet from Necquer's boots, and whatever shoes the woman wore.

He could hear Necquer's voice now, suddenly very clear, as if he were right next to him. His heart lurched, and he swayed in the darkness. The line of warm orange was on a level with his eyes, and he brought his legs up with infinite care, so that he was squatting on the step.

"You should buy better wine," Necquer was saying, apparently just beyond the door. He heard a clink. Goblets? His mouth was dry. "I certainly have enough money to afford some decent wine."

There must have been a reply, because the merchant was silent, but Liam could not hear it.

"No expense too great for my sweet chuck," the merchant laughed.

Your sweet chuck would have been happy to see you rotting in the sea, he thought, grinding his teeth, and wanted to shout to the woman to speak up. The woman in his imagination had a stentorian voice, a voice like a trumpet, a voice that carried across miles as well as attic rooms. She did not even whisper when she stuck daggers in wizards. Why was he so sure?

"You're not going to start that again, are you?" said Necquer, exasperated. "I've told you, she's my wife. There's nothing else for it. You're looked after well enough."

She wanted him to leave his wife. She was pregnant, and he would not leave his wife.

"That's a good girl," Necquer said after another pause, reassured and magnanimous. "No more arguments, then. I've only got one other cheek." He laughed.

One other cheek? One other cheek to bruise. She had hit him, not some nonexistent bandit. When he came back from Warinsford, he went to see her first, before his wife. And she had hit him, hard enough to leave a mark.

"Then you'll be rid of it?" The merchant's tone was more serious; there was uncertainty in his voice, and a shade of apprehension. "There are herbs, I know. See Viyescu, he can get them. You're not so far along, are you? It's not even showing."

Rid of the child he had sired. That was a reason to kill a man, Liam supposed, because he had gotten you pregnant and would not marry you and ordered you to get rid of it. But she had already gone to Viyescu for the santhract. And after Tarquin's death she had frightened him enough to get it for her. So why try to kill Necquer, if she was prepared to do as he wished?

He clearly heard the rustle of skirts across floorboards. She was moving, and, by the sound, towards him. For a moment, he thought irrationally that she was going to open the door and find him, and then he caught hold of himself. She was coming to Necquer, and he heard another sound, the brushing of cloth against cloth. Was she embracing him? Then a loud kiss. Yes. He prayed with all his might, squinting his eyes in the dark with effort. *Please, please, please, speak.*

"I'll attend to it soon," she said, and his eyes sprang open and his mind reeled. "Soon. For now, drink your wine and let's to bed."

Gods, what have I done?

"A fine idea, my sweet," Necquer said, the smug smile practically audible.

Liam heard the merchant's words, but they were meaningless to him.

He knew the voice, though he had never heard it used seductively, the way Tarquin had. A dozen revelations fell on him with stunning force, and his arms trembled so much that he had to lower himself to the stairs, resting his forehead against the damp wood.

She wanted Necquer dead for his betrayal, for refusing

to spurn his wife, because she was fierce that way. She had killed Tarquin, he was sure, because he had threatened to reveal her.

"Finish your wine," she said with an indulgent laugh.

And he had done that because he had discovered that the virgin's blood—so hard to come by, so useful, and Donoé couldn't possibly supply enough, however willing she was—had not been real. How could it be, when she was not a virgin? So when the illusion spell failed because of the faulty blood, the wizard had cast the spell Lons wanted instead and threatened to reveal her. And for nothing, nothing at all. She had agreed to lose the child, to reconcile herself to his wishes, to go to bed with him again.

Liam did not want to move. Self-reproach held him in an iron grip, and he wished the dark would surround him and become complete.

Gods, I have so completely bungled this whole damn thing. His mistakes were beyond repair.

He could not tell Coeccias, he could not tell Fanuilh. He could not tell them, because then he would have to tell them what he had done in his weakness and imbecility.

"When I've more of a thirst, after." After what was clear. Necquer gave the word a lecherous weight. There were footsteps, moving away.

After, Liam thought miserably. *After I've crawled back down these steps and ridden as far away from Southwark as I can.*

"Careful, it'll spill," the beautiful, musical voice laughed. "You'd best drink it now, or it'll end on the rugs."

Would she not shut up about the wine? He did not want to hear her anymore. He wanted to get Diamond from the stables and ride north, to Torquay, maybe, or the Midlands, or maybe further.

"You want me drunk, do you?" Necquer laughed aloud.

Drunk, of course, drunk, Liam thought, shaking his head bitterly, *drink the wine, drunk if she can't have you dead. Drunk is—*

His head jerked up in the dark, and he gaped at the door. Drink the wine—

Because you powder santhract and take it in a cup of wine or cider to hide the bitter taste, and the right amount of santhract will terminate a pregnancy and too much will kill a man.

He scrabbled to his feet and jumped forward, stumbling on the stairs but gaining his balance again as he hit the door.

It burst open and he slid to a halt in his stockings.

"I didn't think—" he began, and stopped, because what he had not thought of was what to say.

Necquer and Rora stood in the middle of an expensive carpet, swaying close to each other, shocked, the merchant's hand on her exposed breast, the cup in his other hand at his lips. A broad bed, with snowy sheets, a wide window to the right. A huge number of candles, shocking after his time in the darkness of the staircase.

"Poison!" Liam shouted. "Santhract!" He pointed at them, and Necquer dropped the cup, still staring. Only a little wine spilled out. Rora's face twisted in rage.

"Questor," Boult gasped hesitantly from behind him. When Liam had suddenly burst open the door, he had hurried up.

Rora lunged at him, her teeth bared in an awful snarl, but Necquer instinctively grabbed her arm and pulled her up short. The momentum carried her around toward the window, but she turned back with a dancer's grace and lunged again, snarling furiously at Liam. No one heard the soft thump that came from the roof above.

"She's trying to kill you," he shouted at the merchant, afraid to let her speak. What would she say? He felt guilty, terribly guilty, as though he had used her. It never occurred to him to think of it the other way around. So he shouted, trying to drown out denunciations she did not try to make. "Santhract in your cup. She killed Tarquin Tanaquil, because he would not help her, and would have told you about it."

He went on, shouting disconnected facts at Necquer, who hauled the hysterical dancer to him. The merchant held her roughly by the shoulders, trying to see her face, and she

suddenly spat furiously at him. Her nails flashed up towards
his eyes. Liam and Boult both started toward the struggling
couple.

The large window shattered, and a dark shape hurtled
towards Rora in a shower of broken glass and wood. It lit
on her back, water gleaming on the scales, and a single beat
of the wings drove Necquer back. Blood fountained from
Rora's neck, where the wedgelike head had buried itself.
She screamed.

Fanuilh rose off her back and darted in the air around
in front of her to plunge at her face. Shouting now, she
flailed her arms at the creature, but it came at her like a
whirlwind, biting and scratching and pushing, silent except
for the flap of its wings. It pulled back for a moment and
then leapt again, forcing her back against the windowpane
with its remnants of glass and wood, and then over.

She fell, and the dragon disengaged itself, hovering in
the window. It turned its head over one shoulder, between
the lazily sweeping wings, and fixed its gaze on Liam.

Done, Master.

Then it dove out the window after Rora.

For long seconds, the three men remaining in the attic
room stared at the shattered window. Gusts of rain blew
in, spraying successive patterns of moisture on the rug,
darkening it.

Numb, Liam could only think of Fanuilh's weakness, its
constant protestations of *soon, soon*. But the dragon had
killed her.

Silenced her, he thought, and stirred to drive the idea
away.

Boult moved as well, and the spell that held them was
broken. "Questor," the Guardsman said shakily, his voice
uncertain.

Liam shook himself, like a dog shedding water, and
looked at Necquer. The merchant's face was white, his
eyes bulging and his lips moving without producing any
sound. Even when he slipped bonelessly to his knees in the
broken glass, Liam took it for shock, but when the merchant

heaved convulsively and clasped his stomach, Liam rushed to his side.

"Go get Coeccias," he barked at Boult. "Get him and make him bring Viyescu. Tell him to tell Viyescu that the Hierarch said he needed an antidote to santhract. He'll understand." He knelt by the contorted merchant, and found the Guardsman at his side. "Go now," he shouted angrily. "Tell him it's santhract—he'll understand. Go!"

After a second's gawking, Boult shrugged—his all-purpose reaction—and darted out the door.

The merchant was feverish, his skin slick and gritty and radiating unnatural heat. He crouched on his knees, one hand splayed out on the ground while the other clutched at his stomach. He took in great lungfuls of air with croaking sobs, as if he was desperate to breathe. His head swung in wide arcs, like a frightened cow.

Glass was digging into Liam's knees and stockinged toes, and he could see trickles of blood run, mingled with rainwater, from beneath the merchant's outflung hand. Grimacing, he put one hand around Necquer's waist and took hold of his chin with the other, probing a long finger between the clenched teeth.

"Stop fussing," he muttered as Necquer tried to roll his head away, and managed to shove his finger down the merchant's throat. Necquer's teeth closed momentarily, and then his mouth and throat opened, and vomit gushed out, lukewarm and thick on Liam's hand and arm.

As he held the spewing merchant, mechanically urging him to get rid of the contents of his stomach, he looked vacantly out the window.

Fanuilh killed her. No recriminations, no heaping on of guilt. She could never reveal what he had done, what he had allowed to happen.

He could not decide how he should feel, and, for safety's sake, felt guilty.

CHAPTER 15

BOULT RETURNED QUICKER than Liam had expected, but without the Aedile. Coeccias, he explained, had gone to get Viyescu, and sent him back to help, if he could.

There was little for him to do. Necquer had gotten rid of everything in his stomach but was wracked by dry heaves, and his breathing was still labored. Liam held him around the waist and shrugged at the Guardsman, who set himself to brushing the broken glass and wood into a pile with his foot. The window had no shutters, and the rain still blew in.

Taking the lantern, Boult edged towards the windowsill, and risked a soaking by leaning far out. He dangled the lantern below him, turning his head this way and that. When he ducked back in, Liam was looking at him.

"She lit not on the ground," the Guardsman said in simple explanation, with yet another shrug.

The idea horrified Liam, but he did not let it show. What would Fanuilh do with her?

Coeccias arrived then, followed by Viyescu, who was carrying a bulging satchel. He did not seem in the least surprised when he saw Necquer's state, but darted ahead of the Aedile and took charge of the situation. They laid Necquer out on the bed at his orders, and then Liam stood aside as the druggist removed several flasks and twists of paper from his satchel.

Concentrating on Necquer, Viyescu kept his head down, as though unwilling to recognize the others around him. Liam kept his eyes and thoughts on the merchant as well, though he spoke a little to Coeccias.

"Boult explained?" he asked without turning his head.

"Some, not all. The maid, though? I'd've never credited it, had you told me before." There was a note of admiration in the Aedile's voice, as if he thought Liam had suspected Rora all along. It set Liam's teeth on edge, but he only grunted noncommittally.

In order to get his antidotes down the merchant's throat, Viyescu needed him upright, and he called Liam to help him. He spooned semiliquid pastes into Necquer's slack mouth while Liam held him behind the shoulders.

Boult had returned to looking out the window, and suddenly called for Coeccias. The Aedile went to the window, and their voices were drowned out by the rain. Viyescu took the opportunity to speak.

"Hierarch Cance," he said in a voice so quiet Liam almost did not hear, "I needs must beg your forgiveness for my sins." He did not look up, staring rigidly at the spoon he was inserting between Necquer's teeth.

Liam had been expecting something else, and it did not help that he had almost forgotten the name he had used. How could the apothecary still think he was a Hierarch? But it seemed he did, because he waited for a moment, and when Liam did not answer, went on, tight-lipped.

"There're things I've done, Hierarch. I'm sure you know—the woman and I—I beg your forgiveness. The woman and I . . ."

Not able to stand anymore, Liam spoke, more harshly than he meant to.

"Save this man and all is forgiven." It sounded silly to him, melodramatic and, worst of all, unpriestly. He cringed, but Viyescu merely paused, and then nodded.

"My thanks, Hierarch," he said after a moment. "Uris grace you," he added. He gave the merchant a few more mouthfuls, and then motioned for him to be let down. Then he waved Liam away and set to checking under Necquer's eyelids and taking his pulse.

At the window, both Coeccias and Boult were leaning out, careful of the jagged glass still left in the sill. The Guardsman was pointing something out. Liam wandered over as the two men pulled their heads back in.

"Something?"

"The maid," Coeccias said. "Caught on a gable, I think."

Liam blanched. Fanuilh had not taken her, of course. It was ridiculous to think he could have. Still, the thought unnerved him. He asked if he could go, and Coeccias nodded after a moment's thought. He and Boult could handle getting her up, or they could get another member of the Guard.

"Will y'attend me at my house? Burus'll let you in. There's still the Uris's Eve fast to break."

Liam refused, as politely as he could, but the Aedile pressed him to come to the feast the next day at his sister's.

"There're matters," he had said in a gruff, strangely gentle tone, "that require our discourse, if not this night, then tomorrow." He was obviously concerned about Liam's distracted air and pale face. "Come to my house at midday tomorrow."

Liam agreed, and left as quickly as he could, ignoring the glance Viyescu threw at him. He sat in the dark on the stairs and pulled on his boots. Miraculously, the broken glass had not cut his feet, but he did not think of this.

He knew that Coeccias had let him go because he thought him a weak scholar who had never seen blood before. It did not bother him: better to appear a coward than face Fanuilh's handiwork, and the corpse to which he had unwittingly led the dragon.

The rain pelted him as he walked slowly back through the Warren, but he only hugged his cloak closer to him. Perhaps the worst of it was that he had not expected anything like this, that the adventure he had so blithely embarked on only a few days before had turned out so very different.

Unable to face the ride out to Tarquin's in the rain, and unwilling to face what might be waiting for him there, he went to his garret. Mistress Dorcas was not in the kitchen when he entered; he heard her conducting the Uris's Eve meal with the other boarders in the dining room. Relieved, he slipped upstairs, not bothering with a candle.

He threw off his cloak and sat in his chair in the dark. The window bothered him, however, with the rain pelting it, and he decided to try his luck with sleep.

His luck held, and he only had time before he slipped off to think one thought three or four times.

I'll have time to think about it tomorrow.

A weak, underwater light filled the room when Liam woke. The rain had stopped sometime in the night, and the clouds, now only light gray, had retreated much higher into the sky. It was almost ten, he guessed.

He was stiff and sore, much sorer than the day before. The tattoo on his chest had begun to turn a sickly yellow at the edges.

Healing well, he thought, and turned a groan of pain into a laugh.

Moving slowly, he dressed and packed his few belongings into his seachest. It was light, even with all his possessions in it, but he managed to bring it downstairs only at great expense to his aching muscles.

The boy from the stables brought Diamond round to the kitchen door, and helped him lift the chest to the horse's withers and tie it tight. The boy's generally merry air and the nonchalant way he accepted a large tip reminded Liam that it was a holiday. It also explained the small number of people in the streets, and the fact that Mistress Dorcas was not up yet. On Uris-tide, she obviously believed she could sleep in.

This suited Liam well; he did not want to see her. He mounted Diamond slowly and set him to a gentle, easy pace. It took almost an hour to reach Tarquin's house, but Liam was not unhappy with the ambling gait. There was plenty of light, even with the clouds, but he knew even if it had been a beautiful, sunny spring day he would not have wanted to approach the house.

Fanuilh, however, was nowhere to be seen, and no thoughts crashed into his head as he walked tentatively from room to room, calling the creature's name. Bemused, he went out to the beach and let the trunk tumble off Diamond onto the sand. Then he half-dragged, half-carried it into the entrance hall.

Feeling he had pressed his luck enough, he left it there, mounted Diamond again and started back for Southwark.

He did not want to see Fanuilh, and was glad he had not. He did not want to see Coeccias at the moment either, but he had promised, and there were things that he would have to explain. He purposefully dawdled on the way back, because he did not want to arrive early.

Coeccias was waiting for him, opening the door himself and ushering Liam in.

"How was your sleep?"

"Good," Liam said, surprised to find it was true. "I'm sore."

The Aedile laughed. "Your friends'll be in hand soon." He led the way to the kitchen and put the finishing touches to a positively monstrous cauldron of cider while they talked.

Liam outlined the story, filling in the details he had learned or figured out the night before. It was remarkably easy.

Rora was pregnant and Necquer would not support her. Kansallus's talk had hinted at a certain pride and vengefulness in her; if anything, he had underestimated them. She had obviously been much more fierce than Kansallus had guessed, even with the evidence of Knave Fitch's mangled ear. And the way she had used Viyescu to get her the poison to murder Necquer and then threatened to reveal whatever had passed between them indicated the depth of the ruthlessness hidden behind her beauty.

"I don't think she was altogether right in the head," Liam commented, and Coeccias grunted his agreement.

So she was set on killing Necquer. Lons must have told her about his deal with Tarquin, and she convinced the wizard to switch the spells, in return for some of her blood. Why she chose the illusion spell was not clear; perhaps she did not want to ruin her brother's arrangement, and thought that as soon as the Teeth disappeared, Lons could claim his reward. It would not matter if Necquer tried to enter the harbor the very next day and was smashed to pieces.

Perhaps she thought it would be fitting, a sort of double revenge: give his wife to another man and then kill him.

"She was clearly somewhat mad, for all her cunning." Liam amazed himself with his own tone of voice. He sounded cold and analytical, describing the events from a pitying distance. He wondered how he was able to do it.

Tarquin had tried to cast the spell she wanted, but it had failed—Rora had had no real virgin's blood to give him—so he cast Lons's original request, maybe as a kind of revenge. When Necquer returned unharmed, she went to see Tarquin, most likely to upbraid him for not casting the spell, not knowing he had figured out her deception. He threatened to reveal her plot to Necquer, so she killed him.

"Of course," Liam said finally, talking to Coeccias's expansive back as the Aedile crouched over his boiling pot like a gnome or dwarf from a story, "there's little pure proof. Much of it's only circumstance, and motive. The santhract she put in Necquer's wine proves something, I guess, and she was pregnant. Really, it just fits best." He paused, reflecting. He knew he had done it. "And Tarquin's familiar certainly thought she did."

"Truth. Curious, that," Coeccias said at last, rising from the pot. "But I grant you all—she must have done it. There's naught else that makes sense. And I've something from Herione, as well: Rora used to dance for her—just dance, you mind—nigh on two years past. We'll say that's when Viyescu met her, and Necquer as well."

For a moment, the stout man regarded Liam intensely, as if trying to pry a secret from him; then his features softened into admiration. Liam realized Coeccias had been wondering how he had figured it all out. In telling the story, he had left out both Rora's visit to him and Fanuilh's part. Thinking back, he realized he had sounded like quite the natural investigator, and the cold, confident tone he had assumed had not hurt. It was Luck, again, the Luck he carried with him, that allowed him to handle something incompetently and somehow come out looking all the better for it.

It made him feel very uncomfortable, and he hung his head to hide his guilty blush. He suddenly thought that he had not said Rora's name once while telling what he knew. He had said "she" or "her." Not her name. It made him feel worse.

"When do you want to tell Lons?"

"I've already done it, last night," Coeccias said. He and Boult had brought Lons his sister's body, recovered from the gable where it had lodged in her fall. Liam was shocked by this, but the Aedile hastened to explain. Fanuilh had not been vicious—scratches on her back, and a single bite at her throat. He and Boult had washed away the blood from her face and hands, and covered the wounds pretty well. "The Golden Orb's company parts Southwark tomorrow for the heath, and Lons'll with them."

There was nothing else to say about the investigation, and Coeccias suggested they go to his sister's. Liam wondered how they would get the cauldron of spiked cider to her house, but it turned out that she lived only a block away, and Coeccias simply filled a smaller pot to bring with them.

"One of the whelps'll run back for more when we've drained this one."

Coeccias's sister was like him, broad and short, with weight to spare but a warm, matronly face. She kissed her brother warmly and made much of Liam. Her husband was a cooper, and they had an uncountable swarm of children. They held Liam, as a stranger, in awed respect, but mobbed Coeccias affectionately at first, and then Burus when he appeared.

Several relatives of Coeccias's brother-in-law soon arrived, bringing huge amounts of food and an army of small children to the feast. The tables groaned under the weight of the food, and afterwards, stuffed to bursting, the whole family gathered around to sing to Burus's piping. They were merry, and Liam felt out of place. There were things he wanted to think about, and though he would have liked to stay, he knew he could not contribute to their celebration, and left soon after the music began.

He spent three days alone at Tarquin's, exploring the house and thinking about all that had happened. He slept on the couch in the library and spent the days idly leafing through the books or examining the items in the wizard's trophy room.

Many times the image of Rora floated in his mind, cursing him, saying all the things he had been afraid she would. She reviled him, called him a betrayer and a fool, a heartless monster. He knew he was not these things, that she had used him, and that he was not responsible for her death. He knew them, but he could not shake a feeling of responsibility.

At other times he thought of Viyescu, whose darkest, deepest kept secrets he had effectively exposed in the guise of a priest. He hoped that the druggist might have taken his hasty absolution in the attic to heart, but did not think that even that excused his deception.

And there were Freihett and Poppae Necquer to consider. He would not be able to see them, to deal with the husband or pass an idle afternoon with the wife. What he knew of them, and their awareness of some of his knowledge, would make such encounters extremely uncomfortable.

Still, what else could he have done? He could not have known things would turn out the way they had.

In the end, he simply acknowledged that he had not handled the whole thing well, and vowed to leave it at that. In time, he thought, he might well be able to.

On the second day, Boult appeared at his door, rousing Liam from a book of history he had found in Tarquin's library. The Guardsman had brought a copy of the wizard's will, as proof of ownership. The diffidence and hang-all attitude Liam had liked in the man was gone, replaced with a sort of uneasy respect.

Coeccias had been telling stories about the investigation, Liam knew, and portraying him as some sort of omniscient seer into men's souls, whose only weakness was a certain queasiness at the sight of blood. He was surprised to find that he did not mind the picture as much as he might have. He felt a little guilty because the result was more Luck than omniscience, but at heart he was secretly pleased.

Boult also brought a note from the Aedile. It was very
short, scrawled wildly across a piece of paper. In it, Coeccias
invited him to dinner the next day, and mentioned that
Necquer had recovered completely from the santhract.
Finally, he wrote that Scar, Ratface and their friend had
been caught, and were currently residing in the Aedile's
jail awaiting judgement.

Liam asked Boult to tell Coeccias that he would come
to dinner.

Between all of this, he stood on the beach, or sat on the
balustrade of the veranda, and scanned the sky for signs of
Fanuilh. The little dragon did not return for three days.

His feelings were mixed about the creature. It had lied to
him when it said it was still too weak to fly, and he knew
that it had followed him to Rora. That bothered him, but
he reflected that there was little he could have done about
it. The dragon could see into his head at will.

That, really, was what bothered him most, and he thought
angrily of their deal. And he had thought of something he
had to attend to, with which the dragon might help.

Wake. Wake.

On the morning of the fourth day after Rora's death, he
was wandering in a dream through the old temple, and the
walls were inscribed again with the single word:

Wake. Wake.

He woke on the couch, and looked deep into the dragon's
glittering cat's eyes.

"You're back," he muttered.

*Yes, Master. I had to hunt, and I thought you would be
angry with me.*

Sitting on its haunches, neck bent, Fanuilh looked like a
dog awaiting a well-earned whipping.

"I was," Liam agreed, putting his feet to the floor and running a hand through his tousled hair. He was much calmer
than he had thought he would be. "You didn't tell me you
were going to kill her."

The thought was a long time forming: *It seemed appro-priate. She killed Master Tanaquil.* Another idea formed, very quickly, and just as quickly disappeared. *When we joined, it came to me that it was something you would do.*

"Me? You mean you got the idea from me?"

Yes. You did such a thing once.

Liam laughed, but it was bitter, the kind of laughter he directed at himself. "Yes, I did. But I was much younger then. Much younger. And I've paid for it as well." He had an insight into the creature's nature, how little it understood of men, and how it must pick and choose its ideas from its master.

I am sorry, Master.

There was a long pause.

"Then you recognize me as your master?"

Yes.

"And you'll fulfill your part of the bargain?"

I will serve you as you wish. I have done what I . . . There was a break in the solid thought, as though Fanuilh had never used the concept in connection with itself before. . . . *what I wanted.*

"You'll teach me how to keep you out of my head?"

Anything you wish, Master.

"Do you know what I want to do now? What I want to take care of?"

Yes. The dragon lowered its head, as if ashamed to admit that it could still read his mind.

"Can you help me with this thing I have in mind?"

Yes.

"You'd best tell me how. I want to do it today."

With Fanuilh's help, it was easy. Liam rode into Southwark alone that afternoon and left Diamond at the stables. He told them he would be keeping the horse with him after that night, and settled his account.

Then he strolled down towards the harbor and the one thing he needed to make sure of. The clouds had rolled away a day before, leaving a bright sky out of which a cold, invigorating wind blew. His soreness was gone, and he felt well.

The harborfront was busy, men and animals straining to move the last of the season's cargo. He walked alone to Marcius's warehouse, and knocked at the smaller door. An unknown face appeared, and ordered him off. There was no activity around the building, and Liam smiled to himself spitefully. There was no activity because Marcius's best hopes were at the bottom of the sea. He found he could not muster much sympathy.

"I think your master will want to see me," he said, and pushed his way past the ugly face into the warehouse proper.

Two new men waited behind the doorkeeper, who now thrust his face into Liam's and growled.

"I think you—" he began, and then his eyes rolled up in his head and he slumped heavily to the ground. Liam stepped back, startled, and saw that the other two guards had dropped as well.

Fanuilh fluttered to the ground behind them.

"They're all right?"

Asleep. It will not last long.

"Then we'd better hurry."

He walked to the stairs, and with a lazy beat of its wings, Fanuilh rose and settled on his shoulder like a bird. It was large, the size of a dog, but Liam barely felt the weight, and he imagined he looked quite fearsome. Fanuilh rocked gently to keep its balance as he hurried along the creaky steps.

Marcius's perfectly coiffed head snapped up as his office door slammed open, and a shout of anger died on his lips as he saw Liam stride into the room with Fanuilh on his shoulder.

From the merchant's sudden pallor, Liam judged that he did indeed look frightening with the tiny dragon in tow.

"Master Marcius. Do you remember me?"

"Yes," the merchant stammered, and before he could recover himself, Liam plowed on, as much to keep Marcius off balance as not to laugh at what he was saying.

"It was not wise of you to fool with a wizard, Marcius. Do you understand that?"

Marcius nodded once.

"The things that can result are unpleasant, you see."

Marcius nodded again.

"And I would not want to have any unpleasantness. Your men are in prison, now, and will remain there. I allow them to escape lightly, because I know they acted on your orders. You will rescind any such orders you may have since given, and will leave me in peace. Do you understand?"

Marcius nodded several times, his eyes on Fanuilh, who was yawning widely, revealing needlelike teeth.

"The maps I sold you are good, and will not be sold to anyone else. I suggest you put them to good use, and forget about me. Is that clear as well?"

The merchant was still nodding when Liam left, because Fanuilh stayed behind.

I will leave here in a few minutes, Master, and wait for you at the beach.

Not used to thinking to the dragon, Liam simply nodded and walked out.

Once on the street, he indulged in a broad smile. He had achieved the effect he was looking for, and knew the merchant would not bother him again. He was pleased with his own performance, absurd as it seemed in retrospect, but knew that most of the merchant's fear had stemmed from Fanuilh's presence.

And the dragon had acted completely in accordance with Liam's wishes. It was truly his servant. The thought buoyed him up, inspiring another secret smile.

Wondering what else it could do, he let his imagination play with the idea as he walked to dinner at Coeccias's.

There was still a great deal of cider left from the Uris-tide batch, but between the heavy meal Burus served and a misguided attempt on the part of the three men to go through all the verses of "The Lipless Flutist," they finished it by midnight.